"It's too risky."

"So what then?" Valerie asked. "You'd rather just move on and pretend like none of this happened? Hope that I eventually let go of this stupid crush I've had on you for years?"

Dismissing any thoughts of Valerie was impossible. He didn't want to forget her. Last night he'd gotten to see past her tough exterior down to her soft, vulnerable side, one that she didn't share often, and the things she'd said had meant a lot to him. *She* meant a lot to him...and always had.

Logan sighed. "No, goddamn it, that's not what I want."

"Then what is?"

His gaze locked on to hers, and a spark ignited in his gut. What the hell was wrong with him? Maybe it was the heat of the moment. Or maybe it was a turning point in his life. Because Logan couldn't stay away from Valerie another minute.

"I want the same damn thing I've always wanted. You."

ALSO BY ALISON BLISS

Size Matters

ON THE PLUS SIDE

ALISON BLISS

FOREVER

NEW YORK   BOSTON

Copyright © 2017 by Alison Bliss
Excerpt from *Size Matters* copyright © 2016 by Alison Bliss
Cover design by Elizabeth Turner. Cover photography by Claudio Marinesco.
Cover copyright © 2017 by Hachette Book Group, Inc.

Forever
Hachette Book Group
1290 Avenue of the Americas, New York, NY 10104
forever-romance.com
twitter.com/foreverromance

First Edition: June 2017

Forever is an imprint of Grand Central Publishing. The Forever name and logo are trademarks of Hachette Book Group, Inc.

The publisher is not responsible for websites (or their content) that are not owned by the publisher.

The Hachette Speakers Bureau provides a wide range of authors for speaking events. To find out more, go to www.hachettespeakersbureau.com or call (866) 376-6591.

ISBNs: 978-1-4555-6807-9 (mass market), 978-1-4555-68055- (ebook)

Printed in the United States of America

OPM

10 9 8 7 6 5 4 3 2 1

ATTENTION CORPORATIONS AND ORGANIZATIONS:

Most Hachette Book Group books are available at quantity discounts with bulk purchase for educational, business, or sales promotional use. For information, please call or write:

Special Markets Department, Hachette Book Group
1290 Avenue of the Americas, New York, NY 10104
Telephone: 1-800-222-6747 Fax: 1-800-477-5925

For Barbara Campbell, the strongest woman I know. You amaze me.

Acknowledgments

I would like to thank my husband for being my rock and always listening to me spin my crazy stories out loud. Your support means everything to me! A big thank-you to my awesome boys for not complaining about pizza night when I have a pressing deadline. No more pizza this month, I swear. Also, thanks to the rest of my family and friends for all of the never-ending love and for keeping me sane.

To my agent, Andrea Somberg, I don't know what I'd do without you. Your guidance and friendship are invaluable. To my editor, Alex Logan, thank you for your editing brilliance and for making my books the best they can be. Thank you to my publicist, Michelle Cashman, for tirelessly helping to promote my books and for always going above and beyond. It's appreciated. Special thanks to Grand Central's art department for giving me another beautiful cover. I can't tell you how many readers have asked me where they can buy the purple dress.

And of course, thank you to all of my readers, fans, blogging friends, PAs, and street team members. Your reviews and the help you offer in spreading the word about my books are the biggest compliment you can give an author. All of you make a difference.

Last but not least, a special thank-you to my boxer, Ecko, for bringing my family eleven years of unconditional love. Unfortunately, we lost him this past year, but he was the best dog, friend, and writing companion a girl could ask for.

ON THE
PLUS SIDE

Chapter One

Valerie Carmichael needed a drink. A strong one. Because it was the only way she envisioned herself getting through the night.

Then again, maybe if she drank enough, the alcohol would sour her stomach and give her a good excuse to bail out and take the first cab home. Sadly, that option sounded the most appealing.

An elbow nudged into her side, bringing her thoughts back to the crowded bar. "I can't see anything through all of these people," Brett said, scanning the room with his eyes. "Come on, let's go to the other side so I can get a better view."

Sighing, Valerie trudged behind him without a word.

When Brett had asked her to attend the grand opening of Bottoms Up, a new bar in their hometown of Granite, Texas, she'd hesitated to say yes. Sure, she was curious what the inside of the recently remodeled bar looked like and had no doubt the place would be jam-packed with handsome, available men. But it was still the last place on earth she wanted to be.

She knew better than to hang out in bars with her older and only—*thank God*—brother. Every time she'd done so in the past, the nights had always ended the same way. Brett would spend the entire evening hovering over her like a rabid pit bull, daring any single guy with a glint in his eye to look her way. And eventually, one of them would.

At least one brave soul, brimming with liquid courage, would be dumb enough—or drunk enough—to risk approaching her while Brett stood guard. Then the potentially suicidal man would quickly find out what a hot-tempered asshole her brother could be. It was inevitable.

Because Valerie turned heads. She always had.

Oh, she wasn't silly enough to believe she looked like some gorgeous supermodel with a lean, trim figure or anything. She definitely didn't. But she had a pretty face, banging plus-size curves, and a lively personality. And that was good enough for her. Valerie was just... Valerie. And damn proud of it.

Unfortunately, that noteworthy self-confidence of hers was akin to a powerful magnet, drawing unassuming male moths to her female flame. Which meant, as with any heat source, there was always a chance someone would get burned. And with Brett around, odds were in her favor that it wasn't going to be her.

As they made their way across the room, Brett's muscular frame easily parted the sea of people, giving her plenty of space to walk behind him without bumping into anyone. But even then, she only made it ten feet before a masculine arm circled her waist and pulled her back against a hard body. "Hey, baby. Wanna dance?"

Valerie winced. *Another guy with a death wish. Lovely.* No, wait. She recognized that voice, didn't she?

Glancing over her right shoulder, she stared directly into Max's playful eyes just as Brett whipped around and shoved Max away from her. "Get your hands off my sister, jackass."

Max released her and held his hands up in surrender. "Whoa! I was just playing around with her. No need to get pissy about it, buddy."

"I'm not your goddamn buddy," Brett sneered, fire flashing in his eyes as he stepped toward Max.

Valerie scrambled into her brother's path to keep him at bay. "Stop it! He's just a friend of mine, Brett. You don't have to go all caveman on him."

"Then tell your *friend* to keep his damn hands off you." Her brother shot Max one of his blue-eyed Taser glares, which usually sent most men retreating.

But Max wasn't like most men and continued to stand there, as if he was throwing down a challenge of his own. One Brett was clearly willing to accept, since he started for Max.

Jesus. Here we go again. Valerie readjusted her position and placed her hands on Brett's chest to stop him. "Knock it off right now. Damn it, you promised to behave yourself tonight. If you can't control yourself, then I'm going home." She almost hoped Brett would throw a punch just so she had a reason to leave. *Sorry, Max.*

"Me?" Brett asked innocently, his eyes widening. "I

didn't do anything...*yet*." He zapped another threatening look in Max's direction for good measure.

Valerie shook her head, annoyed with the whole situation. "Why don't you just go ahead without me, and I'll catch up to you in a little bit?"

Her brother didn't move.

God, why did I come out tonight? Me and my bright ideas. "Damn it, Brett. Just go already. I'll be fine. I want to talk to Max." Her brother planted his feet, as if he planned to wait for her, so she added, "Without my body-guard present, if you don't mind."

Brett gritted his teeth and set his jaw but eventually stalked away. Once Valerie was sure he wasn't coming back, she turned her attention to Max and sighed. "Sorry about that. My brother's a little...intense."

"Who, that guy? Nah." Max's sardonic tone wasn't lost on her, but then he shrugged. "No big deal, Val. You warned me that your brother was an asshole. If I had known he was with you tonight, I wouldn't have grabbed you like that."

She grinned. "You're such a liar."

The corner of his mouth lifted in a tiny smirk. "I know."

Though they'd met only six months before at Rusty's Bucket—a seedy local dive bar that made this place look like some kind of upscale cocktail lounge—she'd had Max's number from the beginning. And she wasn't refer-ring to his telephone digits...though she had those too.

Upon meeting Max, Valerie had quickly figured out two things about him. One, he was a decent guy, even though he was a bit of a troublemaker at times. Two, he hadn't been remotely attracted to her. Which was fine with her, since she hadn't been interested in him either.

She hadn't lied when she told Brett that Max was just a friend. Nothing romantic had ever evolved between them and never would. At the time, they had each unknowingly used the opportunity to set up their best friends, Leah and Sam, by feigning interest in each other.

And it had worked! The lucky couple were now engaged and living together in Sam's apartment while his construction crew built their new house not far from Leah's bakery, Sweets n' Treats. Within three weeks, Leah would have her intimate beach wedding and be moving into her glorious new home with the man of her dreams.

And Valerie couldn't be happier for them.

Especially since the one-bedroom apartment over the bakery was now available for Valerie to rent, thus making Leah not only her best friend and employer but also her landlord.

"I'm surprised to see you here tonight," Max said, steering Valerie toward a surprisingly vacant seat at the small side bar in the corner. "Leah said you weren't coming."

"I didn't plan to," she said, noting how strange it was that there were plenty of seats in the area around them while the rest of the bar harbored wall-to-wall people. She slid onto the black, vinyl-covered stool as Max stationed himself next to her. "I know it's hard to believe I'd miss it though."

"No kidding. Since when do you not enjoy the bar scene, party girl?"

Okay, so maybe I'm not the only one who's got someone's number.

Grinning, she ignored his question and glanced around

the room. "So where are Leah and Sam? I thought they'd be here by now."

"They're here," he confirmed. "They headed over to the main bar to get a drink. The bartenders over there are much faster than this one is," Max said, gesturing to the young man fumbling a glass behind the bar. "If you want something to drink, you better tell me quick. If he has to make more than one drink at a time, you'll die of thirst before I can save you."

Normally, Valerie would have ordered a beer, but the shiny metallic bandage dress she wore showed off her feminine side and wasn't really the kind of outfit a lady would drink a beer in. *Hmm. Something colorful and fruity perhaps?* Besides, the hard liquor would probably help ease some of the tension she'd felt creeping up her spine since she'd entered the building. "Um, how about an appletini?"

"A what?"

She grinned. "An apple martini."

Max nodded. "You got it. Coming right...er, scratch that. You might get it soon, if you're lucky." He grinned and then leaned over the bar and repeated the order to the young bartender.

The barkeep nodded in acknowledgment but seemed a bit unsure of what to do. When he finally made the decision to reach for a glass, it took him three tries before he found the one used for martinis. Even as he chilled the glass with ice, he moved so slowly and deliberately that Valerie wondered if he was pacing himself so he didn't pull a muscle in his hand. If he didn't learn to speed up, the thirsty bar-goers would eat him for breakfast. Because, chances were, it would take him until morning to finish making one drink. *Jeez.*

While they waited for her drink, Max and Valerie lingered at the bar counter chatting about their friends' pending nuptials. Since they were the best man and maid-of-honor, Max and Valerie would soon be walking down the aisle together. Of course, she wouldn't dare word it that way to her brother or he'd jump to conclusions and blow a gasket.

After a few minutes, Sam and Leah emerged from the dense crowd, with a beer bottle for him and a glass of water for her. Apparently, Leah was still on that damn diet and counting calories so she would fit into her wedding dress. Though why she didn't just buy the dress in a larger size was beyond Valerie.

Leah blinked at the sight of her sitting with Max. "Val? What are you doing here? You said you weren't coming."

Valerie shrugged. "I changed my mind."

"Are you feeling okay?"

"Yeah, sure. Why?"

"When you said you didn't want to go out, I assumed you were sick. You *never* turn down a night out. Actually, you're the one who's always asking me to go." Leah placed her palm lightly against Valerie's forehead. "You sure you don't have the flu or something?"

Valerie laughed and pushed her friend's hand away. "Oh, stop it. I just didn't feel like getting dressed up. I'm getting tired of the whole bar scene."

Leah squinted with disbelief. "Since when?"

Since three weeks ago when I found out this place was opening. Valerie gazed expectantly at the bartender, who was using a jigger to carefully measure out the vodka for her cocktail. Damn, she could really use that drink about now. She sighed inwardly. "I'm fine," she told Leah. "I was tired, but the mood passed."

"Good," Sam said cheerfully, clasping a hand on his buddy's shoulder. "Then maybe you can help us keep Max out of trouble for one evening. Lord knows he needs all the help he can get."

Max just grinned.

"Already on top of it," Valerie replied. "A few minutes ago, he met my brother."

Leah's eyes widened. "Oh no. Brett's here? I can only imagine how well that went over."

"Yep, exactly what you're thinking. It didn't. But I managed to send Brett away for the time being. I'm sure he's still watching me from some dark corner though." She leaned over to Max and loudly mock-whispered, "If you want to keep your arms attached to your body, I wouldn't make any sudden movements in my direction."

They all laughed, probably because a truer statement had never been spoken. As the chuckling died down, the young bartender finally slid a green-tinted apple martini on the counter in front of Valerie. *Thank goodness.*

Max reached for his wallet and nodded across the room in the direction Brett had wandered off in. "Think I can get away with paying for your drink, smart-ass? Or should I consult your brother first?"

She smiled up at him, her eyes twinkling with mirth. "Oh no. You don't have to ask his permission for that." Then her gaze followed the same trail Max's had. "Always feel free to pay for my—"

Valerie's heart stopped, along with her lips. *Oh God.*

Across the room, Brett stood there talking to a tall, dark-haired man who had one thumb hooked in the front pocket of his jeans while he leaned comfortably against the wall with his right shoulder. She couldn't see the other guy's face, but she didn't need to. Valerie recognized all six feet, two inches of him.

Jesus. I don't think I can do this.

"Can't do what?" Leah asked, puzzlement filling her voice.

Shit. Had she said that out loud?

Valerie winced. Her friends probably thought Brett's ridiculous brotherly behavior had been the motivation for her wanting to stay home tonight...and that was partly true. But she hadn't told them the real reason—a bigger reason—for wanting to avoid stepping into the hottest new bar in town. And that reason not only had a name, but he was the owner. Logan Mathis.

"Val?" Leah placed her hand on Valerie's shoulder, pulling her out of her thoughts and right back into her noisy surroundings.

She immediately lifted her drink and downed the martini in one gulp then rubbed a flat hand across her queasy stomach. "I *can* do this," she whispered in encouragement to herself.

Sam and Max were no longer paying attention and were busy having a heated football discussion, but Leah raised one suspicious brow. "What the hell are you talking about?" she asked before her gaze fell on the empty martini glass. "How many of those have you had?"

Valerie glanced across the room again at the man who had her insides tied up in knots and sighed heavily. "Not nearly enough."

Leah's gaze immediately followed the invisible trail of

bread crumbs Valerie had left behind. She grinned and pointed across the bar. "Hey, isn't that—"

"Logan Mathis," Valerie groaned, not bothering to hide the contempt in her voice.

"Yeah, that's the one. He was your brother's—"

"Best friend."

She nodded. "Yep, but didn't he move away like—"

"Eight years ago."

Leah pursed her mouth in annoyance. "Okay, how about you actually let me ask the question before you answer it?"

Despite the way her stomach was churning, Valerie couldn't help but grin. "Sorry. Go ahead."

"Isn't he the guy you had that huge crush on back then?"

Valerie blinked rapidly. "Wait. H-how did you…"

"Oh, come on," Leah said, rolling her eyes. "You didn't really think you fooled me, did ya? You mooned over the Mathis boy every chance you got. And the way you always wanted to tag along with the two of them, though Brett frustrated the hell out of you most days. It was obvious."

Great. Just great. Valerie closed her eyes and rubbed at her temples before looking back at Logan. He had shifted his position and was now leaning with his back against the brick wall, which gave her a clear view of his face. Her mouth went dry. *Good Lord. Could he possibly get any hotter?*

He had the same brooding brown eyes from before, but his muscled frame had filled out and taken on a more rugged appearance. A five o'clock shadow now graced his chiseled jaw but gave his face more depth and dimension.

His clothes, however, were a bit misleading from the Logan she remembered. The neutral-toned flannel shirt permitted him an almost respectable, approachable look that was probably good for his business. But then she noticed that he'd only slightly tucked in the front of the shirt, enough to showcase the noticeable bulge beneath his belt buckle. As if he were putting his manhood on display.

There's the Logan she remembered. *That damn subtle arrogance of his.*

Leah eyed her warily. "So that's why you're acting so weird tonight? You still have a thing for Logan?"

"No, I don't," Valerie answered quickly.

"Oh my God. You do! You're practically sweating right now," Leah accused, grinning her ass off. She peeked over at him again. "Hmm. Well, he does look good."

"Really? I haven't noticed," Valerie said, keeping herself from taking another peek.

Leah looked more confused than ever. "But haven't you seen him since he got back into town?"

"No. I've been...busy. I had all that unpacking to do, ya know? And I'm pretty sure that opening a new bar required a lot of his attention."

"Val, you moved into my old apartment a month ago, and I helped you unpack everything the first week you were..." Leah paused. "Hold on. Did you say he opened a new bar? As in *this* bar?"

"Um, yeah. It's his place."

"I didn't know that. I guess all this wedding planning has kept me distracted and out of the loop. I'm surprised you didn't mention it thou..." Leah paused then threw back her head and cackled. "Oh, I get it! So that's why you didn't want to come out tonight. You're avoiding him."

When Valerie bit her lip, Leah grinned wider, apparently enjoying the role reversal they had going on. Then she eyed Logan from across the room once more. "I never thought I'd say this to you, Valerie, but payback is a real bitch."

Before Valerie could stop her, Leah waved her hand in the air, snaring Brett's attention. He immediately recognized his sister's best friend and nodded to her before leaning toward Logan. Brett's mouth moved with inaudible words that had Logan's head spinning in the girls' direction.

Valerie leaned back quickly so that Max's body blocked her from view as Logan glanced over. "Leah, what the hell?" She peeked around Max's shoulder in time to see Brett start in their direction...with Logan on his heels. "Oh God! Why the hell did you do that?"

"Because I'm your friend. There's no point in avoiding him. It's like ripping off a bandage. Just get it over with already."

"Damn it, Leah..."

"Don't be mad. Besides, Granite isn't that big of a town, and you were bound to run into him sooner or later anyway."

"I was good with later."

Leah giggled and then tapped Sam on the shoulder, interrupting his conversation with Max. "Why don't the three of us go grab another round of drinks from across the room? Brett's coming over here, and I'm pretty sure Valerie is going to need a refill...or possibly ten."

"What?" Valerie blinked at her. "Now you're leaving me all by myself? Gee, thanks. Some friend you are."

"I'm doing you a favor. You'll thank me for it later. Besides, you wouldn't want me standing here grinning like a fool when he walks up," Leah said with a wink. "Let me know what happens though. I'm dying to hear how all this plays out." Then she flitted away, taking Sam and Max with her.

Traitor. She'll be lucky if I tell her anything at all.

Brett and Logan wove their way through the crush of people invading the bar, and with every step they took in her direction, Valerie could feel the room growing considerably smaller. Unwilling to make eye contact, she turned her body to the bar and stared straight ahead. Adrenaline raced through her veins, and her nerves surged with anxiety. *Yep, definitely going to throw up.*

The moment the air pressure surrounding her changed, she knew Logan—and his overbearing male presence—was standing behind her. It was as if she could feel the tension rolling off him in waves.

Unfortunately, she couldn't put it off any longer. Straightening her posture, she sucked in a calming breath and crossed her legs, allowing her short skirt to ride up her thighs a little more than was polite. She planted a big smile on her face, spun around on her bar stool, and looked directly at Logan's unsmiling face. He had always towered over her much shorter frame, but somehow she'd forgotten how impossibly small he could make her feel with just one simple look.

Logan's eyes met hers head on, and his lips curved. "Well, well. If it isn't Princess Valerie."

*   *   *

Logan Mathis hadn't seen Valerie Carmichael since he'd skipped out of town eight years ago, but the moment he'd come face-to-face with his best friend's kid sister, he couldn't help himself. He'd called her the one thing he knew would get a rise out of her.

And boy, did it ever.

Just like in the past, Valerie jutted out that perfect pointy chin and narrowed those piercing ice-blue eyes. But instead of shrieking at him like she used to, Val did something he hadn't expected. She lifted one brow in a prominent arch, as if daring him to find out just how much of a princess she really was. *Interesting.*

Her cool, assessing eyes flickered over him. "Logan," she stated calmly, though her pitch held an undeniable amount of irritation, "I heard you were back in town. What happened? Houston got tired of you and decided to kick you out?"

The young Valerie he remembered from years before had always been pretty and blooming with personality, but this girl, this *woman*, sitting in front of him had an air of confidence he hadn't seen before.

He smiled at the hostile edge to her tone, but as his gaze landed on the exposed flesh of her upper thighs, he began feeling a little antagonistic himself. "Yeah, guess that's what happens when a guy makes his way through all their women."

Brett laughed and slapped him on the back. "Good one, bro." Then he nodded toward the empty glass on the bar. "Looks like you're empty, Val. Want another one of those...uh, whatever the hell that thing is?"

A smile tugged on her red-painted lips as she swept her long, wavy blond hair over her right shoulder. "It's an apple martini. And yes, I'd love another." She leaned toward her brother and lowered her voice to almost a whisper. "But you might want to order it from the main bar across the room."

Logan didn't need to ask why. He knew Derek wasn't as fast as the other bartenders he'd hired, which was exactly why he'd started him out at the small side bar, where he wouldn't see as much action. But he seemed like a good kid and had the desire to learn. He'd get faster in time. Probably.

But leave it to Valerie to point out the one weakness in his staff. At least she hadn't been loud about it. Didn't matter anyway. Brett was so preoccupied by a redhead who walked past that he didn't even question why he'd have to get their drinks at the main bar. He just nodded and said, "All right. I'm going to grab a beer while I'm there. Logan can keep an eye on you while I'm gone."

"I don't need a babysitter," she said, rolling her eyes.

Logan considered doing the same. It was as if Brett expected women-eating sharks to start circling if he left his sister alone for even a minute. Then he noticed a guy standing a few feet away with his eyes trained on the hem of Valerie's barely there dress. *Okay, so maybe Brett has a point.*

Shifting his position, Logan used his own body to block her legs from view. Unfortunately, that meant he was practically standing over her, which only gave him a better viewpoint of her never-ending cleavage. His gaze focused between her breasts and slid all the way down to where hardened nipples poked through the thin fabric.

"You want something, Logan?"

Oh, yeeeah. It took him a moment to realize he still hadn't answered Brett's question out loud. "Uh, no. I don't drink on the cock...I mean, clock." *Shit.*

Brett chuckled. "You sure you haven't been drinking, buddy?"

"I'm sure," Logan said, forcing his gaze away from Valerie. "Just give the bartender your name, and they'll put your drinks on my tab. I've already told them to expect you to—"

Brett snorted. "You aren't comping our drinks, jackass. You can't make money by doing shit like that. First night on the job and you already suck as a businessman." When Logan opened his mouth to argue, Brett held up one hand. "I'm serious, dude. Don't make me kick your ass in front of everyone."

Logan grinned. "You could try."

Once Brett disappeared into the crowd, Logan turned back to Valerie, keeping his eyes on hers. His gaze begged him to shift lower, but he wasn't about to let that happen. Even if she was wearing a sinfully tight dress.

Actually, if you asked him, it wasn't really a dress. More like a sparkly, figure-flattering scrap of spandex that outlined the shape of her curvy-ass body. The torturous, high-cut hem practically screamed at him to slide some part of his anatomy under it.

His hands wouldn't have been his first choice, but the nerves in his fingers twitched anyway. The last thing he needed tonight was to see her prancing around in shit like that.

"Nice dress," Logan said, clenching his jaw, though he managed to keep his tone casual. "Where'd you get it—the fabric store?"

She grinned, as if his backhanded compliment pleased her. "I bought it online." She stood, which brought her much closer to him than before, and smoothed her hands down her sides. Her eyes glittered under the flashing neon lights. "Do you like it?"

"Not much to like," Logan said gruffly.

"Well, that's basically the point, isn't it?" Valerie giggled in that sexy, girly way that made a man's balls draw up inside him.

"I'm surprised your brother let you wear that. I figured he would have wrestled you to the ground to keep you from walking out the door in something so low-cut."

"Oh, please. Brett doesn't have a say in what I wear. I don't live with him."

"That hasn't stopped him in the past."

Valerie sighed. "That was a long time ago, Logan. Believe it or not, I'm fully capable of picking out my own clothes. I don't need his approval. Or *yours*." She leaned forward, licking her plump lips, and whispered, "Maybe you haven't realized this yet, but I'm not a little girl anymore."

His stomach tightened. *You can say that again.* But he also knew Brett better than anyone. "How many times did you change before you passed inspection?"

Her lips curved. "Only once. Brett said the first dress would have gotten me arrested...or possibly him."

Damn it. Now Logan wanted to see that one too. It didn't really matter which one she wore though, since he was pretty sure both would look fan-fucking-tastic lying on his bedroom floor. He'd never find out, of course, but he couldn't help grinning for being right about her brother. "Yeah. I thought so, princess."

Her lips pursed as if she was mildly annoyed, but she recovered quickly. "So what are you doing back here anyway? The way you left town so fast, I was sure you'd never step foot within the city limits again."

"I came back to open a business. Or did you forget that you're sitting in *my* bar wearing next to nothing?"

"Yeah, but you could have opened a bar anywhere."

Yep, he could have. But he didn't. "So?"

"So why here?"

"Why not?" he asked, deflecting the question.

She gazed at him curiously and shrugged. "Seems like an odd choice, that's all. Houston is a much larger city. Why would you want to open your business in a small town like Granite?"

Damn. Couldn't she just leave it alone already? "I'm from here, Val. And my mother still lives here, remember?"

"Of course I remember," she said, lifting one inquisitive brow. "I guess I'm just surprised *you* do. Your mom comes in the bakery all the time. I've probably seen her more in the past month than you've seen her in the past eight years."

Ouch. Okay, that stung. But what really pissed him off most was that she was right. He hadn't come home. Not even once. And although he had his reasons, he wasn't willing to discuss them with Valerie. Ignoring the jab, he gave her one of his own. "Yeah, your brother told me you were working in your friend's bakery now. How many people have you poisoned with that endeavor?"

"None yet," she said, giggling. "But I'm certainly willing to make an exception in your case." She grinned again.

God, she had to stop doing that.

The way her sensual mouth curved with that secretive little smile of hers had always driven him up the wall, but it was flat out lethal when paired with the delicate scent of her perfumed skin hovering in the air around him. Sugared oranges and sweet coconut. Like the blond goddess had bathed in a pool of ambrosia. It was enough to drive a man insane.

He needed to wipe that sexy grin off her face before he did something stupid like lean over and kiss it away. "I'm not surprised," Logan said, leaning forward and inhaling deeply. "But then again, I've always been the exception. Haven't I, princess?"

His comment had her temper flaring in those catlike eyes of hers, deepening the color. She crossed her arms, which only succeeded in pushing her breasts higher. "God, must you keep calling me that?"

He shrugged lightly. "It suits you."

Her eyes held his. "Why? Because my brother would love nothing more than to fit me with a chastity belt and lock me away in a tower somewhere? Or is it because you've always thought of me as a royal pain in the ass?"

Stunned, his mouth hinged open. He hadn't expected her to be so...direct. When had that changed? In the past, she'd always been sly with the subtle overtures she'd sent his way. Not that they'd ever gone unnoticed or anything. At least not by him. But even then, he'd done the only thing he could. He'd ignored them. Because if Brett ever found out his sister had made flirty passes at his best friend, Valerie would have found herself locked away, all right. Never to be seen or heard from again.

It would serve her right.

Either way, Logan had no intention of telling her the

reason behind the nickname. That was his business, and if she didn't like it, tough shit. Let her think whatever she wanted. "Both," he lied.

Her eyes narrowed slightly, but her smooth, silky voice had the same drugging undertones he'd remembered so well. "Well, I can see you're still the same cocky jerk you've always been."

Unable to resist, he stepped closer to her. "Sweetheart, you have no idea how *cocky* I can be."

Logan knew better than to say something like that to her, but her sultry eyes were playing tag with his and had forced all rational thought out the window. And watching her tongue dart out to swipe across her full bottom lip only made things worse. An image of him taking her back to his office, bending her over his desk, and finding out exactly what was under that damn slinky-ass dress had his dick hardening almost to the point of pain.

But then he spotted Brett making his way through the crowd with a drink in each hand and cringed inwardly. *Sonofabitch.* Logan quickly moved away from her and ran a frustrated hand through his hair. *Damn it. What the hell am I doing?* He'd gotten so caught up in their exchange that he hadn't realized he was toeing a very dangerous line, one he wasn't willing to cross.

Brett was the closest thing to a brother Logan would ever know. Which meant that, no matter how eye catching the guy's sister was and no matter how many times she flung herself in his direction, Logan wouldn't risk giving up a lifelong friendship for one night of pleasure. It wasn't worth it.

His gaze traveled down to her crossed legs, and he imagined those smooth, sexy thighs gripping his hips as he shoved into her. He swallowed hard. *Damn, it would be one long-ass night with a whole lot of pleasure though.*

As Brett approached, he scowled and handed Valerie a half-full green apple martini. "Here, take this fucking drink. Do you know how hard it is to walk through a packed bar with one of those things?" He pulled his shirt away from his body, showing them a wet spot that had darkened the front. "I spilled it on myself twice, and that fruity shit is sticky."

"I've got a box of T-shirts with the bar's logo on them in the back," Logan told him. "I'll get you one, and you can change into it."

"Thanks, man. But only if you let me pay for the shirt."

Logan grimaced. As if he wasn't already feeling guilty enough about accidentally flirting with the man's sister, Brett had just unknowingly twisted the knife. "Damn it, Brett. You don't have to pay for the fucking—"

"Don't go there with me, Logan. I said I'm paying for it." Brett straightened his posture, as if to show how firm he stood on the idea. "If you have a problem with that, then I'll just go home and change. Up to you."

Logan sighed. "Fine, get your shirt from Paul. He's the head bartender. He can ring you up and grab one from the storeroom."

As he watched Brett head out in search of Paul, Logan shook his head. *Stubborn asshole.* Then he grinned because the big, lovable jerk knew the dire situation Logan was in and was obviously damned determined to help in any way he could.

Logan needed money. And he needed it now.

"Want to explain what that was all about?" Valerie asked. The sound of her voice alone had Logan furrowing his brow. He needed to get away from her before he did something stupid. "Nothing. It's just a damn T-shirt."

"I wasn't talking about the shirt. I was talking about...the way you were looking at me before my brother walked up."

His eyes drifted over her face, and his throat tightened, but he said nothing.

Valerie smiled, as if the thought of silencing him had shifted the winds in her direction for a change. She slinked over to him with a feline grace that disturbed the air around him and held a man's attention.

"What's the matter, Logan?" Her sharp eyes focused on him with an intensity that heated his blood and made his heart hammer against his rib cage. "Cat got your tongue?" The words hissed past her parted lips and sizzled in his ears.

He'd love nothing more than to stroke Valerie's...ego and see how many times he could make her purr. But he didn't have time for games. Especially not with *her* of all people. She was off-limits. A distraction. One he didn't need or want in his life.

Logan took a step back. "I've got to get back to work. Why don't you go find your friends and let one of them babysit your ass for a while?" Then he turned and stormed away.

He hadn't meant to be so harsh and imagined her staring after him in confusion, but he refused to look back. One minute, he'd been flirting with her. Then the next, he'd come to his senses and snapped at her...like it was her fault. *God, I'm a fucking idiot.*

Maybe it was better this way. Safer even.

Logan remembered all the times she'd flaunted herself

under his nose, teasing and taunting him. And memory served him well. She'd damn near tortured him back then, and he wasn't about to let it happen again. He'd just do what he had done years before—avoid her...even if it was difficult to do since the girl was impossible to ignore.

He wasn't going to look at her, think about her, or imagine what she looked like naked. Been there, done that. And all it had ever done was get him into trouble. He knew better than to get anywhere near Valerie, and he was washing his hands of her. For good this time.

Dismissing all thoughts of her from his mind, Logan crossed the room and searched for Brett. He found him standing at the main bar, waiting to get Paul's attention. Along with about twenty other people crowded around the bar with money in hand.

Logan sighed. He'd been afraid of that.

Grand opening night was the worst time to be under-staffed, but it couldn't be helped. Logan had hired the only three bartenders he could find on short notice—Paul, Derek, and James.

Paul and James both seemed to know their way around a bar, working fast and efficiently, but Derek was younger and didn't have the same level of experience as the other two. At least his pours were accurate and the cocktails were well made.

Though some of the customers were moving away from Derek's section to order their drinks from a waitress or traipsing over to the main bar to order for themselves, there wasn't much Logan could do. If he hadn't been forced into opening the bar sooner than he'd expected, he would've had time to find another qualified bartender or two. *Lesson learned, for sure.*

Logan stopped beside Brett and caught him scoping out a brunette wearing a tube top at least two sizes too small for her ample breasts. "Hey, Romeo, put your tongue back into your mouth before you step on it."

Brett grinned. "I think I just died and went to heaven."

Chuckling, Logan said, "Yeah? Well, then where do you want me to bury your body?"

"In her cleavage."

Logan shook his head at his buddy. Some men acted like such fools when it came to women. All they thought about was sex. Thank God he wasn't perverse like that.

Brett watched the woman join a group of her friends and then smirked. "So where do you want to be buried?"

Logan sighed. *Balls deep in your sister.*

Chapter Two

Valerie was at a loss for words. Not that it really mattered since Logan hadn't stuck around to hear any of them anyway. The jerk.

She hadn't predicted the sudden dismissal, nor had she expected him to storm off like he couldn't bear to look at her for another second. Did he really loathe her that much? And if so, what the hell had she done to deserve it?

Letting out a frustrated breath, she sank onto her stool. For a moment, she could have sworn she'd seen interest blazing in those dark brown eyes of his. But it was like he'd flipped a switch and then hightailed it out of there without looking back even once. And he'd been angry, as if he resented Brett for leaving him behind to "babysit" her.

God, she hated when they called it that.

Unlike Max, Valerie didn't need anyone to keep her out of trouble. Not Brett. And certainly not Logan. Besides, how could she get into any mischief when she only had eyes for one guy in the room and he wouldn't give her the time of day?

Valerie didn't get it. She was putting out plenty of sexually charged signals, but for some odd reason, Logan didn't seem to be picking up on them. Almost as if she'd flown under his radar completely undetected. God, she must be losing her touch or something.

No. That couldn't be it. She'd never before had a problem pinging other guys'...instruments. Maybe Logan just had a defective transmitter. But if that were true, what was with the heated look he'd given her? Had she misunderstood?

She didn't think so, but Logan had always been impossible to figure out. It wasn't like this was the first time she'd noticed an underlying male awareness to her sexuality while in his presence. Or was it possible that she had seen only what she'd wanted to see?

Valerie sighed.

Damn it. She'd worn this slinky dress for one reason: to knock his socks off...or his pants, whichever came first. Yet her plan to dangle herself in front of him, to prove once and for all that Logan Mathis wouldn't be able to resist her, hadn't worked at all. Not only had he resisted her, he'd flicked her aside like an unwelcomed ant at a picnic.

Was the man blind or what?

She thought she looked pretty damn good. No, actually she looked great. So what the hell was his problem? She knew damn well she'd caught his gaze sliding down the length of her dress more than once tonight. But for some reason, he'd seemed almost irritated that she had worn something so sexy and low-cut, as if—

Oh God!

It had been the same reaction her brother had had when he'd picked her up tonight and got a load of what she was wearing. Was that it? Was Logan thinking of her as some sort of adopted kid sister? *Eww. Gross.* Valerie couldn't—and didn't want to—look at Logan like a sibling. And she hoped like hell he wasn't thinking of her in those terms either.

But it would explain why he continued to treat her like a child though. Older brothers were notorious for that. *Oh yuck! Did I just refer to Logan as my brother? Kill me now.*

Aggravation percolated inside her, but she straightened her shoulders and held her head high. Whatever. If Logan wasn't interested in her, then there was nothing she could do about it. It was fine. Better than fine, actually. It was *his* loss. There were plenty of other men who were willing to date a fun, down-to-earth girl like her. She didn't need a guy like Logan to boost her ego, thank you very much. Her ego didn't have a damn thing wrong with it.

In fact, she wasn't going to waste another minute of her time on a guy who patted her on the head and told her to run along and play like a good girl. If he was stupid enough to let her get away, then so be it. *Good riddance.*

Annoyed with the whole situation, Valerie rose and headed out to find her friends. She weaved through the packed room, squeezing through tight spaces and ducking under elbows, until she neared the main bar on the opposite side of the room where the wooden counter ran almost the length of the entire wall. The two bartenders were taking order after order and working fast to fill them.

She didn't see her group of friends anywhere, but she

spotted Logan and Brett parked at the end of the bar. Ah, hell no. The last thing she wanted was to chance another run-in with either of them so she veered a quick right and circled behind a wall of men who unknowingly blocked her from view.

When she came out on the other side of the entourage of men, she stood about ten seats away from her original position at the bar. Valerie glanced around. Where the hell were Leah, Sam, and Max? She'd only been looking for them for a few minutes, but she was already tired of searching in the cramped room. The bar was jam-packed, the music was too loud, and the more the patrons drank, the rowdier they seemed to get.

Maybe she should just ask Brett to take her home.

Of course, that would mean facing Logan again. Valerie's gaze landed back on her brother, who was now sitting alone. Puzzled, she glanced around his vicinity until she found Logan behind the bar talking to a middle-aged bartender with a bald head, beady eyes, and tattooed sleeves.

She couldn't hear what they were saying, but it didn't take long to figure out that Logan was talking to Paul, the head bartender. Especially after Logan gestured to the man's black T-shirt with Bottoms Up's logo emblazoned on the front, said something in his ear, and then pointed at Brett, who held up a twenty-dollar bill.

Paul nodded, picked up a set of keys off the back counter, and motioned for Brett to follow him through a set of swinging doors that read EMPLOYEES ONLY. Logan started to trail after them but ended up getting sidetracked by the other bartender—a scrawny, older gentleman wearing a black leather vest and sporting a goatee—who was beating the crap out of a blender that didn't seem to be working properly.

Valerie gazed back at the swinging doors. With Logan temporarily detained, it was the perfect opportunity to ask her brother for a ride home without having to come face-to-face with Logan again. So she circled back around the large group of men blocking the path and picked her way through the crowded room until she made it to the swinging metal doors and pushed her way through.

The two men stood in front of a door halfway down the narrow hallway. As Paul unlocked the door, she overheard him telling her brother that the T-shirts were in a box on the back shelf and that he could grab one and change inside the storeroom. Brett handed the bartender the twenty-dollar bill and disappeared into the room.

As Paul closed the door behind Brett and turned to leave, Valerie began moving in his direction. But she'd barely taken two steps when Paul did something she hadn't expected. He pulled a brown wallet from the back pocket of his jeans and slid the money inside with all the coolness of someone who'd done something like that many times before.

Valerie froze, unable to believe what she'd just witnessed.

She would've normally given him the benefit of the doubt, especially since Paul was a stranger to her and all, but the moment his gaze lifted and connected with hers, she knew her first inclination had been an accurate one.

Paul jerked to a stop, his whole body stiffening, as he stared at her with an *oh fuck* expression, apparently realizing he'd been caught with his hand in the proverbial cookie jar. A few seconds ticked by before he recovered and tried to conceal his obvious guilt with a broad smile. "I think you're lost, honey. Employees only back here. The bathrooms are on the other side of the bar."

Maybe he thought hinting that he worked there would throw her off, but she wasn't about to let him get away with what he'd done. Not when he'd stolen money . . . and from Logan of all people. "I'm waiting for Brett."

He shrugged nonchalantly. "Never heard of him."

She nodded to the door behind him. "He's the guy in that room changing his shirt."

The color washed out of Paul's face, but he somehow managed to control the tempo of his voice. "I see. So you're another one of Logan's friends, huh?"

Um, not really. "Yes. So close we're practically family." *Ugh. Damn it, Val. Stop it with the family shit!*

"Good to know," Paul said with a grin, moving closer and stretching out his hand. "Any friend of Logan's is a friend of mine."

She stared at his offered hand but didn't accept it as her eyes lifted back to his. "I think I could do without a *friend* like you in my life."

The bald-headed bartender eyed her warily. "Why's that?"

She crossed her arms. "I saw what you did."

"Yeah? And what was that exactly?"

"You put Brett's money in your wallet."

The muscles in Paul's neck tensed, but he chuckled softly. "Oh, that? Well, I was just keeping it safe until I got back to the cash register. Didn't want to drop it, ya know?"

Valerie rolled her eyes. "As sticky as your fingers seem to be, I'm pretty sure you wouldn't have had that problem."

"Just what the hell's that supposed to mean?" Paul took another intimidating step toward her.

Uneasy, she glanced around. For a moment, she considered calling out for her brother, but she didn't want to alarm him. Especially since Brett had a tendency to punch first and ask questions later. *But seriously, what the hell was taking him so long?*

Paul continued to stare at her with beady eyes. "You trying to accuse me of something?"

"I'm not trying. I *am* accusing you of something," she said with a waning bravado. *Come on, Brett. Hurry up.*

The bartender advanced on her so Valerie stepped aside to let him pass. But he didn't continue straight ahead like she thought he would. Instead, he followed her movements until he had effectively backed her against the wall. The second she realized what he was doing, she tried to maneuver around him, but he flung his arm up to block her motion.

She flinched so hard that her teeth chattered together, and she accidentally bit the inside of her cheek. Anxiety swam through her veins while fear took a record nosedive straight to her gut. If he was trying to scare her, he was doing a damn good job of it.

When Paul placed both of his palms against the wall on either side of her body and leaned in, she flattened herself against the hard surface at her back to get as far away from him as she could. Unfortunately, it wasn't far enough. His hot, whiskey-fueled breath practically singed the split ends off her hair.

That's just great. Not only was Paul a thief, but he was a drunk one at that. And she doubted Logan knew anything about it, since she'd already heard him tell Brett earlier that he didn't drink on the job. It would only make sense that he wouldn't want his employees to either. "I wonder what Logan will say when I tell him that I caught you stealing his money and that you've been drinking on the clock."

Paul's mouth went slack. Then he narrowed his eyes in warning. "Darlin', you don't want to go there with me. I can get real nasty if someone starts spreading lies about me. Real nasty," he repeated, twirling a strand of her hair between his fingertips. "You remember that, honey, and we won't have any problems."

Although her stomach tightened and panic welled up inside her, she stood her ground. "Are you threatening me?"

He chuckled under his breath. "Now why would I do that to such a beautiful young woman?" His finger trailed leisurely across her collarbone.

She slapped his hand away. "Don't touch me, you jerk."

"Why? Afraid your boyfriend will get mad?" he asked, gesturing back to the closed storeroom door.

"Brett isn't my boyfriend."

"Good to know," Paul said, his gaze flickering with something sinister.

Valerie didn't like what she saw in his eyes. She needed to get out of there. Now. But as she tried to leave once more, Paul wrapped his arm around her waist and hauled her up against him and then pressed her into the wall to pin her in place.

She pushed her hand against his chest to keep him from leaning in to kiss her. "If you don't let me go, I'm going to scream. Then Brett's going to come out here and wipe the floor with your ass."

He hesitated a moment, then his gaze fell to her cleavage before lifting back to her mouth. "So you're a screamer, are you? Hmm, that could be fun." Then his thumb grazed the length of her jaw.

She wasn't sure what he was about to do, but she sure as hell wasn't going to just stand there and let him do it. Without a second thought, she reached down with her right hand and grasped his balls in a viselike grip. "This is your last warning. Let. Go." She squeezed harder just to show him she wasn't playing around.

He winced, and his hold on her immediately loosened. "You're going to pay for this, you bitch."

Her heart beat faster as dread trickled down her spine. If he managed to get away from her before Brett showed up, she would be in deep shit. He was much bigger than her and a hell of a lot meaner. So she shifted her right leg between his and was prepared to lift it into his balls if that happened.

But then she heard a door swing open and a male growl filled the air. She nearly cried out in relief. *Brett! Thank God.* She released her hold on Paul immediately, happy to remove her hand from any part of this disgusting man's anatomy.

The moment she freed him, Paul pushed away from her so fast and forcefully that she spun sideways with dizzying speed and had to grasp on to the wall to keep from sliding to the floor. But when she turned and opened her mouth to stop her brother from murdering the drunken bastard who'd been holding her captive in the hallway, she realized it wasn't Brett who had come to her rescue after all.

* * *

Logan had never been so pissed in his life.

The moment he'd walked in on Paul and Valerie, a red haze had fogged his vision and molten lava had bubbled in his veins. Just seeing their bodies pressed so tightly together up against the wall with her hand down below had sent Logan into a blind fury.

Paul quickly moved away from Valerie, who let out a long, slow breath and braced her hand against the wall, as if to steady her weak knees. *Christ.*

He glared at Paul. "What the hell is going on in here?"

"Nothing," the bartender answered gruffly.

Yeah, it looks like nothing all right. Asshole.

Logan threw his hands in the air. "Goddamn it. We've got a packed bar, and we're already shorthanded as it is. We don't have time for my head bartender to be...trying to score in the back room."

"Trying to score?" Valerie repeated, surprise registering in her voice. "I would hardly call that—"

"Stay out of it," Logan sneered, his lip curling in disgust. "I'll deal with you in a minute."

She blinked at him. "Deal with *me?*"

Good God. Is she deaf or something? Why the hell does she keep repeating everything I say? "Yeah, that's right. You heard me the first time, princess."

The pet name once again had her narrowing her eyes, but she shook her head. "Logan, I don't think you understand—"

"Damn it, Valerie! I don't need this crap right now. The POS system just went down, two kegs are empty, and one of the blenders isn't working. So excuse me if

I'm a little upset that my employee is hooking up with some random girl in the back room while he should be working."

Her eyes widened. "Some random girl?"

Jesus. Not again. "Well, I'm assuming the two of you don't know each other. Or maybe I'm wrong about that. Either way, I don't really give two shits."

She crossed her arms. "Yeah, that's always been your problem."

Logan wasn't sure what the hell that meant, but he wasn't going to worry about it right now. Valerie had always done what she could to gain his attention, and this time, he wasn't falling into the trap. He turned his attention back to Paul. "I don't pay you to fuck around with women on the clock, nor do I appreciate you doing so in my bar. Do that shit on your own time and at your own place, or you'll be looking for a new goddamn job."

"I don't have to put up with this," Paul spat out. "This job isn't fucking worth it. And neither is she," he said with a smirk, tossing Valerie a look.

Anger exploded through Logan, and he clenched his fists at his sides. "Say what you want about the job, but you watch how you're talking about her."

"Fuck both of you," Paul said, throwing the storeroom keys on the floor. "I quit." Then he stormed out, banging the swinging door against the wall as he left.

Logan ran his hands through his hair. "Well, great. That's just fucking great."

"What's great?" The deep voice echoed down the hallway.

Logan snapped his head up to see Brett exiting the storeroom. He was wearing a new bar T-shirt and had his soiled one draped over his right shoulder. "My head bartender just quit on me."

"Why?"

"Good question." Logan glared at Valerie before looking back at his buddy and sighing heavily. "Whatever. It doesn't matter. Do you know anything about bartending?"

Brett shook his head. "I can make a beer, but that's about it."

"The fact that you referred to it as 'making a beer' just told me all I need to know about your bartending abilities. Shit. Okay, do you think you could cover the floor for me while I jump behind the bar and pitch in?"

His buddy shrugged. "Yeah, sure. What do I need to do?"

"Just walk around the room and keep an eye on things. Check the bathrooms to make sure no one's in there vomiting, having sex, or trashing the place. Look around on the tables and floors for spills or broken glass, and then let the waitresses know if you spot any. And if you see anyone getting too rowdy, show them the door. Got it?"

"No problem. Anything for you, man." Brett squeezed Logan's shoulder then headed out the door, letting it swing back and forth on its hinges behind him.

Valerie stood there with a strange, unreadable expression on her face. It was as if she was contemplating something heavy, but then she finally said, "I can help too."

"I don't want or need *your* kind of help," Logan said, bending to swipe the storeroom keys from the floor and dangling them from his fingertips in front of her face. "I believe you've done enough already."

His harsh words made her visibly wince, and his stomach twisted in response. Damn it. He shouldn't feel guilty for snapping at her like that. Not when she deserved it.

Back in the day, Valerie had pulled all kinds of crazy stunts to draw attention to herself, and she'd always gotten away with it. It was about damn time someone finally taught her a lesson. So Logan did the only thing he could think of. He moved in the direction of the door to get the hell out of there before he did something idiotic...like apologize to her.

"Logan?" she whispered.

God. He didn't want to stop walking, but he couldn't help himself. It was as if the hallway were a black hole and Valerie was the gravitational pull inside it that held him firmly in place.

Fine. He just wouldn't look at her then. "What?" he muttered, not bothering to turn around.

"W-we need to talk about what just happened with Paul."

That comment not only had him glancing at her over his shoulder but shooting her a dirty look for even suggesting something so ludicrous. "Why? Like I need to hear all the sordid details?" He shook his head. "No, thanks. You keep 'em."

"God, you're such a stubborn asshole." She shook her head with disgust. "It wasn't what it looked like. I wasn't—"

"I don't care."

She scowled. "Yes, you've made that perfectly clear."

"What do you want from me, Valerie? I already told you I don't have time for this," he said, gritting his teeth.

"If you want to play games, do it elsewhere. I've got a bar to run."

"Games?"

Jesus. There she goes repeating what I say again. Like she's clueless to what I'm talking about. This time, Logan turned to face her with his whole body. If she wanted him to spell it out for her, then so be it. "Yeah, games. Like the one you play where you throw yourself into a guy's path and see how long he can hold out. You've been doing that shit for years. When the hell are you going to grow up?"

Not saying a word, Valerie stood there blinking at him while wearing the strangest expression on her reddening face. He'd never seen her get embarrassed by much so he didn't think that was it. Was she pissed? And if so, what the hell did *she* have to be pissed about? If it wasn't for her, he wouldn't have just lost his best bartender on the one night he needed him the most.

Okay, so maybe it wasn't *all* her fault. Logan had over-reacted after finding the two of them together. But damn it, seeing someone else touch something of his had blown a fuse in his brain and . . . *Wait. His? What the fuck?* Since when had Valerie ever been *his*? It wasn't like he had dibs on her or something. *Christ.*

As a young teenage girl, Valerie had always short-circuited his system, but the curvy blond goddess standing in front of him was apparently warping his feeble, testosterone-charged mind. It was as if she made him want to claim her luscious body and brand his name all over her every time he got near her. Something he needed to rectify immediately. In fact, starting right now.

Logan didn't wait to see if she would respond. Instead, he threw open the door and marched toward the main bar to give James a hand behind the bar. Lord knows he would need it with this unruly crowd, which was only growing louder and more demanding by the second.

Unfortunately, Logan had known from the beginning that opening Bottoms Up early was a bad idea, but it wasn't like he'd had much of a choice. If his mother would've told him about the foreclosure notice on her home *before* he'd signed all of the papers on the bar, he wouldn't have used all of his savings to buy the damn place to begin with. But since he had, his only way to help her now was to make Bottoms Up as profitable as he could, as fast as he could.

Or sit back and watch his mother lose everything.

Chapter Three

Valerie couldn't believe it.

Not only had Logan refused to listen to a word she said, but then he had the nerve to accuse her of playing games and thought it was *her* fault that his head bartender quit.

Maybe she should have made Logan hear her out from the beginning. But the accusatory things spewing out of his mouth in anger had hurt her. More than she cared to admit. And even when she pushed the hurt deep down inside of her and offered her assistance in his time of need, he'd once again cast her aside as if she were a child.

Valerie shook her head in disgust. *Whatever.*

Her heels clicked on the tile floor as she made her way over to the swinging doors and shoved her way through them. She hadn't noticed it while in the hallway, but the entire bar had grown considerably louder. She could still hear the bass of the rock music pumping out of the mounted speakers, but the singer's faint words were drowned out by the noise level of the crowd.

People yelled out drink orders and waved their money into the air, though it didn't seem to do any good. Other fed-up groups complained openly about the lousy service, which only seemed to rile up the calmer customers. Even the ones who already had their drinks were griping about how long it took to get them. Then Valerie noticed several people vacating their tables and heading for the exit.

If Logan doesn't do something soon, he's going to lose a lot more business.

Glancing around, Valerie found him behind the bar hitting buttons on the screen of the POS system. He must've finally got it running again because he fistpumped the air and spun toward the counter. Logan began rolling his sleeves farther up his well-toned forearms, which only punctuated the size of his large manly hands. Ones he immediately put to good use.

Logan began pitching in, slinging beers at a fast-paced rate and pouring shots like a champ. He obviously knew his way around a bar and had done this many times before. But when it came time to make a strawberry daiquiri, his efficiency went down the drain. Logan and the other bartender were apparently sharing the only working blender, which had them invading each other's workspace and slowing one another down.

Someone stepped up beside her. "Damn, it's a madhouse in here tonight."

Valerie glanced up into her brother's eyes and nodded. "Yeah, it is. And it's probably going to stay that way unless

Logan gets it under control. I told him I could help, but he doesn't want me to."

"You know he's not the type to ask for help, Val."

"He asked *you*."

Brett shrugged. "Yeah, but that's different."

She narrowed her eyes at the negative undertone. "Why? And if you say it's because I'm a female, I'm going to kick you in the shin."

He chuckled. "That's exactly what a girl would do. Guys don't kick each other in the shins...unless they're playing soccer."

"Don't make me call Mom and tell her what a chauvinistic pig you are."

"Retract the claws," he said with a chuckle. "You know I'm just playing around. I believe in women's rights and all that shit."

All that shit? Really? She sighed. "I'm being serious, Brett. I know how to make cocktails. Logan's short-handed and could use me behind the bar. At least until he finds another bartender."

Brett shook his head. "You don't want to work here. Besides, you already have a job at the bakery."

"What about the bakery?" Leah asked, approaching them from behind.

Valerie spun around. "There you are! I was looking for you earlier and couldn't find you. I thought you left without telling me."

"Nah, I was just on the dance floor with Sam. I got tired of stepping on his feet though so I told him to go play pool with Max for a while. Now what is this about the bakery? Did something happen?"

Valerie waved her hand through the air. "Oh, it's nothing.

The bakery is fine. Logan's head bartender quit on him, and he's already understaffed so I told him I could help out. At least temporarily."

Leah shrugged. "Sure, it's not a problem. I can change up our schedule so that you don't work any morning shifts on the nights you work here. No biggie."

Brett grimaced. "Valerie doesn't want to work here."

Funny how he keeps saying that. Valerie scoffed. "You mean *you* don't want me to work here," she corrected him, poking her finger into his chest.

He rubbed at the spot. "Well, yeah. That too. But you also can't inconvenience Leah with a last-minute schedule change. It's rude."

Yeah, like Brett has ever been concerned about being rude.

Leah shook her head. "It's actually not an inconvenience at all. Changing up the schedule would work better for me too. Sam and I have so many wedding details to finish up over the next few weeks, and his construction site is really hectic in the morning. Makes it harder for him to get away. Having him take off early in the afternoon to work on this stuff with me would be better. Perfect, really."

Valerie smiled. "See, Brett? It works for everyone."

"Yeah, I see that," he said, sounding almost disgruntled. Then his face broke into a wide grin. "Except for the guy who said he doesn't want your help. Remember him?"

Shit.

She chewed on her lip as she glanced over at Logan. He was making change for a customer while simultaneously wiping up a spill on the counter. Sweat beaded along his brow, and he looked every bit as frustrated as she felt. "We'll see about that," she told Brett and then stalked toward the bar.

Spouting apologies and excuse me's, Valerie quickly squeezed her way to the front of the counter, where Logan had lined up six beer bottles and was popping the metal caps off each of them. He glanced up, but the moment he locked eyes with her, he looked down and returned to his task. As if he planned to ignore her.

Valerie sighed inwardly. "Logan, I need to talk to you for a moment."

"I'm busy," he said, leaning away to pass out the beers he'd opened.

She waited until he righted himself so she wouldn't have to scream over the noisy crowd. "I know you are. But that's what I need to talk to you about. I can help you—"

"No." Logan put both hands on the counter and firmed his stance. "I've already told you I don't want your help."

She smirked. "You may not want it, but you *need* it."

"No, I don't." He turned away from her to hand the other bartender the money he'd received for the beers.

Though his stubbornness pissed her off, she wasn't going to take no for an answer. Valerie had always had a bit of a rebellious streak in her. The more someone told her she couldn't do something, the more she wanted to do it.

"I've already made arrangements with my other job. I can work here temporarily until you find someone to replace me."

"I said no."

Valerie blew out a hard breath. "Would you stop being unreasonable for just one second? I have some bar skills that could be put to good use. If nothing else, I could at least distract everyone and keep them from focusing on how long it's taking to get their drinks while you guys catch up on the orders."

Logan stopped what he was doing and leveled a sardonic gaze at her. "What are you going to do—dance on the bar?"

"Damn it, Logan. Just give me a chance to show you—"

"I said no. Now leave it alone. I've got work to do." A scuffle behind her had Logan leaping over the bar in order to break up two guys who were shoving each other.

Right there. *That* was the reason he needed her help. He might not like the solution she'd offered him, but it wasn't possible for him to manage Bottoms Up effectively while being stuck behind the bar serving drinks. On a slow night perhaps. But not with this many people vying for a bartender's attention. If only he'd listen to reason.

Valerie released a frustrated sound from deep within her throat. God. Why did he have to be so darn pigheaded?

A soft hand touched Valerie's shoulder, and she turned to see Leah frowning at her. "Sorry he's acting like that."

"You heard?"

"Yeah. But I'm sure it's nothing personal. I'm guessing Logan knows that Brett wouldn't want you working here and doesn't want to step on your brother's toes. Otherwise I don't see why he's so adamant to turn down the extra help. He obviously needs it."

As sad as it was, Leah was probably right. Brett had always hated Valerie hanging out in bars, even though she only did so with her friends. "God, this sucks. Brett ruins everything for me."

Leah shook her head. "Well, you can't blame it all on him. *You* are the one who puts up with him interfering in your life like he does."

"Yeah, but only because he's my brother."

"I have a brother, but I don't let him have a say in my life."

"But Ethan is your little brother. It's different with Brett. He's older than I am." Valerie didn't want to explain why she put up with Brett's behavior, but she felt like she needed to defend her brother to some degree. "And, well, something happened in the past that made him this way."

Leah squinted at her. "So that's the past. Aren't you an adult now?"

"Yes, but—"

"No buts. Every time my mom criticized me, you encouraged me to stand up to her. Yet here you are not taking your own advice. Come on, Val. When are you going to grow up and stop letting your older brother run your life?"

As disheartening as it was to hear someone else tell her to grow up, Valerie couldn't be upset with Leah. After all, she was right. Valerie wasn't the same awkward girl in pigtails who'd needed her brother to defend her honor on the playground after a boy decided to use her hair as horse reins. Nor was she the silly lovestruck teenager who'd cried into her pillow over the stupid guy who'd left town and never looked back.

Valerie was twenty-six now, which meant she was a grown, mature woman. A capable, intelligent adult who was able to handle her own affairs and make her own decisions. No matter what happened in the past, it was time to stand on her own two feet.

"You're right, Leah. Maybe I just needed to hear that it was okay to feel this way. Brett doesn't have to like what I do, and he shouldn't get a say in it. Not anymore anyway. The only three people that should be allowed to make decisions in my life are me, myself, and I." Right then, Valerie made a unanimous decision. "Even if Logan's mad at me right now, I know I'm the best person to help him out. So that's exactly what I'm going to do."

Leah held up a hand. "Wait a minute. But didn't Logan already say no?"

"Yeah. So?"

Leah must've seen determination flashing in Valerie's eyes because she grinned and said, "Um, Val... You aren't about to do what I think you're going to, are you?"

"Damn straight."

Every situation she'd ever been in that involved Logan Mathis had always ended badly. Chances were good that tonight probably wouldn't be any different. But she wanted Brett to see that his sister was much more than just a pretty face. Almost as much as she wanted to prove to Logan that she wasn't a princess. If she had to do something drastic to open the eyes of both of them, then so be it.

And with that, Valerie hiked her leg up onto the closest stool, climbed over the bar, and hit the ground running.

*   *   *

Logan wanted to beat his head against the nearest wall.

He'd barely gotten things settled down between the first two guys when another fight broke out a few tables away. Thankfully, Brett had been nearby at the time and managed to grab one of the men while Logan held firmly on to the other. Although no punches had been thrown, Logan knew it was only a matter of time. Alcohol and frustration were never a good combination, especially when it came to a bar full of ornery men. If he didn't get a handle on things soon though, he was going to have a full-blown riot on his hands.

They escorted both guys to the exit and asked Steve, the doorman, who was still checking IDs, to call them a taxi and keep an eye on the two men until their ride showed up. Logan didn't really expect any more problems out of them since it seemed showing them to the door had taken all the fun out of their fight.

With Brett on his heels, Logan went back inside to make sure no one else was about to throw down and cause another ruckus. Almost immediately, he noted that the crowd had simmered down considerably and that the noise level was now that of a regular nightclub. *Thank God.*

Breathing a sigh of relief, he gave his buddy a friendly slap on the back. "Thanks for helping me get those two clowns out of the bar. As rowdy as this crowd was, the last thing I needed was people to start brawling in here."

"No problem," Brett said, grinning. "I didn't mind. It's fun throwing people out."

Yeah, it had been kind of fun. Logan chuckled. "Reminds you of old times, doesn't it?"

"Yeah, except this time we were the ones doing the throwing instead of the other way around."

"Well, if you hadn't been such a little shit back in the day, we wouldn't have gotten tossed out of so many places. You know, you were a bad influence."

Brett laughed. "Me? Look who's talking. It was *you* who hustled that guy and his friends in that little pool hall we went to in South Padre all those years ago. If you hadn't gotten us into a fight, we wouldn't have spent the night in jail."

Yep. Logan remembered that night all too well. It was the night he'd decided to leave Granite, Texas, for good. "Okay, so that was my fault. I'll own that one." Then he elbowed Brett. "But the rest were all yours."

Brett barked out a deep laugh. "You wish."

Logan was just about to say something else when, out of nowhere, customers in the distance began whooping and hollering like crazy. He exchanged puzzled glances with Brett, and then gazed around the room, realizing that most of the cheers were coming from the people crammed up to the bar. But there were too many bodies in the way for him to see what the hell they were excited about.

For a moment, he hoped Paul had reconsidered his resignation and returned to help out. Then Logan remembered how Paul's body had been pressed tightly against Valerie's lush figure in the hallway. Right then and there, Logan decided that, if the bastard hadn't quit already, he would've fired him on the spot. The fucker.

"What the hell is going on at the bar?" Logan asked, trying to peer over the crowd.

Brett shook his head. "You're taller than me, dumbass. If you can't see, how the hell do you expect me to tell you what's going on over there?"

When another round of clapping sounded, Logan couldn't stand it any longer. Something was definitely happening, and he wanted to know what the hell it was.

"I'm going to go check it out. You coming?"

"Nah, you go ahead. I haven't checked the bathrooms yet. I'll catch up to you in a bit," Brett said, heading in the opposite direction.

Logan marched across the room, wedged himself into the crowd, and forced his way to the counter to see what the excitement was all about. But when he caught a glimpse of a blond-haired, blue-eyed rebel waltzing around behind his bar, Logan didn't see a damn thing to cheer about.

Goddamn it. What the hell is she doing?

Logan tried to move from his position, but the crowd had already closed in behind him and were packed together like a bunch of linebackers. There was no getting through. So he did the only thing he could. He called out Valerie's name and waved his arms to get her attention. Unfortunately, she was too far down the bar and couldn't seem to hear him over all the surrounding chatter.

Or maybe she was ignoring him? Because that definitely seemed like a likely scenario as well. Didn't matter though. When James passed by a moment later, Logan managed to snag his attention and nodded toward Valerie. "What the hell? You know only employees are allowed behind the bar."

The bartender held his hands up in surrender. "Hey, she said she was a friend of yours and that she was helping out. We definitely needed it so I thought you knew. Either way, it's not like I asked her to climb over the bar."

"She climbed over the..." Logan ran a frustrated hand over his face. "Damn it. She could have hurt herself. What the hell is she doing back there anyway?"

"Well, frankly, if you ask me, she's putting on quite the show."

"Show? What are you talking about?"

"From the moment she jumped back here, she's held a captive audience. The lady's damn good. She changed two kegs on the fly, fixed the blender, and has been making drinks faster than I can and with a hell of a lot more flair."

Logan rolled his eyes. "I'm not surprised. Valerie has always had a flair for the dramatic. But that doesn't mean she can—"

"No, not that kind of flair. I mean she's a flair bartender. You know, bar tricks. Extreme bartending. That sort of thing. A few minutes ago, I watched her balance two bottles with a pint glass on top, using only one hand. The crowd went nuts."

"That's what people were cheering about?"

"Yeah, among other things. Seems like she's a big hit with your customers."

Logan blew out a hard breath. That's just what he needed. For Valerie to be using his bar to show off and gather more attention for herself. And where the fuck had she learned that stuff anyway? Brett hadn't ever mentioned her working in a bar before. Then again, Logan had always avoided the topic of Valerie whenever Brett was around.

Logan watched closely as Valerie quickly lined up six shot glasses, flipping each in her hand before setting them down. Then she called out, "Who wants a free shot? Make some noise." The crowd went crazy.

Sonofabitch. "No wonder she's got everyone's attention. She's giving away drinks to the customers? I can't make money like that."

James shook his head. "I beg to differ. Those shots cost

three times more than the beer, and every time she gives out a few, she sells five times that amount. She's pacifying the natives *and* making you money while doing so." He nodded in Valerie's direction. "Here she goes. Just watch. It's entertaining as hell."

Logan couldn't believe he was going along with any of this, but he craned his neck to see what she was going to do. He could always strangle her afterward.

Valerie tossed the stainless steel Boston Shaker into the air with one hand and caught it behind her head with the other. Without hesitation, she flipped it up again and let it land on the back of her hand before spinning it once more and snatching it out of the air. Then she placed it on top of the rubber drip mat and tossed a scoop of ice inside.

From his side view, Logan couldn't see what kind of liquor she grabbed, but his eyes stayed glued on her as she juggled three bottles, then poured some of each into the tin shaker. Slapping a clear mixing glass on top, Valerie spun the entire canister upside down in her hand and shook the hell out of it. When she was done, she smacked her palm against the rim to crack the seal and went down the line, filling each shot glass with a creamy beige liquid. Then she began spraying each with a dollop of whipped cream.

Okay, so maybe that was pretty cool to watch. Valerie obviously had the charisma and focus of a professional bartender and clearly knew her way around behind a bar. But those fancy moves of hers were probably nothing more than parlor tricks. The real test was whether the drinks tasted like they were supposed to.

Logan nodded at the shots. "Are her drinks accurate?"

James snorted and said, "I'll let her clue you in on that." He headed down the bar, not stopping until he reached Valerie. He whispered something in her ear that caused her to grin sadistically, and then he took her place at the bar.

She lifted one of the shots from the counter and carried it back to Logan, setting it in front of him. "Bottoms up."

Logan eyed her warily. "What?"

"This is a test, right? You're wondering if I made the drink properly? Well, I can tell you that I did, but somehow I don't think that's going to satisfy your curiosity. The only way to know for sure is if you taste it. So go ahead."

"I already told you I don't drink on the clock."

Valerie shrugged. "I know, but one isn't going to kill you. Besides that, it's almost closing time, and you still need another bartender for tomorrow night." She smiled and lifted one haughty brow.

Damn it. She had him there.

He made it a habit never to drink on the job, but he needed to know whether she made the drink correctly. Because if she didn't, then she had no business being behind his bar in the first place.

Logan lifted the shot to his lips and threw it back in one gulp. The moment the creamy liquid hit his taste buds and slid down his throat, he nearly groaned out loud. *Christ. She's giving out fucking Orgasms.*

And damn good ones at that.

Unable to help himself, Logan let his mind wander and imagined lifting her onto the bar, sliding that tight skirt up her voluptuous thighs, and giving her an orgasm of her own. Then he would find out what other talents those magic hands of hers may hold.

God, I'm an ass for even thinking it.

Brett would kill him if he knew that Logan was having those kinds of dirty thoughts about his friend's sister. Remembering his oath to stay away from the girl who had grown into the sexy young woman in front of him, Logan strengthened his resolve. Looking at Valerie was the closest Logan was ever going to get. He knew that. It was just that his dick couldn't seem to comprehend the notion.

Yes, everyone in the place was mesmerized by her performance, including him. But that was just another perfectly good reason to stay far away from her. He couldn't hire Valerie. It would never work.

Pride shining in her eyes, she smiled at him from across the bar. "So what do you think?"

"I…uh…" God, he was pathetic. How the hell was he going to give her the bad news when she was looking at him like that?

The truth was, he would've hired her on the spot if she had been anyone else. Actually, if he were just thinking with the proper head, he would be smart enough not to let her slip through his fingers. But no. Instead, he was planning to ignore her skills in mixology, which meant he was screwing himself over and letting his cock run his business. But then he remembered something important.

It wasn't only *him* that he was screwing over. Shit.

Logan had only three weeks to come up with enough money to pay off the default balance on his mother's home or the bank would foreclose on it. He couldn't possibly let that happen when a solution to his problem was staring him right in the face.

A feeling of desperation came over him, and his stomach tightened in response.

Damn it. He didn't have a choice.

Valerie's drinks were dead on, his customers were happy, and his staff needed the extra help... at least until he could find someone qualified to replace her. Which would have to be soon. And by qualified, he was simply referring to someone he wasn't attracted to. Because he would let a bum off the streets take her place if that meant he didn't have to torture himself this way for the next few weeks.

He sighed. "Okay, you're hired."

A smile spread across her face. "Really?"

God. Deep down, he knew he was going to regret this decision. It was as if he'd opened a can of worms that he wouldn't be able to close later. But it was too late to do anything about it. *Or was it?*

"Yeah, really. But only if you can get Brett to agree to it."

Chapter Four

It was unfair.

Valerie had passed Logan's taste test with flying colors and earned her right to work at Bottoms Up, yet he still insisted that her brother have the final say. As if she couldn't possibly make her own choices. Then Logan had taken her place behind the bar with a smirk on his face, knowing damn well what Brett's answer would be.

And she knew too.

Well, she had news for both of them. She wasn't going to take this lying down. Or standing still, for that matter. Sweeping her gaze back and forth in search of her brother, Valerie navigated the room until she finally found him near the pool tables, where he was leaning on a rail and keeping an eye on the crowd from his position.

She marched right up to him and tugged on his sleeve. "I need to talk to you."

He grinned down at her. "Hey, sis, I've been looking for you. Where have you been?"

"I was tending bar...and kicking ass at it, I might add."

His smile melted. "What? I thought Logan told you that he didn't want your help?"

"Yeah, well, I changed his mind. In fact, he just hired me."

Brett gritted his teeth. "Damn it. I thought I made it perfectly clear to him that I didn't want you in his bar."

Valerie's eyes widened, and she felt like her head spun in a complete circle. "You did what?"

Not looking the least bit sheepish about it, Brett said, "Oh, calm down. I just told him that I didn't want you hanging out in here every night. And I don't know why you're so surprised. You know I don't like you going to bars."

She couldn't believe what she was hearing. "But *you* were the one who asked me to come tonight!"

He shrugged. "Yeah, because you were with *me*. But it's not like I can be here every night, and Logan doesn't have time to babysit you. He's got a bar to run."

There's that stupid word again. *Babysit.* "I've already told you a hundred times that I don't need someone to watch over me. I'm not a child. And for your information, I don't need your permission to work here either." *No matter what Logan says.*

"Damn it, Val," her brother growled. "Be reasonable."

She crossed her arms and glared at him. "I *am* being reasonable. Logan is understaffed and needs me to help him out."

"Well, he can find someone else."

"Like who? He hasn't lived here in years, and most of the friends he grew up with have already moved away. The only people he probably even knows in town are the two of us and his mother, and I seriously doubt her Bingo friends are going to be lining up to work here."

Brett rolled his eyes. "Very funny."

"Okay, fine. Then *you* get behind the bar and serve drinks to his customers."

"If I knew how, I would. But you know damn well that I don't."

"Exactly. But I *do* have some bartending skills, so that makes me Logan's last resort." *God, that sucks to hear out loud.*

Brett's suspicious eyes narrowed. "And just where did you get these so-called skills? Just because you've made drinks for us doesn't mean you know what you're doing at a bar. You've never worked in one before."

"No, but Dave taught me some great bartending tricks."

"Who the hell is Dave?"

Damn. Why did I have to open my big mouth?

"Dave was...someone I know that happened to be a bartender. He taught me some pretty cool moves before he moved away last year. He was just a friend." *Who also happened to be my ex.*

Valerie had dated Dave for only a short period of time, and she'd never mentioned anything about him to Brett. She didn't want her brother giving the poor guy the third degree. Dave was...sensitive and a bit scared of her brother. Besides, as far as she was concerned, the less Brett knew about her love life, the better.

Though Brett was still glaring at her, he must've decided to let the Dave information go. For now. "Well, that doesn't mean you need to work *here*."

Yeah, actually it did. She'd always wanted to work in a bar and thought she'd be great at it. But she also knew Brett would worry about her. Working for Logan was her best chance at being able to do what she wanted with Brett's approval. But either way, she wasn't going to let Brett ruin this for her. "You know, I thought Logan was your friend."

"What are you talking about? You know he is."

"Then why are you standing in the way of me trying to help someone who you *claim* is your friend? Don't you want me to do what I can for him? Isn't that what you do for friends?"

Hesitating, Brett lowered his head. "It's not that, Val. It's just . . . well, you're my sister."

"So?"

"So I can't protect you if I'm not here."

"Oh God. How many times do we have to go over this? I'm a big girl and can take care of myself."

From across the room, Logan hollered out last call.

Valerie glanced over at him and then back to Brett. "Don't you trust Logan? Do you really think he would let anything happen to me? I'm probably safer in this bar than I am at the bakery."

Brett's brows dropped low over his eyes. "Did something happen at the bakery that I should know about?"

Oh, jeez. "No. You're missing my point entirely." Valerie tossed back her head and stared at the ceiling in frustration before leveling a hard gaze at her brother. "Okay, enough is enough. I'm not going to keep arguing with you about this. You're just going to have to learn to deal with it. It's only a temporary position, and whether you like it or not, I'm going to work here until Logan finds someone to replace me."

Irritation flashed in Brett's eyes. "I don't like it."

"Well, that's just too damn bad."

Stunned, Brett blinked at her but didn't say anything. She had never spoken to him like that before and was pretty sure he didn't know how to respond to her blatant defiance. She almost felt bad for him. Almost. But he needed to finally face the fact that she didn't have to check in with him. He was her brother, not her damn parole officer. *Sheesh.*

Besides, this was her big chance. Not to get closer to Logan—although that was definitely a bonus—but to try the bar business on for size. Her full-time job at the bakery was a good one, but the truth was, Valerie was a night owl who hated getting up early. The only reason she'd even taken the job at the bakery was because her best friend, Leah, owned it so she knew Brett wouldn't have a conniption about it.

But she'd always had an affinity for the bar industry and thought bartending would be the perfect job for her. There weren't many places a girl could clock in broke and leave at the end of her shift with a wad of cash in her pocket from all the tips she'd earned. Well, unless that girl worked as a stripper.

Um, yeah. No thanks.

Valerie loved getting dolled up and hanging out in a nightclub environment, but she wasn't keen on the idea of taking off her clothes for a bunch of strangers. There was only one guy who she wanted to remove her clothes for, yet he didn't seem to have any interest in seeing her naked. The idiot.

Maybe she was narcissistic, but there was no way in hell she would admit that the only guy she'd ever wanted was the one guy she couldn't have.

Brett's grim mouth softened, and he released a long, slow breath. "Okay."

She lifted a brow. "Okay what?"

"I won't pitch a fit about you working here."

Valerie stared at him in shock, waiting for the punchline. "Well, not that it would've mattered if you did, but... what's the catch?"

"There's not one. You're right about one thing. Logan is not going to let anything happen to you. When I'm not here, I know he'll look out for you like I would. I mean, he's practically a second brother to you."

Ew. Did he really have to go there? "Um, yeah. Sure."

"But, Val, if you need me for anything..."

She smiled and lifted onto her tiptoes to kiss his cheek. "Don't worry, brother dear. I know where to find you."

"I'm serious. Anything at all, and I'll be there for you."

Valerie nodded. "You always have been." She glanced around the room, which had started to clear out. "Well, I guess I'll go give Logan the good news. You want to join me?"

"Nah, that's okay. I'm going to make another pass around the dance floor to make sure everything is good out here. It's not much, but it's the least I can do to make sure opening night ends well for him. He's had enough problems for one night."

"Okay. I'll see you in a bit." With that, Valerie moseyed over to the main bar wearing a smug grin. She couldn't wait to see Logan's face when she told him that Brett was okay with her working there. Well, maybe not *okay* with it, but he wasn't arguing about it anymore. That was progress, wasn't it?

Many of the customers had already vacated the premises, which made maneuvering toward the counter much easier. But as she approached Logan from behind, she heard him tell James, "I can't hire someone who has never worked in a bar before. I need someone with experience."

Valerie cringed. Crap. Was he talking about her?

She knew a thing or two about bars, but most of that experience came from dancing and drinking in them, not working behind them. A fact that Logan probably wasn't aware of when he'd hired her.

"That's okay," James replied with a shrug. "It was just a suggestion. My cousin is looking for a job, but he doesn't have any knowledge of the industry. If you get desperate enough, let me know and I'll send him in to fill out an application."

Logan nodded. "Will do."

Whew! Okay, so they hadn't been talking about her. Thank goodness. She couldn't think of anything better than spending her nights here, making all kinds of new drinks and entertaining the crowd with her natural flair for mixology. Not only was it fun, but she loved being the center of attention.

James slung a white bar towel over his shoulder. "Anyway, I'm going to close out my remaining tickets, clean up my station, and head home. I'll see ya tomorrow."

"Yeah. Tomorrow," Logan said, not sounding the least bit enthusiastic about a busy Saturday night crowd. He watched James walk away and then turned and almost immediately locked eyes with Valerie. "Back already, huh? I take it that it didn't go well for you with Brett?" He grinned.

Valerie smirked. "Actually, he said he was fine with it." Okay, maybe that's not exactly what he said. At least in so many words.

His smile collapsed. "Really?" He sounded more confused than relieved.

She crossed her arms and huffed out a breath. "If you don't believe me, you can ask him yourself."

"I wasn't saying I didn't believe you. I'm just a little…surprised, that's all. I thought for sure he would tell you no. But what do I know? Judging by all those expert moves of yours, you've clearly worked in a bar before."

Valerie could've corrected him. And maybe she should have. But the thought of losing her one real chance to work in a bar, and with Logan no less, had her keeping her mouth shut and her eye on the prize.

She might be asking for trouble, since her brother knew that she'd never worked in a bar before and might unintentionally out her, but she didn't see any other way around it. Besides, it wasn't her fault that Logan falsely assumed she had bartending experience, was it?

She smiled and steered the conversation in a different direction. "So when do I start?"

"I guess that's up to you. I know it's short notice and that you have another full-time job. I don't want to overload you."

Valerie waved her hand through the air dismissively. "It's fine. I've already spoken to Leah, and she said she would change the schedule at the bakery and take my morning shifts. I can be here any night you need me, for as long as you need me."

"Well, in that case, be here tomorrow by six o'clock. It's earlier than usual, but it would give us time to get you logged into the POS system, let you get acclimated, and set up your speed well before the crowd piles through the door."

"Okay, sounds good." *Yes! Nothing is going to stand in my way now.*

Logan started to walk away but stopped himself mid-stride. "Oh, and Valerie, be sure to bring in a copy of your TABC certification. I'll need it for my files."

Damn it.

* * *

The next day, Logan was awakened by a light tapping on his bedroom window. At first, he thought it might be a bird pecking at the glass so he ignored it. But when the tapping became louder, he groaned and rolled over to check his alarm clock on the nightstand. It was already past noon, but thankfully the blackout curtains covering the window blocked out the bright midday sun. Unfortunately, they couldn't block out persistent people with their annoying tapping fingers.

"Logan?" a woman's muffled voice rang out. "Are you awake?"

Oh. "I'm up, Mom. Go around to the front door. Give me just a second, and I'll let you in."

"Okay, dear."

Logan sat up and ran a hand through his unruly hair

before pulling on a pair of jeans and heading to the living room. He squinted in the bright room, allowing his eyes to adjust, as he unlocked the front door and swung it open.

His mother stood in the doorway, patting her light brown hair into place. She smiled and then moved past him, her flowery sundress swishing in her wake. "Sorry. I rang the doorbell, but you didn't answer. I didn't mean to wake you."

"Says the woman who knocked on my bedroom window." He gave her a teasing grin and shut the door. "What are you doing here so early anyway?"

"I wanted to hear how things went for you last night with the bar's grand opening. You were really starting to pack them in when I left."

Logan chuckled. "Mom, you left at eight o'clock. I think there were only thirty people in the bar at that point."

"That's not a lot? It seemed like a good amount to me."

He grinned. His mother had never been one for bars, and he was pretty sure she'd never stepped foot in one before. At least not until last night. And she'd only done so as a show of support...for her son. But he could tell it had made her uncomfortable being there, and he didn't blame her one bit for leaving early.

Logan hit the button on his coffeemaker and reached into the cabinet for two ceramic mugs. "We had a full house by ten. Standing room only. And the place stayed packed all the way up until closing time."

She gave him a genuine smile. "That's great, honey. I'm so proud of you. I have no doubt it's going to be a huge success."

He didn't know about that, but last night's figures were

definitely promising. Even with the couple of small hiccups they'd had, the numbers were still looking better than he'd expected. "I lost my head bartender last night. He quit on me in the middle of the shift, but thankfully I found a last-minute replacement." An annoyingly persistent, doesn't-take-no-for-an-answer replacement at that.

His mother gazed at him in confusion. "Um, is that a good thing?"

"Sure. Why wouldn't it be?" He turned to pour them each a cup of piping hot coffee.

"You tell me. You're the one scowling something fierce."

Logan hadn't realized he'd made a face, but knowing he was thinking about his newest bartender, he had no doubt his mother was telling the truth. Only Valerie Carmichael could get under his skin this much.

He passed his mom a steaming cup. "I was just thinking about the foreclosure notice on your house," he lied.

His mother shook her head. "Logan, I already told you that it's not your responsibility. I'll figure something out."

"And I already told you that I'm taking care of it. I don't want you worrying about it. I'm going to come up with the money to reinstate your loan, and then I'm going to make the rest of the payments until it's paid off. That way, you won't have to worry about it ever again."

Her eyes misted over, and she blinked rapidly, as if trying to force the tears back. "Son, I love you, and I appreciate that you want to help. But it's a lot of money to come up with in a short amount of time. I don't think anything is going to keep the bank from taking my house."

"I will," he said firmly. "You're not going to lose your house, I promise. I won't let it happen."

His mom sighed. "You're not going to do what I think, are you? Because if so, Logan, I can tell you right now that I would rather live in a ditch than to watch you go down that path again."

He looked straight into her eyes, hoping his sincerity would reassure her. "Mom, have I ever lied to you?"

"No."

"Well, I don't plan to start now. I made you a promise, and I'm going to keep it."

She smiled. "Good." Then she took a quick sip of her coffee. "I just don't think I could handle it. Not after what your father—"

Logan raised his hand to stop her. "You don't have to say any more. I know. And you don't need to worry about me either. Unlike Dad, I won't do anything to disappoint you."

He moved away from her and poured some coffee down his throat, letting the hot liquid sear it closed to keep the overwhelming guilt from spilling out. Because even though he *had* made her a promise and was doing everything he could at the bar to bring in enough money to help her out, there was no doubt in his mind that he would break the damn promise before he ever let his mom lose her home.

Chapter Five

Valerie arrived at Bottoms Up a few minutes early. Not only did she want to make a good impression, but her nerves were getting the best of her.

After Brett had dropped her off at home last night, she'd spent hours stressing out over the TABC certification that Logan had asked for—the one she didn't actually have—then spent the rest of her sleeping hours on the Texas Alcoholic Beverage Commission's website, researching how to obtain one.

Since it was only a two-hour class and the fee was relatively small, it shouldn't have been a hard problem to solve. But there were several issues. Big ones. The course was only held twice a month and the testing site was almost a three-hour drive away from Granite, Texas. Which meant she would need at least eight hours of free time to sneak off and take the class.

Unfortunately, free time wasn't something she was going to have a lot of now that she would be working two jobs. And that didn't even begin to cover the issue of the certificate having the date the course was taken plastered right on the front. Something Logan would surely notice.

So she was forced to come up with another plan. One that consisted of not taking the class at all and holding Logan off about the certificate for as long as possible. Chances were good that he would replace her before she had time to take the course. And it was just a temporary position anyway. Who was going to know?

Valerie hated the idea of lying to him, but she couldn't resist the idea of having him all to herself without her brother hovering between them. Brett worked throughout the week at the mechanic shop, and she doubted he would be able to spend his weeknights hanging out at the bar and watching her every move. Sure, there would be a bar full of other people around them, but she planned on keeping Logan's mind on her as much as possible. She wasn't about to lose the only real chance she'd ever had with him...even if she had to use false pretenses to keep from doing so.

Taking a deep breath, Valerie threw the bar door open and sashayed inside wearing a tight little black number with matching heels. Logan stood behind the counter going over a sheet of paper attached to a clipboard while a slow song, low and sexy, hummed from the speakers mounted on the wall above him.

As she crossed the room, her heels tapped a staccato tune on the tile floor and echoed in the empty bar, announcing her arrival. Logan raised his head, and his brooding brown eyes landed on her, darkening in color. *Hmm. Interesting.*

"You're early," he said, his voice sounding a bit strained. "None of the other employees have arrived yet."

So it was just the two of them? Alone? *Good.*

Valerie smiled. "Well, I thought it might be smart to get a head start on setting up my station and learning where everything is before the crowd arrives." Her right hand curled beneath her hair and slid a thick blond strand off her shoulder to show off her ample cleavage. "You don't mind, do you?"

Logan rested a hip casually against the opposite counter and shrugged nonchalantly. "It's fine. Since you're here early, you can fill out your paperwork." He pulled a couple of papers from beneath his clipboard and slid them across the bar in front of her. "Did you bring in the copy of your TABC certification? I still need that for my records."

Damn it. She knew he wasn't going to let that go so easily. "Um, no. I just moved and haven't unpacked yet. I'll have to find the box that it's in." Her stomach tightened. She didn't make it a habit to lie, but he'd backed her into a corner.

"Oh yeah. Brett mentioned you had moved into a new place recently. An apartment over the bakery, right?" He waited for her to nod in confirmation and then continued, "All right. Then bring the certificate in as soon as you find it. In the meantime, grab a chair somewhere and fill these out."

"Okay." Valerie slid onto the black stool in front of her, crossing her legs. She pulled a pen out of her purse, clicked it, and began to write her name in the first box.

"Uh, you're going to fill them out right here?"

She glanced up and smiled. "Yeah, is there a problem with that?"

Logan gazed around the room at all the empty tables and chairs, and the corners of his mouth pulled downward. "No, I guess not." Then he turned, putting his back to her, and began counting the liquor bottles lining the shelf behind the bar.

Valerie cocked her head to the side and arched one eyebrow. She wasn't sure why, but he clearly hadn't wanted her to sit near him. As if she were some pesky gnat flying too close to his open liquor bottles. Did he think she was going to disturb him or something? Because, if so, he would be absolutely right. She planned on disturbing the hell out of him as much as possible while working here. Just not necessarily while filling out paperwork.

She put her head down and got to work, finishing the forms in record time. "I'm done."

Logan glanced over the forms and then laid them down. "Looks good." He reached for a set of keys next to the POS terminal and tossed them on the bar in front of her. "These are the keys to the storeroom. You can find everything you need in there." Then, as if he were done talking to her, he went back to counting the bottles.

Puzzled, Valerie stared at the keys and then back at him. "Um, but aren't you going to show me around?"

Not bothering to turn around, Logan said, "I don't have time. I got here later than usual because I had a visitor show up at my house earlier. She kept me detained all afternoon, and I really need to get this inventory done before we open."

She? A woman had been at his house earlier? Valerie's heart sank. "Oh. Well, I thought maybe you would help me get acquainted with the place. You know, since you are my new boss and all."

He glanced over his shoulder. "If you have any questions, you can ask James. He'll be here soon. Besides, you've worked in a bar before so this isn't your first rodeo. You did just fine on your own last night. I'm sure you can manage to find your way around again."

"Yeah, but that was only the bar area. I haven't been to the storeroom yet."

Finally, he spun around to face her, his eyes narrowed. "I'm pretty sure you'll have no trouble finding it, princess. We both know you're already familiar with the employee hallway."

She cringed and bit her lip. "Logan, about that..."

He held up his palm to stop her from saying anything else. "You don't owe me an explanation, Valerie. It's not like it's any of my business anyway."

"Yeah, but—"

"I'm really busy. I have to get this inventory done before we get slammed tonight." He nudged the keys toward her. "Go ahead and get started. I'll send James to help you out when he gets here." Without waiting for her to respond, he lowered his head and started putting figures into a calculator.

Frustrated, Valerie snatched up the keys and headed through the swinging doors. She marched down the hallway until she stopped at the storeroom door. It took her only two tries before she found the right key. Then she shoved open the door, flipped on the lights, and headed inside what looked like an oversized walk-in closet.

A half-dozen kegs stood in formation on the right side of the room while a large, commercial-quality ice machine leaned against the wall on the left, humming quietly to itself. Huge wooden shelves lined the back wall, holding a substantial array of glass liquor bottles, bar equipment, a few office supplies, and a big cardboard box with a few black bar T-shirts spilling out over the sides.

Knowing damn well her messy brother had probably left the shirts in their current state, the first thing Valerie did was straighten them and fit them neatly back inside the box. Then she spent the next half hour memorizing the different types of liquor Logan kept in stock and even made mental notes to look up some drink recipes for the ones she wasn't familiar with.

When James finally showed up, they loaded their arms with supplies and headed toward the main bar, where Logan was still working on the inventory. James helped her stock her speed well, answered a few questions about their routine procedures, and showed her how to use the POS system. Since Leah's bakery was equipped with a similar one, it didn't require much training on her part. Thank goodness. Because Logan had been standing not even ten feet away and she was supposed to know what the hell she was doing.

They'd just finished the tutorial when the young bartender who'd made her drink the night before swept through the front door and rounded the bar. The moment he saw her behind the counter, he grinned wide. "New bartender?" he asked James.

"New bartender," James confirmed with a nod.

"Hi, I'm Valerie," she said, offering her hand.

"Derek," he said, taking her outstretched hand and shaking it gently. "I'm the slow one. But you probably know that already since I made your drink last night." He gave her a friendly wink. "I'm still learning."

Not wanting him to feel bad, she smiled warmly. "Aren't we all?"

The smile reached his eyes. "That's nice of you to say, but it's hardly true. I saw those awesome moves you had behind the bar last night. You're going to have to show me how to do that sometime."

"Sure, I'd be happy to."

Behind her, Logan cleared his throat. Loudly. "Will you guys excuse us for a minute? I need to speak to Valerie about something. Alone." Though he'd politely asked them to leave, his tone wasn't all that friendly.

Once the other two men made themselves scarce, she tilted her head back and glanced up at Logan. His dark gaze sent shivers running up her spine, but she fought the urge to take a step away from him. She wasn't sure why he looked like he was about to deliver some bad news, but she forced herself to smile anyway. "So what's up?"

"I hate to say this, especially since I know how you love fashionable attire, but you...uh, might want to consider wearing something a little different to work in the future."

She stared at him point blank and then glanced down at the minidress riding high on her bare thighs. She smoothed her hands down her sides and planted them on her hips. "You don't like my outfit?"

His gaze followed the same path as her hands. "Um, no. I mean, yes." Logan sighed and then shook his head, as if he were just as confused as she was. "Although I do think your brother is going to kill you if he sees you wearing that, I wasn't talking about your dress. I was referring to your feet. They're going to be sore after standing on those spikes for so many hours."

"Oh, these?" Valerie lifted one foot off the ground and pointed her toe, showcasing the sexy, three-inch skinny heels she'd worn.

"Yes, those. I think a pair of sneakers would probably be a better option. Less slippery that way too."

She smirked. There were so many racy things she could say to that, but instead she went with a bland, "It's okay. I think I can manage."

"If you say so, princess. Don't say I didn't warn you though." Then, without another word, he headed off across the room at a brisk pace.

Valerie let out an irritated sigh. Why did he always call her that? And what the hell was his problem anyway? It was bad enough that he hadn't wanted her to sit near him while filling out those forms and then he'd basically ignored her. And now he couldn't seem to get away from her fast enough. Weird.

His apparent lack of interest was ego-deflating, to say the least, but Valerie knew none of it was because of her. Couldn't be. She hadn't done anything to cause him to avoid her like this. At least nothing *he* knew about anyway.

But so much for thinking she would have Logan's undivided attention while working for him. Even when she had him alone, she didn't have his attention, undivided or otherwise.

* * *

Logan crossed the room as fast as he could.

Valerie was wearing another one of those tiny dresses that clung deliciously to her shapely figure, and it was all he could do to stifle the urge to reach down and rearrange himself. He should probably have his head examined for agreeing to let her work here while wearing shit like that.

Who knew it would be so hard. *Literally.*

He glanced back at her standing under the bar's relaxed lighting. She wore an innocent smile on her angelic face, but all those breathtaking curves and that dangerously high hemline forced all the blood to rush to his damn head. And he wasn't meaning the one on his shoulders.

If he'd had it his way, Valerie Carmichael wouldn't be allowed to wear anything less revealing than a potato sack. A long one. Because although she'd always been feminine as hell, in this barely there outfit, she looked like a walking version of a wet dream. One he never wanted to wake up from.

As if she'd known he was staring, her eyes darted in his direction, and a delighted smirk lifted her cheek. She'd always been a stunner, but over the years, she'd somehow perfected that flirtatious smile of hers. Like the blond she-devil knew lustful memories of her had filled his teenage spank bank on way too many occasions.

Even though it had been eight long years since he'd been this close to her, the sound of her loud, playful laughter and the soft, bell-like tone of her voice had always stuck with him. But now there was something even more intriguing about her.

He'd never met anyone who oozed sex appeal like Valerie did. It was as if a bright sexual aura hung permanently in the air around her and saturated his skin whenever he got near her. The kind of excruciating tension that started in the balls and drove men like him to the nearest bathroom to yank their dicks in order to establish some modicum of control.

Actually, sexy didn't even begin to describe her accurately. It was more like she was a work of art, and her gorgeous body was the canvas. One he'd happily paint over again and again using only his tongue. Take that, Leonardo da Vinci.

Logan let his gaze trail over her once more, appraising her voluptuous figure. Just the thought of how she would taste or the mere notion of him burrowing himself deep inside her swirled heat in his gut and had stale air backing up in his lungs. *Jesus. Get a grip already, man. She's off-limits.*

Yeah, that was no shit. He couldn't keep thinking about Valerie in that way. There weren't many guys Brett would trust to be alone with his little sister. In fact, Logan couldn't think of anyone else that would be considered safe enough to watch over her, which meant he was probably the only one. And that only made it even more important not to abuse the trust her brother had put in him.

Besides that, he couldn't stand around eye-fucking Valerie all night long. He had shit to do. There was only one way to make this easier on himself. As long as she was working here, he just wouldn't look at her anymore. That was simple enough, wasn't it? *Yeah, right. And I might as well stop breathing while I'm fucking at it.*

Maybe someday he'd be able to look at her without desperate need and fierce desire tying his gut into knots. But that day wasn't today. And chances were good it wouldn't be tomorrow either. But possibly after a few nights though...

Yeah. That might work. Once he spent a couple of non-stop evenings with her, he was bound to develop a thicker skin. Until then, he'd have to do everything in his power to keep her from getting under it.

Hunching his shoulders, Logan set out to find the waitresses, Sally and Trisha, to make sure they had everything they needed. Then he swept the entire bar with his eyes, checking that everything there was ready to go. Derek had already positioned himself at the side bar while James and Valerie stood behind the main counter eagerly awaiting customers.

Logan peered out the front door and gave Steve the nod to start checking IDs. An even bigger line had formed than last night and stretched around the side of the building. Damn. If business continued to be this good, Logan would have the money he needed to save his mother's house in no time.

Chapter Six

The initial rush had kept Valerie busy for over an hour, but she finally received a respite between customers. Good thing too because both of the waitresses were heading her way at the same time.

Trisha got there first and swept her brunette locks off her shoulders. "I need three Buds and two margaritas on the rocks."

"On it," Valerie said, pivoting away from her as she reached for the large margarita glasses with the stepped diameter.

She barely had time to salt the rims when Sally arrived and set down the tray she carried. "Hey, Valerie. Two Dos Equis with lime. And please tell me you know how to make a Nuclear Reactor...whatever the hell that is."

"Don't worry, I've got you covered," Valerie said with a grin. Well, technically Google and the cell phone in her back pocket had the waitress covered. Close enough.

Sally smiled. "Damn, you really know your stuff."

Valerie tossed some ice in the shaker. "Not really. I've just picked up a few things here and there." She winked at the waitress as she flipped a bottle of tequila up in the air and caught it upside down, letting it pour the correct number of ounces into the shaker below. Then she did the same with the triple sec and lime juice.

"Well, you're doing great."

"Thanks," Valerie said, her chest swelling with pride. "I'm just glad that I've been able to keep up with you girls. I've never seen anyone move so quickly." She topped off the silver shaker with a clear glass tumbler and spun the conjoined pieces in her hand, giving it a good, hard shake.

Trisha snorted. "That's not what I hear."

Valerie paused mid-shake. She wasn't sure what that meant and was almost afraid to ask, but her curiosity got the better of her. She smacked the side of the container to release the suction. "I'm not sure what you mean."

"I'm talking about Logan, you know...our boss. Rumor has it that he's got a reputation for being pretty fast with women. I figured you would know all about that."

Yeah, she'd heard the rumors years ago. But she'd hoped none of them were true. "Not really." Valerie poured the margaritas into the two salt-rimmed glasses, filling them to the brim. "Logan and I have never, um..."

"Oh no," Trisha said, leaning into the counter and lowering her voice. "I wasn't implying that you've ever done anything with the man. I wouldn't do that." A smile lifted her rosy cheeks. "He just told us last night that he had hired his best friend's little sister. I guess I assumed you might have had a front row seat to all the action since the two of you grew up together."

God. If the other employees only saw her as a tag-along after that short statement, then what hope did she have of Logan seeing her as something else? "Sorry. I can't really help you there. My brother is four years older than me so I didn't hang out with his friends much." *Only every chance I had.*

Hoping to let the conversation die a slow and painful death, Valerie busied herself by pulling three bottles of Bud from the beer cooler and setting them on the counter. Then she quickly flipped off the caps using her bottle opener and set all the drinks on Trisha's tray. "There you go."

But the waitress didn't leave. Instead, she nodded toward Logan standing at the opposite end of the bar, leaning in to whisper something to a pretty redhead wearing tight jeans and an olive green halter top. "Well, I hope for that poor girl's sake that he's not as fast in the bedroom."

Trisha and Sally giggled, but Valerie cringed. The last thing she wanted to do was think about Logan in a bedroom with a woman...at least one that wasn't her. *Thanks a lot for that mental image, Trisha.*

Sally shook her head furiously. "I can't imagine him being bad in bed. I mean, I just don't think it's possible. Not with that fine body of his. The man's built in all the right ways."

Oh, come on! Not her too.

Valerie sighed. She didn't want to listen to the waitresses moon over Logan, nor did she like the idea of watching him flirt with the redhead. So she did the only thing she could do and quickly changed the subject. "Sally, what did you say you needed again?"

The swooning waitress sighed, her gaze still on Logan. "One night with him would be good."

Trisha laughed, but Valerie pursed her lips together. *Seriously? Were they trying to torture her?* "No, I meant what drinks did you say you needed?"

"Oh," Sally said, coming out of her trance. "Two Dos Equis with lime, please. And wait a few minutes on that Nuclear Reactor. I want to make sure the guy still wants it first."

"Okay." Valerie opened two of the Mexican beers and stuffed a lime wedge into the tops of each before sliding them across the bar to her. "They're ready to go."

While Sally and Trisha ventured away to serve their customers, Valerie asked James to keep an eye on things and excused herself to go to the bathroom. She didn't really need to go, but she locked herself in the stall and pulled up Google on her cell phone to see how to make the drink Sally requested. After quickly reading up on it and memorizing the ingredients, Valerie washed her hands and headed back toward the bar. She hoped like hell the guy actually ordered one of these drinks from her because it looked like it would be a cool cocktail to make.

By the time she'd made it back to the bar, Sally had returned as well with a guy on her arm who looked to be in his mid-twenties and wearing a college jersey. "Hey, Val. This is the one who asked about the drink. He wants to watch you make it."

"Sure." When Sally walked away, Valerie gave the customer her friendliest smile. "You ready to get radioactive?"

"Definitely." He slid onto a stool and leaned on the bar with his elbows. "I was actually surprised to hear that you knew how to make a Nuclear Reactor."

Valerie picked up the metal tin and did a palm spin with it before setting it down with a clank and tossing a scoop of ice inside. "Oh yeah? Why is that?"

He watched her as she flipped the bottle of melon liqueur in the air and let the green liquid trickle down into the metal cup, and then he said, "Because I didn't know there was such a thing. I made the whole thing up."

Huh? Without adding any flair to her move, she poured some sweet and sour mix into the metal cup and eyed him warily. "I don't get it. Why would you do that?"

"Well, usually when a bartender doesn't know how to make a drink, they call the person who ordered it over to the bar to ask them what's in it." He smiled wide as his gaze slid over her chest. "Basically, it was supposed to be my one-way ticket over here, but you were too smart for my own good."

Oh, jeez. He was flirting with her. God, she must really be off her game tonight if she hadn't even seen that one coming. A bit of harmless flirtation came with the job, especially since a bartender's income was based mostly on tips, but that didn't mean she couldn't distract him in other ways.

To keep Casanova from staring at her boobs all night, Valerie reached for the next bottle and tossed it behind her back before catching it in her opposite hand.

"Impressive," he said, nodding.

She winked at him. "Oh, you haven't seen anything yet." Then she tipped the bottle of Everclear over into the shaker and grinned. After drinking this potent concoction, the poor dude would probably be seeing double.

Valerie shook the lime green mixture and strained it into a slender shot glass, which she then inserted into a short, wide tumbler that she held upside down. Then she flipped both over simultaneously, encapsulating the liquid inside the smaller container. After trickling in some lemon-lime soda and adding a splash of blue raspberry vodka and a touch of Blue Curaçao for color, she carefully set the cocktail in front of him. "That'll be eight dollars."

He handed her a ten-dollar bill. "Keep the change."

"Thanks."

She rang him up and threw the ones into the tip jar next to the register. He lifted the inner shot glass slowly, allowing the inner green fluid to flow out and mix into the blue moat surrounding it. He set the shot glass to the side, lifted the tumbler to his lips, and downed the whole thing in one swallow.

His eyes hardened into a sheet of glass, and he coughed. "Damn, that's toxic."

Valerie giggled. The funky cocktail looked and apparently tasted like hazardous waste. Still, maybe she should talk to Logan about making it one of their signature drinks. It was bound to be a big seller.

"I didn't catch your name," he said, holding out his palm. "I'm Ryan."

"Valerie," she said, sliding her hand into his.

His fingers stretched over hers and closed around them. "So, Valerie, what are you doing after work?"

She started to withdraw her hand, but he tightened his grip to keep it in place. "Well, I have to be at my other job by noon. So I'm going home and crawling into bed."

One of his brows lifted. "Alone?"

"Well, I, um…" She didn't necessarily want to announce to a strange man that she lived alone. Granite was a small town where most people knew each other, but she'd never seen this guy before.

A strong, well-muscled arm slid around her waist, yanking her free from Ryan's grip. "Actually, *I* was planning on putting her to bed tonight. Right, princess?"

The moment she heard the pet name pass over his lips, her spine straightened and her head snapped up. Her gaze landed directly on Logan's bitter glare, and she sucked in a hard breath, her mind reeling from the sudden burst of oxygen flooding her lungs.

Too stunned to speak, she stared at him in silence. Did he really just say what she thought he did?

Ryan verbalized his disappointment with a sigh. "Damn. I should've known you had a boyfriend lurking around here somewhere. You're too damn pretty to be single."

Though she didn't think he meant it as an insult to single women everywhere, Valerie couldn't stop her eyes from narrowing slightly. Maybe she was channeling her inner feminist, but she didn't particularly like this young guy's assumption that all single girls were ugly. It was the farthest thing from the truth. "Actually, there are plenty of beautiful women in this world who are single…by choice."

Logan's arm tightened protectively around her, intense heat emanating from his body. "She's just not one of them."

"I got it, man," Ryan said, swaying to his feet. "She's off the market." His words had begun to slur a little.

Valerie opened her mouth to say something, but Logan's

fingers dug into her side and a muscle twitched in his jaw. "That she is," he told the other guy. "But you're a handsome fellow. I'm sure you'll find someone else to procreate with."

She didn't know whether it was due to the amount of alcohol he'd consumed or the idea of having children, but Ryan's face sheeted white. "That's not quite what I had in mind for tonight," he said, chuckling a little.

"I didn't think so." An amused grin played on Logan's mouth. "Is there anything else we can get for you?"

"Nah, I'm good." He gazed over at Valerie with glossy eyes. "I'll be back in a little while to get another one of those drinks from you," he said, wearing a goofy, half-lit grin.

She nodded and watched him stumble away. The dude was clearly a lightweight. Unfortunately, she would have to cut him off after the next drink and call him a taxi. By morning, he would be in hangover city. *Safe travels, little buddy.*

Logan removed his hand from her waist and glared at her as if she'd done something wrong. "I need to talk to you in the back room. Now."

* * *

Logan waited for her in the hallway.

Arms crossed, he tapped his foot impatiently on the tile floor until she swung through the doors. Then he spun on her with flared nostrils. "Don't ever do that again," he growled out.

Valerie flinched at his sour tone. "Um, okay," she said. Then she squinted at him and scratched her forehead.

"But you might need to be a little more specific. Don't ever do *what* again?"

Was she kidding?

"If some drunk asshole is hitting on you, don't try to take care of him on your own. Next time, let me know immediately. That's what I'm here for."

"Don't you think you're overreacting a bit? It isn't like the guy was pawing me or something. I was perfectly fine."

"Yeah, well, then what do you call him grabbing your hand? I saw you trying to pull away from him and him not letting you go."

She rolled her eyes. "Oh, come on. It's not like I was trying all that hard to get my hand back. Trust me, if I really wanted him to let it go, he would have. Otherwise, I would have kicked him in the balls so hard, he would have been tasting them for a week."

Logan grinned. "Still fighting dirty, I see."

"You shouldn't be surprised. After all, you and Brett are the ones who taught me that move."

"That's because you were bound and determined to go to prom alone. All your friends had dates, and three boys had asked you to go with them, but as usual you were being stubborn. If your friends weren't around and something happened, you needed to know how to defend yourself."

Her eyes widened. "You remember that?"

"Who could forget it? You were wearing that sparkly blue dress with a slit up the side that had your brother seeing red for a week."

Valerie laughed. "He saw what I was wearing when I left the house. I'm pretty sure my mom had to tackle him to keep him from going after me and hauling me out of the prom over his shoulder." She paused and then tilted her head toward him. "My brother told you what I was wearing that night?"

"No, I saw you when I . . ." Logan let the words die on his tongue.

Her eyes focused directly on him. "You saw me that night? When? Where?"

Damn. He hoped she wouldn't catch his slip-up, but as usual, Valerie immediately latched on to it like a dog with a bone.

"You know, I don't really recall."

"Bullshit." She shook her head, not buying a word of it. "You're lying to me."

Logan sighed. "Okay, fine. I saw you from the high school parking lot."

Valerie blinked. "What? No, you didn't."

"I damn sure did." But leave it to Valerie to accuse him of lying when he had actually told the truth this time. Go figure.

"That doesn't make any sense. Why would you be in the school parking lot that night?"

"I was . . . in the area so I thought I'd stop by."

She rolled her eyes. "Granite is a small town, Logan. Everyone who lives here was in the area that night. What's the real reason? If Brett sent you to spy on me—"

"Whoa," he said, raising one hand in surrender. "He didn't, I swear. In fact, he doesn't even know I was there. And to be honest, I don't know why I drove through the parking lot that night. I guess I wanted to check up on you myself."

Valerie lowered her gaze to the floor, unwilling to look him in the eyes. "You said you saw me. Where was I?"

"You were sitting by yourself on a concrete bench outside of the high school's side entrance."

Her whole body tensed. "I, um...I didn't know you were there."

"That was kind of the point."

"Why didn't you say something?"

Logan shrugged a shoulder. "I figured you would be mad if you knew I was checking up on you. I know how much you hate it when Brett does it. And because I didn't want to embarrass you."

She flipped her hair, obviously unaware of the nervous gesture. "Why would I have been embarrassed?"

"Because you were crying."

"N-no, I wasn't." She rubbed absently at her arms as if a chill had slid down her back.

"Don't lie to me, Valerie. I had a good view of you that night. I know you were crying." But now, seeing her with her arms cradled together and her wide eyes filled with such vulnerability, he almost wished he had kept his big mouth shut. He ran his fingers through his thick hair and sighed. "I'm sorry. I shouldn't have said anything. It wasn't my place."

"It doesn't matter." She glanced toward the door. "I should get back to work," she said, taking a step.

"Valerie?"

She stopped in place and turned back to him. "Yeah?"

For once in his life, he needed her to tell him the truth. "Why were you crying that night?"

Her shoulder lifted. "What difference does it make?"

"I just...want to know what had you so upset." She

hesitated, as if she was going to make up some story that would satisfy his curiosity so he added, "The truth, please."

Valerie licked her lips nervously but stared directly into his eyes. "I was crying because I finally realized that the guy I wanted didn't want me back."

Don't do it. Don't ask her. "Who was the guy, Val?"

She didn't hesitate to answer. "You."

The verbal sucker punch slammed into Logan's gut with the same force as a champion boxer's fist, threatening to double him over. All those years ago, it had been *him*. He had been the one to put sadness in her crystal blue eyes and sent tears trailing down her cheeks.

Logan wasn't even sure how, why, or even what specific thing he'd done to upset her at the time, but in the end none of that really mattered. The useless knowledge wouldn't make it any less his fault. And really, why was he so surprised?

He knew better than to ask her that question. Hadn't he always suspected that he was somehow to blame? That night, he'd spent nearly an hour watching her sob and silently stewing in his own fucking guilt.

So yeah. Logan had known. He just never thought in a million years that she would confirm it. But now that she had, it only made him want to protect her more.

From him.

Chapter Seven

Valerie didn't get it.

After the intimate conversation in the hallway, she'd thought she made some progress with Logan. But four days had passed, and he'd done nothing but steer clear of her. If anything, now he seemed more distant than before.

Every time she tried to get close enough to talk to him, he dashed away to handle something important. Or so he'd said. Then he would make up some lame excuse as to why it took him so long to return and how he didn't have a minute to spare for her. It wasn't the usual reaction she got from men, and the whole situation grated on her last nerve.

When James had asked to cut out early last night, Valerie jumped at the chance to stay late and close up the bar for him. She'd planned to use that opportunity to corner Logan and force him into having another conversation while no one else was around. But Brett had showed up half an hour before closing and her chance to talk to Logan was flushed straight down the drain.

The only good thing that had come from staying late last night for James was that he'd promised to cover part of her shift today in return and had said she could come in late. Even still, she'd arrived early hoping to catch Logan alone and unaware. But that hope disintegrated when she saw him standing behind the bar with James while going over their inventory order.

She still had time to spare before her shift started though. So when she spotted Leah sitting at a small, round table watching Sam and Max shoot pool, she headed in her direction.

As she approached, Leah raised her head and smiled. "Hey, Val. How's the new job treating you?"

"It's fine," Valerie grumbled, plopping into the chair across from her friend.

"Well, that doesn't sound good. What's wrong?"

Valerie picked a piece of fuzz off her black slip-style dress. "Nothing. I'm fine. Actually, everything's fine. Couldn't be better."

"Come on, Valerie. I know we've both been busy lately, with me working on wedding plans and you working two jobs. But I've also known you long enough to know that when you say everything's fine, then it's the exact opposite of that. Spill it. What's going on?"

She sighed. "Nothing. It's..."

"Fine?" Leah asked with a smirk. Damn, that girl didn't give up easily. "Don't you like working here? You seemed to."

"No, it's not that. I do like working here. Actually, I love it. More than I ever thought I would."

Leah cocked her head. "Then is it Logan? How are things going with him?"

"They're not," Valerie said with a heavy sigh. "He spends most of his time avoiding me, and even when I do pin him down, he seems aggravated...like I'm bothering him or something. I think it's pretty much a lost cause."

"What? It's not like you to give up so easily on something you want."

"Yeah, well, I've wanted him for years, and it's gotten me nowhere. I don't know why I thought things would be different this time around. It's never been this hard for me to get a guy's attention before." She frowned. "I don't like it."

Leah grinned. "Now you know how I felt in the past."

Sam stepped over to take a swig of the beer he'd left on the table next to his fiancée. "Actually, sweetheart, you had my attention from the get-go." He winked at Leah. "I just didn't let you in on that little secret until later."

Leah rolled her eyes. "Well, if you had told me sooner, we could have avoided all that unnecessary drama with my family. I'm pretty sure they thought you needed medication to balance out your crazy mood swings."

"Unnecessary, my ass," Sam said with a laugh. "That was just plain fun. In fact, we should do it again sometime. How about at the wedding?"

"Um, no. With the way my diet is going, there's probably already going to be enough drama with me not fitting into my dress."

A muscle worked in Sam's jaw. "Baby, do you really think I give a damn what size your dress is? I've seen you naked more times than I can count." His eyes smoldered in Leah's direction. "It's not like you're going to be wearing it long anyway. The first chance I get to pull it off that beautiful body of yours, I'm taking it. Count on it."

Leah grinned. "There isn't a doubt in my mind." She waved him away from the table. "Now go play with Max and leave us girls alone to talk."

Sam leaned in, brushing his lips over Leah's. "Fine. But later tonight, I get *my* alone time with you...and I guarantee we won't be doing much talking." Then he kissed her again, letting his mouth linger over hers for much longer than was polite.

"Get a room," Max hollered, standing there with a pool stick in his hands.

Sam lifted his head and wiped the corner of his mouth. "What the hell do you think I'm trying to do?" He grinned at his woman and then crossed to the other side of the pool table to take his next shot.

A blush crept into Leah's cheeks. "Um, so what were we talking about?"

Valerie giggled. It was adorable that Sam could still fluster her like that. "Logan...and how uninterested he apparently is in me. Unlike your man."

Leah giggled. "Sam's interested in you?"

"What?" Valerie sat back and slapped a palm over her face. "Oh, God no. That's not what I meant. I was talking about *you*. He's definitely interested in you. Not me."

"I was just playing. I knew what you meant." Leah reached across the table and placed her hand on Valerie's. "You really need to calm down. He's got you so wound up that you are absolutely freaking out."

"Who? Sam?"

"See what I mean? You can't even follow the conversation. Just breathe already." Leah waited while Valerie took a calming breath. "Okay, now let's think about this rationally. Men normally flock to you so what's Logan's problem? Why would he not be interested?"

"Beats the hell out of me. I don't mean to sound arrogant, but I've never had this happen before. At least not with other guys."

"Are you sure he's not gay?"

Valerie laughed. "Are you trying to make me feel better?"

"Did it work?"

"Well, yeah. But I don't think he's gay. Otherwise he's so damn deep in that closet that he'll probably never find his way out."

Leah glanced over Valerie's left shoulder and furrowed her brow. "Um, does he have a girlfriend then?"

Well, that was something she hadn't even considered. Especially since he'd just moved back into town a few weeks ago. Then again, he had said a woman showed up at his place. "Not that I'm aware of. Why?"

Nodding toward the bar, Leah said, "Because there's a woman over there talking to him with her arms around his neck."

Valerie rotated in her seat to get a look and cringed. "Damn, I know her. She lives in the next town over, but she ordered a cake from me last month for her mom's birthday. That's Shirley Peterson."

"I take it that's a bad thing?"

"Well, no. I mean, not necessarily." When Leah lifted a brow, Valerie sighed. "Shirley is a local barfly who also hangs out at Rusty's Bucket. I don't know her all that well, but from what I hear, she's known around town for being fast, loose, and a bit wild in bed."

"Who told you that?"

"Um, actually, Shirley did," Valerie said with a smirk.

That made her friend chuckle. "No kidding? You mean that woman just came out and told you something like that about herself? That's a bit strange, don't you think?"

"Well, she was drinking at the time and was probably half-lit so maybe it's not really true. You never know about drunk people."

Leah bit her lip. "So do you think Logan is sleeping with her?"

Her heart lurched, igniting an ache deep in her chest. "The thought hadn't really crossed my mind...until now. Thanks for that."

"Sorry. I was just asking."

"Well, just because they're having a conversation doesn't mean they're having sex. Logan is the only person that Brett confides in. If talking equaled sexual relations, then my brother would be hiding out in that closet with him."

"True."

"I don't know. Maybe they're just friends."

Leah leaned back in her chair, grinning. "Logan and your brother?"

"Oh, don't start that again. You know who I'm talking about."

"Okay, okay. But I don't think it's likely that Logan and Shirley are just friends. At least not if she has it her way. I just saw her run her hands down his chest, and then she reached around and pinched his butt. I would say that's not very friend-like."

"Great," Valerie said, peeking over at them again.

Shirley had her hands curled around Logan's bicep, and though his face was slightly flushed, he was smiling at her. Valerie sighed. "Well, if that's the kind of woman he's into, then I have no chance in hell with him anyway."

"Why do you say that?"

"When I first started working here, I thought he only saw me as Brett's annoying kid sister. Now I think he thinks of me as more the spoiled princess type. I mean, that *is* what he calls me. But either way, he doesn't even see me as a grown woman."

"So show him the grown-up side of you."

"You're assuming I have one," Valerie said, grinning. "Look, I'm pretty confident in myself—in and out of the bedroom. But I'm not nearly as wild or sexually adventurous as Shirley seems to be. So if that's what Logan's looking for, then he's probably better off with her."

"I bet you're wilder in bed that you think. In fact…" Leah reached for her purse and pulled out a pen. She grabbed a bar napkin from a small stack on the table and passed both items toward Valerie. "Let's find out."

"Um, find out what, exactly?"

"How crazy in bed you are."

Valerie looked down at the pen and napkin. "I don't get it."

"We're going to play a game. I want you to list all the sexual acts that you would never do."

"What? No way!"

"Oh, come on. It's just for fun. I'm curious to see if your list will be shorter than mine."

"You did this already?"

Leah nodded. "I read about it in a magazine and thought it might be important to know these things up front about Sam. So we both did it. Our lists were pretty similar, but we surprised ourselves on a few things. You might do the same."

Valerie smirked. "I bet having sex in a bakery wasn't on your list, was it?"

A pale shade of pink invaded Leah's cheeks once again, and she glanced over at Sam. "Damn it, Valerie. I'm never telling you anything else. Now start writing."

She lifted the pen but stared down at the blank page in front of her. "This is stupid. I can't think of anything to put down."

"Come on, Val. The first few are the easiest ones." She paused thoughtfully. "Okay, for instance, would you have sex in a public place?"

"Are you kidding? God no. I would die if I got arrested for indecent exposure. And chances are good that Brett would be the one to kill me...after the little rat bastard tells my mother what I did."

"Okay, so there you go. I gave you the first one. I'm sure you can think of a few more sexual things you wouldn't want to ever do."

Valerie wrote *public sex* at the top of the page and almost instantly thought of two more things to add below it. She grinned. Okay, maybe this wouldn't be as hard as she thought. "I added *bondage* and *dirty talking* to the list."

Leah's eyebrow rose. "Really? But those seem so tame."

"I know, but I'm not very good at talking dirty. At least not while having sex. Weird things pop out of my mouth, and then I feel stupid afterward. And the idea of someone tying me up and having that much control over me is terrifying."

"Okay, what else then?"

"Well, there is another I can add. Promise you won't laugh?" She waited for Leah to nod, wrote something down, and turned the napkin around for her to read it.

Leah bit her lip, but a giggle slipped past anyway. "Any particular reason you don't like that one?"

"I don't know. Maybe I've seen *Sleepless in Seattle* too many times and don't want to pull a Meg Ryan. Besides this is almost the same as having public sex, which I've already added to the list. I don't see what would be so fun about getting fingerbanged in a movie theater anyway. I'm fine with having my orgasms in my bedroom, thank you very much."

Leah laughed. "I should probably ask Sam if he wants to go to the movies when we leave here." She waggled her eyebrows. "I bet he'd be all for it."

"That's because the two of you are perverts."

Leah shoved the napkin back to her and motioned for her to keep writing.

After a few minutes of deep thinking, Valerie added *spanking*, *indecent proposals*, *stripping*, and *anal sex* to her list. Then she added *glory holes* and grossed herself out enough to put an end to the dumb game they were playing. "Okay, I'm done. All I'm doing is depressing myself more."

"Aw, I'm sorry, Val. You know, maybe Logan just doesn't know you're interested in him."

"Oh, he knows. Actually, I'm sure everyone here knows by now. I've been flaunting myself in front of him for days now, but he's barely flinched."

"Then he's an idiot. But he's a man so you can't really blame him for that one."

Sam's head poked out from behind the beer light hanging over the pool table. "Hey! I heard that."

Leah giggled. "Sorry, honey. I'll whisper my insults next time."

"That's better," he said with a wink.

God, they were too cute together. Why couldn't she have that same kind of awesome relationship too? Valerie lowered her head. "The only thing I can come up with is that maybe Logan is worried about Brett finding out. I mean, I am being pretty obvious about my attraction to him."

"Well, it can't be too damn obvious. You've felt this way about Logan for years, and Brett still doesn't have any idea."

Valerie grinned. "Okay, that's true."

"Then again, your brother also thinks that every guy who says a simple hello to you is trying to get into your pants. So obviously, he sees only what he wants to see. Maybe the mere idea of you and Logan is out of the range of possibilities in his mind. Like he's totally blind to it or something."

"You think?"

"It's possible. But that doesn't mean he won't eventually figure it out though. And knowing Brett, he's going to go through the roof when he does."

"Doesn't matter. It's never going to happen anyway." She glanced across the room at Logan, who was now sitting at the bar alone. "Okay, enough of this," she said, crumpling up the napkin as she rose to her feet. "My shift is about to start, and I still have to get a couple of bottles from the storeroom before I can start working. If you're still here in a little while, I'll stop by and chat more with you guys."

"We'll be here for a bit. Actually, I'll come up to the bar and grab our next round. That way you can throw some bottles around and wow me with your brilliance."

Valerie sighed. "Well, at least I'm wowing somebody with something."

Leah's laugh echoed behind Valerie as she took off across the room. She stopped behind the bar long enough to see which liquors she needed to restock. James nodded at her, acknowledging her presence though he was busy helping a customer at the end of the bar. Logan, however, never looked up from his inventory list.

They were already starting to get busier as more people wandered through the door and took up residence at several tables. Nothing James couldn't handle on his own. At least for now. Once the crowd multiplied and started to grow restless, it would take two bartenders to keep up with the demand.

After quickly checking her speed well, Valerie snatched up the keys to the storeroom and realized she was still holding the crumpled bar napkin in her hand. *Stupid-ass list.* She didn't need to write down sexual things she was never going to do. That was about as pointless as writing out a grocery list of things you never planned to buy.

And she really didn't need to come up with excuses as to why Logan might not be interested in her. He hadn't so much as spoken a word to her although she'd already passed by him twice. He was doing a good job of demonstrating his disinterest all on his own. So much for getting him to notice her.

But she'd had enough of feeling sorry for herself. If Logan didn't realize what a great thing he was missing out on, then screw him. There were plenty of men who would stumble over each other to get a chance to date her. She didn't need Logan to make her feel like the sexy, capable woman she knew herself to be.

The noise level in the bar rose to a new level, and Valerie glanced up to see more people entering through the front door. Crap. She needed to hurry and get those bottles before James had a maddening rush on his hands.

But she didn't want to give Logan the satisfaction of knowing that she'd seen him sitting there while actively ignoring her. So as she sashayed past him once again, she tossed the wadded-up napkin into the trash while in motion and kept her focus straight ahead.

He wasn't the only one who could play that game.

* * *

Logan tried to keep his eyes to himself but failed miserably. As Valerie made her way past him, he glanced at her rear and watched it sway from side to side. She had a remarkable ass on her. One he would love to get his hands on.

But as she passed the trashcan, she tossed a wad of paper into it that bounced off the rim and landed directly on the floor behind her. Without bothering to stop to pick it up, she continued on her way through the swinging doors.

Oh, sure. I'll get it for you. He rolled his eyes as he got up and rounded the counter. He knew he'd pissed her off by avoiding her for the past few days, but leaving something on the floor for him to pick up was just plain childish.

Logan lifted the balled-up napkin from the floor and started to throw it away, but a word at the top of the napkin caught his attention. *Pubic? What the hell?* He took a cursory glance around to make sure no one was paying attention and then peeled back an overlapping corner of the tiny napkin.

Pubic...six? *What the fuck does that mean?*

God, her handwriting was terrible. Calling it chicken scratch would definitely have been a compliment. And a lie. The symbols she had written looked more like ancient hieroglyphics from some lost civilization.

Though he knew it was wrong to read something that wasn't his, curiosity got the better of him, and he couldn't stop himself from unfolding it and straightening the napkin out so he could see the rest of the words.

But after reading the next few lines, which were written a little more clearly, he blinked. Dirty talk and bondage? Okay, so pubic six, dirty talk, and bondage? Wait, no. There was an *L* in the first word. And the more he studied the second one, he realized the middle letter was a weirdly shaped *E*.

Okay, so public sex, dirty talk, and bondage? Yeah, that made way more sense.

No, wait. Actually it didn't. Logan turned the napkin back and forth in his hand. *What the hell is this thing?*

At first, he thought it might be a grocery list or something. But after reading a little farther down, he'd quickly realized this was not a list of things you could get at the local Food Mart. Unless, of course, it was run by a dominatrix.

It looked more like a list of...sexual fantasies?

Christ. Really, Valerie?

He should've expected her to pull something crazy like this. Not only had Valerie always been impulsive, but she was always coming up with little stunts to get him to sit up and pay attention. And sadly, most of them worked.

He had to give it to her though. This was definitely the most creative one she'd come up with. While public sex could suggest almost anything, there was no mistaking what the hell she wanted with bondage and dirty talk.

That delicious mouth of hers held a slew of unspoken promises for a man, but she wouldn't need to say anything to turn him on. Hell, she could just show up naked. The thought alone made his dick harden against the seam of his jeans.

Logan ignored the ache in his pants and lifted the list to continue on. Maybe it was a foolish thing to do since she was obviously baiting him, but after getting a sneak peek of her naughty little list, he couldn't stop himself from stepping into her trap. Like it or not, the only way that napkin was leaving his hand before he finished reading it was by amputation.

As his fingers moved down the list and found the next item, a ball of heat ignited in his groin. She wanted to have an orgasm in a movie theater and try anal sex? *Fuck.* He closed his eyes, breathing slowly through his open mouth in order to tamp down the flames licking at his balls. *Damn it, this woman is going to be the death of me.*

Moving on down the list, he saw a few that were more interesting than erotic. Electricity sizzled under his skin, and an aching tension settled into the base of his rock-hard cock. Without a doubt, he was going to be in pain the rest of the night, but if you asked him, it would be worth it.

Until his eyes fell on a word that had him holding his breath. *Nuh-uh. No way. She's got to be kidding if she thinks she's going to participate in an orgy.*

A vein throbbed in his temple, and a bead of sweat formed on his brow. He didn't know what she was thinking by adding that one to the list, but it wasn't going to happen. Not on his watch. Logan wasn't normally such a prude, but he damn sure was starting to feel like one.

Then Logan read the last item on the list and braced himself against the counter while sucking in a gasping breath. Okay, now she was fucking delusional. Because if she thought for one second that he would allow her to go to a glory hole, then she had another think coming.

At the thought, fire lit through his veins, and a raging inferno coursed through him that had absolutely nothing to do with his libido. If Valerie wanted a reaction from him, then that was exactly what he would give her.

Logan stormed in the direction of the back room to give her the verbal spanking of her life...though he doubted it was what she had in mind when she added that one to her list.

The storeroom door was wide open so he stepped just inside and glanced around. Valerie stood facing the wall in the back of the room with that fine ass of hers pointed in the direction of the door. As if she'd fucking planned it.

Rock music coursed in the background as he waited for her to turn around and say something, anything. But instead, she lifted herself up on her tiptoes, her short dress rising in the back as she reached for a bottle of premium whiskey on the top shelf. Pissed that she was ignoring his presence, Logan slammed the metal storeroom door shut.

She startled and fumbled the bottle in her hand before dropping it to the floor. A crash sounded, and glass shattered, scattering across the tile. "Damn it, Logan! What the hell did you do that for? You scared the shit out of me."

"Good."

Valerie cocked her head and gazed at him warily. "What's wrong?"

So that's the way she wanted to play this? Really? "I know what you did," he said, slowly stalking toward her.

For a moment, she stilled and stared at him in silence. Then she said, "Oh yeah? And what's that?"

But her hesitant smile and the panic flashing in her eyes spoke volumes. Whether she wanted to admit it or not, she knew exactly what he was talking about. And sadly, she didn't even have the decency to look ashamed or remotely embarrassed by any of it.

"Goddamn it. Don't play dumb. You know what I'm referring to."

Not bothering to deny it, Valerie offered him an exaggerated eye roll. "Look, I don't know what your problem is—"

He stopped in front of her. "You. Right now my problem is you."

She shrugged as if she didn't give a shit. "So what else is new? But if you'll excuse me, I have a mess to clean up now." She took a step away from him and bent down to assess the damage as her dress tightened across her rear end.

Logan's gaze slid over her ass cheeks, and his palm twitched. "You might want to think twice about turning your backside to me."

She glanced back at him. "Are you threatening me?"

"You're damn straight I am. I have a good mind to bend you over my knee right now. Might be wise for you not to tempt me."

With narrowed eyes, Valerie rose to her full height and shifted her body to face him directly. Then she did something he couldn't believe. She gave him a one-finger salute. "That's what I think about your threat."

Losing the last thread on his control, Logan grabbed her by the arms and pulled her toward him. So close he could smell the sugared vanilla perfume wafting from the erratic pulse in her neck.

Her eyes widened. "W-what are you doing?"

His fingers threaded into her silky hair, tilting her face up to his. "Making damn sure you don't wake up next to someone whose name you don't remember."

Then his mouth was on hers.

Chapter Eight

Valerie didn't know what the hell had come over him.

Without any warning, Logan had charged into the storeroom with a volatile look on his face and a reckless glimmer in his eyes. She'd almost immediately felt the tension emanating from him, but it wasn't until he stalked toward her like a jungle cat ready to pounce that a chill had skidded up her spine.

The blur of events had happened so fast that she barely remembered what the hell had set him off. It wasn't like she'd meant to break one of his more expensive bottles of imported whiskey. But damn. If that was all it had taken to gain his attention, she should've knocked down the entire shelf days ago.

Because that was the only sensible explanation as to why his lips were suddenly on hers. And frankly, it was about damn time.

Valerie didn't hesitate. She met his mouth with all the

enthusiasm of a stranded woman in the desert who was taking her first drink in days. The hot, openmouthed kiss warmed her blood and sent electricity sizzling beneath her skin. Desire burned through her at the speed of light, and she whimpered softly into his mouth.

A husky and very male groan tore from Logan's throat. His muscled arms banded around her, drawing her closer, and her body responded automatically by arching into his. He slanted his demanding mouth more firmly over hers, his tongue delving deep. She hummed with pleasure as she memorized the way his lips felt on hers and savored his unique flavor—cool mint and something that could only be described as sin.

Logan slid his knee between her legs and twisted his fingers into her blond hair, angling her head to the side as his lips blazed a trail down her neck. With his free hand, he quickly swept the slim strap of her dress down her arm and gently sank his teeth into the sensitive skin on her left shoulder.

Her breath hitched.

Somehow she'd always known it would be like this with him. Possessive. Manic. Aggressive. Her fantasies hadn't even come close to the real thing. But just when she thought he was going to make her dreams a reality, James's voice echoed from the hallway.

She tensed, sucking in a deep breath, as Logan released her and immediately backed away. Loud rock music blasted from the bar's sound system, drowning out most of what James said, but it sounded like he was talking to a woman. Trisha perhaps?

Wordlessly, Logan and Valerie stared at the storeroom door, both apparently waiting for the inevitable. But then

James fell silent on the other side of the door. After a minute passed and the door didn't open, Valerie breathed out a sigh of relief. "Man, that was a close one."

She stepped toward Logan and twined her arms tightly around his neck as she skimmed her lips over his. "Now where were we?"

Logan grasped her forearms and lifted his head. "No. We need to stop."

What? Oh, hell no. There was no way she was putting an end to something between them that had barely gotten started.

Rubbing desperately against him, Valerie rose onto her toes and captured his lips with hers. But with the way he stiffened reflexively, she might as well have been making out with a statue. She could almost hear the gears grinding in his head as his brain worked against her. "Don't think," she whispered, kissing him again. "Just feel."

"Valerie…" He sighed, and his fingers dug into her forearms, as if he were about to stop her.

So she bit him. Her teeth latched on to his lip with one quick, sharp nip. Not hard enough to hurt him, but with enough pressure to get his attention. And boy, did it ever!

Nostrils flaring, Logan grasped her waist and spun them around with dizzying speed until her back landed with a soft thud against the ice machine. The cold from the metal door instantly bit into her back, but she didn't care. Her heart stopped as his dark, narrowed eyes zeroed in on her. She breathed in his warm scent. Dangerously sexy and so utterly male.

Then he was on her.

His mouth took hers with a searing kiss that was anything but gentle as he quickly peeled her dress down, letting the stretchy fabric fall away from her breasts. Hot hands roamed over her, plucking at her hard nipples. Logan lifted his head slightly, and one strong eyebrow rose. "So the princess likes to bite, does she?"

"Y-yes," she said shakily, unable to concentrate on his words.

He nodded. "Good. Now it's my turn." With that, he lowered his head, took one rigid bud into his mouth, and nipped it gently, sending shock waves all the way down to her core.

Valerie squirmed, but he cupped her breasts with large hands and held her steady as he continued the onslaught. His mouth switched back and forth, carefully tweaking her nipples with his teeth before soothing the ache with his tongue, the exquisite combination driving her wild with need. Without warning, her entire body convulsed against him.

"Whoa, easy," he said, bringing his mouth back to hers and ravaging her all over again. Even when he pulled back to look at her, his persistent hands continued to move over her breasts, his fingers pinching lightly in all the right places. "Fuck. You don't know how good you feel right now."

Wanna bet? But it wasn't enough. Nowhere close to being enough. She wanted more, and she wanted it now. Valerie thrust her hips forward and rubbed her pelvis against the bulging ridge she found in the front of his jeans. Thick and long, and hard as steel. "I need you, Logan. Please..."

Without hesitation, he angled his body more into her so his cock rode up against her cleft. Right where she wanted him most. She moaned something encouraging although she was sure her words weren't all that intelligible. But his eyes glittered with awareness. He knew exactly what she wanted and where... and the smirk he wore held promises to deliver. "You want me, baby?"

"Yes."

"You want to feel my dick throbbing inside you?"

His words dampened her thighs instantly. "God yes," she gasped out.

He rubbed his thumb over her bottom lip and grinned. "Then be a good girl and take off your panties."

Holy hell. She'd never known Logan Mathis had such a dirty mouth on him. But his commanding tone sent heat swirling through her, coiling into a tight ball. One that threatened to burst wide open at the thought of him being inside her. But there was something bothering her that she hadn't thought of before.

He was her boss, damn it. Her very sexually aroused boss with a hard cock in his fucking pants that he was going to use on her... and, dear God, she wanted him to. But she also had a feeling that, by having sex with him, she would be putting her job at the bar in jeopardy.

Even if it was only a temporary position, the last thing she wanted to do was get fired from a job that she loved so much. And screwing the boss would probably guarantee it. After all, it wasn't like any of this was in her job description. *Otherwise, I might've showed up to work a little more prepared.*

Logan leaned closer, gaining her attention. "Maybe you didn't hear me the first time," Logan growled, his impatience showing plainly on his face. "Take. Off. Your. Panties."

Her heart hammered against her rib cage as chills raced

over her body. God, she couldn't breathe. The rough hands on her breasts. The authority in his sexy voice. The way his eyes smoldered and darkened with desire as he looked at her. All of it combined knocked every bit of oxygen from her lungs.

So Valerie did the only thing she could do in this situation. She licked her dry lips and opened her mouth to speak, her words barely a whisper as they slid past her tongue. "I can't. I'm not wearing any."

* * *

Logan bit back a groan.

For years, he'd dreamed about what it would be like to be with Valerie. Yet his lame-ass dreams had had nothing on the real, flesh-and-blood woman standing in front of him. Because out of all the fantasies he'd ever had, not a single damn one of them had anything to do with her not wearing panties. And as strange as it was, he was almost disappointed that he wasn't going to get a chance to see her take them off.

But the mere idea of her curvy body pressing against him with nothing under her skirt had rigor mortis settling into his cock and lit a fire in him that burned hotter than anything he'd ever known. *Oh yeah, she's definitely trying to kill me.*

His hands skimmed down her sides, grasped the hem of her dress, and hiked it up until the fabric stretched tight across her upper thighs. "Spread your legs."

She tensed and blew out a deep breath before parting her feet and doing exactly what he'd asked. To reward her for her good behavior, he found her, cupping her mound with his palm while slowly circling her clit with his thumb.

Their mouths were close but not quite touching as Logan thrust one long finger inside her, glided it through her wetness, and then added another. Her body jerked, her hips bucking forward, and she gasped directly into his open mouth. Her breath was like sweet honey, and the erotic sound she made traveled straight to his balls.

Moving his nimble fingers in and out, he worked her faster and then curled them inside her and found her G-spot, stroking it back and forth. Hot and tight, her inner muscles began to squeeze around him.

Damn. She was close. "You ready, baby?"

"Not yet," she murmured, panting harder. "I'm not quite...there."

He grinned. The fuck she wasn't.

Gentle persuasion turned into mad coercion as his hand brought her vibrating body closer to the edge of completion. "Now, Valerie. I want you to come all over my fingers right now."

The look she gave him was a mixture of confusion, arousal, and possibly a bit of irritation. "What are you talking about? It's not like I can come on command," she muttered, her voice trembling. "That's...not...even...poss—"

And with that, he shoved her off the orgasmic cliff.

Her body clamped down on his fingers, and her head lolled back against the ice machine as she panted out heavy breaths. She clenched her teeth together and rode his fingers through each wave of pleasure until the scent of her arousal perfumed the air around them. Then, with a shiver, her spent body went limp. "Holy shit," she muttered, her tone lazy and breathless.

He grinned and slid his fingers from between her legs, automatically reaching for the button on his jeans. The need to be inside of her was just too great to ignore...even if the noise level in the bar was growing by the minute. Logan freed himself, and his hard dick twitched with excitement, glad to be invited to the party.

But apparently he wasn't the only one who noticed the increasing outside chatter.

Valerie glanced in the direction of the storeroom door and bit into her bottom lip. "Um, how about we lock the door?"

In answer, Logan lifted her leg and pinned it to his waist. He sure the hell wasn't about to let the sound of distant laughter deter him from getting inside her as fast as he possibly could. "How about we don't?"

She stilled for a moment, as if contemplating what he had said, and then took a deep breath and let her body relax. "Someone might come in though."

He wasn't sure why that was suddenly a problem for her, but he couldn't help the amused grin that spread across his face. "Then they're going to owe us an admittance fee for the show we're about to put on."

"Logan..."

He leaned in and kissed her. "This was your idea," he whispered, bending his knees and positioning himself at her entrance. Her warmth and wetness were just begging for him to take the plunge.

She squirmed as he increased the pressure and began to enter her. "What are you...talking...about?"

God, why the hell are we still talking? "This is what you wanted, right? Someone to talk dirty to you," he replied, his heart pounding relentlessly, urging him to take her hard and fast. Trying to keep his eyes from rolling into the back of his head, Logan swallowed and looked her square in the eyes. "But I'm warning you, princess, as far I'm concerned, this is the closest thing you'll ever get to having sex in public."

Every muscle in her body stiffened, including the one around the head of his cock. She blinked. "W-what did you just—"

But Logan couldn't hold back any longer. He thrust fully into her, muscles tensing, and a groan ripped from his chest. Valerie gasped and braced herself against him, her thighs trembling. He held her steady and allowed her time to adjust to the sensation of being filled, then once her body relaxed again, he slowly began to move.

The grip she had on him was unbelievable. God, she was fucking tight. Way tighter than he'd ever imagined. If he was smart, he'd work on those fantasies of his. Because nothing in his imagination had ever been as good as this.

Logan angled his body into hers, the shallow thrusts maximizing her enjoyment yet minimizing his dick's need to race to the finish line. He kept that direct stimulation on her clit until her inner core softened around him. Then he begin to pump faster, harder, deeper. Valerie moaned and arched her back, grinding her body against his.

"You like the way my cock feels inside you?" he asked, increasing the pace once more.

Her eyes closed, and she breathed out a strained, "Yes."

"Then take all of it," he commanded, lifting her other leg off the ground. He wrapped it around his waist, which left her suspended in air, her back supported by the ice machine. His hands slipped under her ass cheeks, holding her over him as he rolled his hips, reaching deeper inside her. "Oh yeah. Take more of me. Just like that."

Her body jolted with every thrust. "Oh God, Logan...please..."

The desperate cry warned him of her pending release so he sped up, driving into her with long, primal strokes, more fiercely than before. "Here we go. Fast and hard, baby."

Her nails dug into his shoulders, and his fingers dug into her ass. His blood heated to a volcanic degree, and sweat beaded on his forehead. Moments later, she shattered, squeezing around him so hard that he couldn't see straight.

He was exhausted, and his limbs were completely numb, but there was no way in hell he was about to stop now. The thought of sating himself with her and relieving the painful ache in his balls had once only been a dream. Now that it was happening, he wasn't about to lose his chance to make his dream come true. Fierce and hungry for more, his libido took over, and his body went on cruise control.

His rock-hard dick was like a heat-seeking missile, homing in on her warmth and locating its target with ease. She'd been teasing him with that delicious body of hers for years, and he needed to fill it with every last inch of him.

After a couple more solid strokes, Logan's breath finally bottomed out. He held himself inside her, and the room whirled around him. Animalistic sounds tore from his throat as he grunted and groaned his release. Seconds later, the room stopped moving and sharp relief washed over him. He felt like he'd died and gone to heaven.

But then a man's voice rang out from somewhere in the hallway, and Logan knew that this wasn't heaven after all. It was definitely hell.

Valerie's head snapped up. "Shit. That's Brett. Hurry, put me down."

She squirmed in his arms, trying to get free, but he was still semi-hard inside her. "Hold on, damn it. Be careful with that thing," he scolded, sliding out of her and quickly setting her on her feet.

He stuffed his junk back into the safety of his pants and zipped up while Valerie pulled up her straps and covered her breasts. Then she yanked the hem of her skirt back into place and headed for the door.

"Where are you going?" he asked.

She smoothed her hands over her hair. "Brett's not looking for you...at least not yet." She glanced at the broken glass and whiskey puddle on the floor. "You stay here and clean this up. I'll go head him off."

"No, Valerie, I—"

But she slid out the door before he could stop her.

Breathing out a sigh, Logan grabbed one of the five-gallon buckets from the top of the ice machine and knelt down to pick up the large shards of glass at his feet. Christ, what a mess he'd made of things.

He wasn't really referring to the one on the floor, but since it was his fault that she'd dropped the whiskey bottle, the most he could do was help clean it up. And while he was at it, he would dispose of the condom too.

Wait, what condom? Logan's body went rigid. He gave his crotch a cursory glance, as if he were consulting parts of his anatomy on something he already knew to be true. They hadn't used a damn thing. "Fuck," he breathed out.

Logan closed his eyes, guilt sloshing in his stomach. He'd screwed up in so many ways tonight that he was starting to lose count. But this one? Yeah, this one definitely took the cake. He knew better, goddamn it. His head obviously wasn't in the right place since he never even thought of protecting them.

Then something whispered in the back of his mind. If he would have been using the right head to think with, he wouldn't have had sex with her to begin with.

Chapter Nine

Valerie hurried to wipe down the last of the counter.

Sweets n' Treats didn't close for another five minutes, but she'd been working hard for the past twenty to get everything done before five o'clock. Her shift at the bar didn't even start for another hour, but if she had any hope of speaking to Logan before the other employees arrived, then she would have to go in early. After what had happened between them last night, they definitely needed to talk.

Without a doubt, she knew things would be weird between her and Logan after her brother had come close to catching them in the storeroom, half-naked and in each other's arms. Had Brett actually walked through that door though, things would've been much worse.

To say her older brother was overprotective was putting it mildly. He was out of control and had been for years. She imagined that, if she had been fathered by the president of the United States, Brett would have been the secret service agent assigned to the task of keeping her virtue intact. But she wasn't the first daughter, nor was he an agent... and she lost her virtue a long time ago.

Valerie was twenty-six, for goodness' sakes. And now that Logan was finally seeing her as a woman instead of a child, the last thing she needed was her brother screwing it up. Besides, if last night had been any indication, she could apparently do that all on her own.

She breathed out a frustrated sigh.

If only she hadn't left the storeroom so abruptly last night. At the time, it had seemed like the smart thing to do to make sure Brett didn't find her and Logan together. But by the time she'd finally shaken her brother loose and made it back to the storeroom, Logan had completely disappeared, along with the broken glass.

It had been James who told her that Logan took the rest of the night off, citing a pounding headache that the loud music only made worse. But if you asked her, it was the dumbest fucking lie he could have come up with because, moments before, the only thing that had been pounding was his body into hers.

Irritation bubbled up inside her. Damn it, she needed to know why he had left like that... and if he'd seen the stupid list she'd written up with Leah. She didn't know how he would've possibly gotten a hold of it, but it was too much of a coincidence that he'd mentioned public sex and dirty talk mere minutes after she'd written them down.

Then she remembered something else he'd said. *This is what you wanted, right?* A strange realization dawned on her, and Valerie froze... then she laughed. Logan apparently thought it was a list of things she wanted to do rather than a list of things she would *never* do. How the hell had he screwed that one up?

Valerie giggled again as she glanced up at the clock on the wall and fistpumped the air. Two minutes until closing. Close enough, if you asked her.

She was just about to round the counter to lock up when, out of the corner of her eye, she spotted a figure pass by the front window, moving fast in the direction of the bakery door.

Shit. No, no, no. The last thing she wanted to do was miss out on talking to Logan, all because she had to stand around after closing time and wait fifteen minutes for a customer to decide what kind of damn pastry they wanted.

If I can get to the door first and lock it though . . .

Not willing to let anything hold her back from talking to Logan, she hurried around the counter and bustled for the door. The other person must have seen her coming through the frosted glass because they also picked up in speed. Each of them covered ground fast, both gaining on the door. Definitely a close one. But at the last second, Valerie launched herself forward and snicked the lock in place.

But the door opened anyway.

What the hell?

Mrs. Howard poked her head inside, breathing heavy. "Valerie Carmichael, were you trying to beat me to the door so you could lock me out?"

Valerie shook her head. "No, of course not. I wouldn't do that, Mrs. Howard. I was just, uh . . . coming to open it for you."

The old woman glared at her as if she didn't believe a

word of it. "Well, I won't take but a minute of your time." She stepped inside and tapped at her wrist. "Though technically I still have two available by my watch."

Valerie wanted to smile but didn't dare. "What can I do for you?"

"I don't need anything. I just wondered if you would deliver a message to your mom for me. Can you tell her that we're playing poker again next week? Same time, same place."

"Sure, that's no problem. I'll text her the info before I leave for my other job."

"Okay, good. And be sure to let her know I can spot a bluff from a mile away," Mrs. Howard said, eyeing the turned lock on the doorknob.

"Um, I'll be sure to do that."

"Thanks again," Mrs. Howard said, then turned and walked out, shutting the door behind her.

The giggle bubbling up in Valerie's throat broke free, and she shook her head. She had no doubt that her mom was going to get an earful on poker night about how her daughter tried to lock poor Mrs. Howard out of the bakery. She probably needed to give her mother a heads-up about that one.

Valerie turned to walk back to the counter when the door behind her opened again. She spun on her heels to see Logan's mother stepping inside. What the hell? Had the door not shut all the way or something?

"Hello, Valerie. I hope I'm not keeping you from closing up."

"Um, no. Of course not," Valerie said, eyeballing the open door and shaking her head. "What can I do for you, Mrs. Mathis?"

"Nothing much, dear. I just stopped by to pick up the dozen glazed doughnuts for our Bible study group tonight. Edna said she ordered them yesterday, but she came down with some sort of stomach bug this morning and asked me to help. Unfortunately, I wasn't able to get here any earlier than now."

Valerie smiled warmly. "That's okay. Let me run to the back and grab them for you. Give me just a second."

She headed into the kitchen and grabbed the box of glazed doughnuts she'd seen sitting on the order cart. She'd noticed them a few hours ago, but Leah had apparently forgotten to tell her what or who they were for. Now it all made sense. She strolled back out through the swinging doors and set the box on the counter. "Here they are, Mrs. Mathis."

"Oh, good."

Valerie hit a few buttons on the cash register and glanced back at Logan's mom. "With the normal discount the Bible study group receives, the total comes to four dollars and forty-eight cents."

"Oh. I...um, didn't realize that Edna hadn't paid for them yet."

"We normally only take deposits on wedding cakes or on large orders for an event. Most everything else is paid for during pickup."

Mrs. Mathis blinked, and then her cheeks reddened. "I see. I...um, don't really have any cash with me at the moment." Her hands shook slightly, and her eyes misted over. "I'm sorry, Valerie. I guess I won't be able to pick them up after all."

The woman looked so embarrassed that Valerie couldn't help but feel bad for her. "That's okay, Mrs. Mathis. Tell you what, the doughnuts are on me tonight." She pushed the white box toward her.

"Oh, no, dear. I wouldn't dream of letting you pay for them."

Valerie smiled at her again. "I don't mind at all. Besides, if you don't take them, I would just have to throw them out. You would really be doing me a favor. I hate wasting perfectly good doughnuts."

Judging by the look Mrs. Mathis gave her, the woman clearly didn't believe a word of it. Everyone in town knew that the bakery made fresh products every day and anything that didn't sell that same day would be marked down to half price the following morning. And that included day-old doughnuts. It wasn't as if there would be anything wrong with them.

Although Mrs. Mathis clearly knew Valerie was fibbing, she said, "Are you sure, Valerie?"

"Absolutely." Valerie lifted the box and placed it into her hands. "You ladies enjoy them."

Mrs. Mathis hung her head. She looked weepy, as if the sweet woman was trying not to burst into tears. Then she sighed with resignation and lifted her head. "Thank you. That's very kind of you."

"You're welcome. Have a great evening."

"You too, dear." She turned and headed out the door, closing it firmly behind her.

Valerie glanced at the knob, noting that the button was twisted into the locked position. Thank God. Now she could stop worrying about anyone else coming in. She slid her hand deep into her pocket and fished around until she pulled out a five-dollar bill and then used it to pay for the dozen doughnuts.

She didn't know why Mrs. Mathis had gotten so upset about forgetting her cash. Hell, most people have done something like that before. Sure, it was a little embarrassing, but it was definitely nothing to cry over. Either way, Valerie didn't mind helping her out. Logan's mother was such a sweet lady and had always been so nice to her.

Now that she was gone and the bakery was officially closed, Valerie could hurry and get to the bar. After what happened last night, she really needed to talk to—

The front door of the bakery swung open again, and Logan stepped inside wearing blue jeans and a beige flannel shirt with his sleeves shoved up to his elbows.

She blinked at the still-locked door. "Seriously?"

"Uh, I'm not bothering you, am I? I waited to come until closing time so you wouldn't be busy."

She walked over to the door and leaned down, examining the doorknob thoroughly. "No, it's fine," she said, peering closely at the lock. "I was just closing up." She tried to turn the knob, but it wouldn't budge. It was still locked, yet it wasn't keeping anyone out. *What the heck is wrong with this thing?*

"Are you sure? I could come back another time…maybe when you're not distracted."

"I'm not distracted." Valerie shut the door and pulled it right back open. *Ah, there's the problem. The door isn't catching.* She would have to call Sam to come over and fix it before she left for the day.

"You sure?" Logan asked again.

She closed the broken door once more and turned to face him. "Yes, I'm sure. Did you see your mother on your way in? You just missed her."

"My mom was here?"

"Yep. And is everything okay with her?"

He stiffened. "Um, yeah. Sure. Why do you ask?"

"I don't know. She just seemed . . . off. Like something was bothering her. She was picking up the doughnuts for her Bible study group, and she got really upset that she didn't have any cash on her. So I paid for them, but I got the feeling that bothered her even more than—"

"How much?" Logan said, whipping his wallet from his back pocket.

"It's okay. I already took care of it."

"No, I'll pay for them. How much do I owe you?"

Valerie shook her head. "Logan, I didn't tell you any of this so you would pay me back. I was only concerned about your mom's welfare. She wasn't acting like herself."

"She's going through something right now." Logan pulled a ten-dollar bill from his wallet. "Will this cover it?"

"Are you listening to me? I don't want your money. Put it away."

"All right then," Logan said, putting his money and his wallet away. He looked very uncomfortable as he shifted his weight from one leg to the other. "I came by to talk to you about something else anyway. You have a few minutes?"

Her heart beat faster. "Sure," she said, leaning her hip against the counter.

"I . . . I wanted to apologize to you for being a selfish bastard last night."

She gazed curiously at him but didn't say anything. Was he referring to the sex they'd had? Because if so, she didn't think anything he'd done to her would be considered selfish by anyone. Ever.

"Look, I've never had sex without protection before. But with you... well, I was so hell-bent on getting inside you, I didn't use a condom. I never even considered it. I screwed up, and I'm sorry. I should've taken better care of both of us in that regard."

Oh, that. "It's okay," she said calmly.

His eyes narrowed. "The fuck it is. Look, Valerie, I know I messed up. But if you end up pregnant, I want to know about it. I mean, you won't have to go through it alone. I'll be there for you and the ba—"

"Logan, I'm on the pill."

He paused for a moment and then nodded. "Okay. Well, then the least I can do is go get tested and give you a copy of the results. I don't want you to worry about anything."

"I'm not worried, but that's fine. In fact, I'll do the same if you want." Then she grinned. "But honestly, if I was worried that you had something or weren't a responsible person, then I wouldn't have had sex with you to begin with. I am careful about who I sleep with, you know."

He shook his head. "I'm sorry. I wasn't trying to insinuate anything. And I know I should never have touched you last night. I can assure you that it won't happen again."

Her heart stuttered in her chest, but she managed to step toward him with her hands on her hips. "The hell it won't!"

Logan reeled back, seemingly surprised by the outburst, but he recovered quickly. "No, I mean it, Val. It can't happen again. It shouldn't have happened this time." Before she could open her mouth to argue with him, he raised his hand to stop her. "I know what you're going to say. But you know as well as I do that we shouldn't be doing this. It's wrong."

She paused. "Are you kidding me? We're two single adults who are apparently attracted to one another. There's not a damn thing wrong with that." She shook her head. "If you're worried about my brother—"

"Damn it, Valerie. You know Brett's going to be pissed when he finds out."

"He's not going to find out."

"Yeah, he will." Logan released a heavy breath. "I'm going to tell him."

Her stomach dropped. "What? No! You can't."

"I have to. I'm not going to lose my best friend over this shit. I need to be up front with him about it. It's the right thing to do . . . even if he ends up hating me for it."

She shook her head. "If he had some time to get used to the idea of us, then he'd—"

"There's no *us*, Valerie. There can't be. Your brother isn't the only issue here, and you know it."

Damn. Did he find out that she'd lied about the certification? "I . . . uh, don't know what you're talking about."

He rubbed the bridge of his nose. "I'm your boss, remember?"

"Okay," she said, hesitating. She couldn't blame him for having the same thoughts that she'd had last night. But there was an easy solution to that problem. "Fine, then I quit."

Logan's head snapped to her. "You can't quit on me like that. You know I'm in a bind right now. I need you."

His words sent a shiver through her though she knew he hadn't meant them the way she took them. She stepped toward him and placed a hand on his chest, running it up toward his shoulder. "Logan..."

He stilled her hand with his much larger one, and a muscle ticked in his jaw. "We can't. I'm sorry, but there's just too much at stake to give this a go. If things were different, then maybe it would work. But they're not."

The look he gave her was heartrending and forced her to take a deep breath. He was serious about the two of them not taking this any further. Dead serious.

Then he added, "There's one more thing too. I want you to take tonight off from the bar."

She blinked. "What? Why? You just said you needed—"

"I know what I said. And I do need you. But after what happened last night, I think it would do both of us some good to steer clear of each other for one night. You know, in order to gain some perspective. It's only Thursday, and I don't think we'll be all that busy. I can help James if we get a run on customers. Besides, you're working two full-time jobs, and I don't want you to get burned out."

Damn it. He was treating her like a child again. "Logan..."

"I'm not going to argue with you about this, Val. Just take tonight off, and I'll see you tomorrow."

"So that's it then?"

He nodded firmly. "It has to be. Let's just chalk last night up to a weak moment and forget about it."

There wasn't a damn thing weak or forgettable about last night. No matter what he said. But thank God she hadn't done something stupid like profess her undying love for him or tell him how she'd been in love with him for years. She would have felt stupid as hell spilling her heart out to him only to be turned down in the end.

"Fine," she said.

His eyebrow lifted, clearly not expecting her to agree with him.

And really, she didn't want to. But she deserved a man who would drag himself through fire to be with her. Not one who was dragging his feet after sleeping with her.

"You're not going to argue with me about this?" he asked.

"Nope."

If Logan didn't see what he was giving up, then that was his problem. There was nothing she could do about it. Yes, she wanted him. But he was the one damn thing she was apparently never going to have.

*   *   *

Logan thunked his head on his desk.

He'd been sitting in the same spot for five straight hours and hadn't gotten a damn thing accomplished. There was inventory to order, sales reports to check, invoices to go over, and employee checks to write, but he just couldn't seem to get his head into the game.

Thankfully, James had a good handle on the bar, which was fairly quiet though there were several groups hanging out around the pool tables and a few couples sitting at the counter. A few of their regular customers had come in as well, but it was getting late and most of them had already headed home for the night...unlike Logan.

If he didn't get this paperwork finished soon, he wouldn't be getting any sleep at all. The bank manager wanted to meet with him early so they could go over the documents on the foreclosure of his mom's house, but while Logan was there, he planned to convince the bank to give them an extension on the deadline.

He needed it. Badly.

Open for less than a week, the bar *was* actually making money. But as with any new business, Logan was also paying out a hell of a lot to the vendors in order to keep it going. All he needed though was enough to cure the default and reinstate the mortgage. Then he would make all future monthly mortgage payments until the house was paid off and the title was free and clear. If everything went the right way, by this time next week, his mom's home would be safe from foreclosure.

Unfortunately, Logan knew from past experience that things had a way of not always working out...just like with him and Valerie.

He hated himself for hurting her. When he'd told her they couldn't be anything more than a one-night stand, the utter devastation on her face had kicked him hard in the left nut. And if her brother had seen the look on her face and had known it was Logan who'd put it there, Brett would've taken out the right one.

And Logan would've let him. Because he deserved every bit of it for putting his hands where they didn't belong. Every time he even thought about how he'd touched her in that storeroom, his dick hardened to the point of pain. But that was exactly the kind of shit that had gotten him into trouble in the first place.

He was surprised that Valerie hadn't argued with him more than she did. Maybe she thought it was a lost cause at this point. Or maybe she'd gotten what she'd wanted from him and the excitement of the chase had quickly worn off.

Logan chuckled to himself. It was usually women

who worried that they had been used for sex. Not men. But then again, the idea had merit. When he'd showed up at the bakery, Valerie *had* seemed way more interested in the door than him. He still didn't know what the hell to make of that one.

But none of this really mattered. It wasn't like Valerie was in love with him or something. And he didn't love her either. It was just a teenage crush that had carried over into their adult years. A simple, mutual attraction between two people who ended up having sex. Actually, it was more of a half-naked quickie. In the storeroom. Against the ice machine. With him pumping into her tight, hot body over and over and...

Fuck. Logan reached down and adjusted the swelling in his jeans. When the hell had his pants gotten so tight?

He needed to stop thinking about her and finish his work though so he shoved her voluptuous image from his mind and picked up the invoice in front of him. He needed to concentrate on her figure. No, wait...not *her* figure. His figures. Numbers, damn it.

Shit. With a sigh on his lips, Logan got back to work.

Logan had barely made it through half the stack of papers when his cell phone rang and Valerie's name popped up. He shook his head. Sonofabitch. How the hell was he supposed to get his mind off her if she wouldn't leave him alone? But he hit the button and placed her on speaker-phone anyway. "What do you want, Valerie? I'm busy," he said, his tone not all that friendly.

"Um, this isn't Valerie," a woman on the line said. "My name is Dawn, and I'm one of the waitresses over at Rusty's Bucket. Valerie left her phone inside, and I'm calling you because she...uh, well..."

Panic flashed through him, and he fisted his hand on the desk. *God, if anything had happened to her...* "What's wrong? Is she okay?"

"Oh, sorry. Yes, she's fine. But she needs someone to come and get her. I tried to call her brother first, but he's not picking up. Since Valerie mentioned that she works for you and your number was in her phone, I thought you could help."

Help? Confusion filled him. "Where's her car?"

"It's outside in the parking lot. Valerie's just not in any condition to drive it right now. I've already taken her keys from her, but she's sitting in her vehicle right now with no place to go since I can't get a hold of Brett. But I know you said you're busy. I could try to call her brother again, if you want."

Logan groaned inwardly. It's not like he could just leave Valerie there. "No, that's okay. I'll come get her. Should take me ten minutes tops. Just don't let her go anywhere until I arrive."

"Um, I can assure you that she's not going anywhere," the waitress said with a giggle, "but I'll keep my eye on her just in case."

Logan ended the call and headed straight for the door. Because no matter how many times he tried to convince himself that he didn't have feelings for Valerie, he wasn't about to stop himself from running to her rescue when she needed him.

After giving James a heads-up that he was leaving, it took Logan only eight minutes to get down to Rusty's Bucket. Since there weren't many cars parked out front, he immediately spotted Valerie's red Mercedes.

It was a late-model sedan, but it had a kick-ass engine

and was flashy as hell. Brett had bought it at an auction for a great price, overhauled the engine, and had given it to her as a graduation present. Man, Logan loved that car. Brett did most of the engine work, but Logan had been there helping every step of the way.

Well, until he wasn't anymore. He'd left town two days after her graduation so he never actually got to see her driving it. The day he packed his things into his truck, he considered going by to see her one last time. But he hadn't been able to do it. Something had told him that she would ask him to stay. And the last thing he'd wanted to do was disappoint her by leaving anyway.

And he would have. Because staying hadn't been an option.

As he approached Valerie's car, he heard a sniffle and gazed through the open window to see tears in her eyes. "Are you all right?"

She glanced up at him, and her mouth fell open. Then she snapped it shut. "Um, yes," she said, her voice cracking slightly.

"Are you sure? What happened?"

"I...lost my keys."

He shook his head. "No, you didn't. The waitress said she took them from you so that you wouldn't drive anywhere. Your keys are still in the bar with her."

One solitary tear rolled down her cheek, and Valerie quickly wiped it away with the back of her hand. "Yeah, but they're in there, and I'm out here."

He didn't really understand why that was a problem. "Okay, so I'll take you inside to get them."

Valerie gazed at him with glassy eyes, her face completely serious. "And just how are you going to do that, Logan? I'm locked in."

Amusement tugged strongly at the corner of his mouth, but he didn't dare smile. Instead, he reached through the open window of the car, lifted the lock with his fingers, and opened the door, catching her arm before she fell out.

Her eyes went wide in amazement. "You're like a magician or something," she slurred.

Logan shook his head and helped her out of the car. "Sweetheart, exactly how much have you had to drink tonight?"

"I don't really know. I lost count. Some man inside told me I drank enough to fill a fish tank. But I told him I don't even have any fish."

Huh? But before Logan could wrap his brain around what she said, Valerie staggered in the direction of the bar.

He caught up with her easily and grasped her arm to keep her from falling on the steps. Once they'd grabbed Valerie's keys and cell phone from the waitress, they stopped by her car long enough to close the windows and lock the doors. Then he ushered her into the passenger seat of his blue Z71.

"I don't like hanging out at Rusty's anymore," she said, hiccuping a little as he started the engine. "Nothing but old drunks and desperate perverts in there."

He pulled out of the parking lot. "Well, since we were both just in there, what the hell does that make us?"

She grinned. "An old drunk and a desperate pervert, I guess." She paused for a moment and then said, "But which one am I?"

"I've got dibs on the drunk since I'm older than you."

A slow grin cradled her cheeks. "Yeah, but I'm drunker than you. Besides, I'm not desperate. And I'm definitely not a pervert."

"You're going to have a hard time convincing me of that last one, princess." He glanced over at her with a smirk on his face. "I saw your naughty list, remember?"

She glanced out the passenger window. "Um, yeah. About that..."

"Sorry. I shouldn't have brought that up. It's really none of my business." Though he'd make it his business if he found out she was doing any of that other shit on her list with some stranger who wouldn't protect her and take care of her like he would.

Then he remembered the forgotten condom. Okay, like he *should* have.

She licked her lips. "So you didn't, um...like what we did the other night?"

Was she fucking kidding? "I liked it just fine."

"Then why can't we do it again?" A soft hand fell onto his thigh.

The truck swerved, and Logan jerked the wheel to get back into his lane. He swallowed hard and quickly brushed her hand away. "We just...can't, that's why." *Jesus. Way to explain things to her, idiot.*

Her lip poked out. "So I'm right then. You didn't like it after all?"

Frustration surged through him, and his hands clenched the steering wheel to keep from reaching for her and showing her just how much he wanted to do it again. "I already told you I liked it, Valerie. It's not that."

She ignored what he said though, and her glazed eyes filled with curiosity. "No, seriously. Tell me the truth. I'm a big girl. I can take it." When he didn't answer right away, she continued. "I mean, did I come too early or something? Maybe too late? What was it?"

"No, Goldilocks, you came just right. Now can we drop this, please?"

Valerie crossed her arms and huffed. "Fine."

"Look, if you really want to talk about this, we will. But not while you're drunk. You're going to have so many regrets tomorrow as it is. Trust me, you don't want to add any more to your list."

Thankfully, she stayed quiet until minutes later when he pulled up in front of her brother's small two-bedroom house and shut off the engine.

"Why are we here?"

"I don't think you should be alone tonight, and it's not like I can stay with you. If you drank as much as I think you did, you're probably going to be throwing up at some point. Brett will keep an eye on you."

Valerie peered at the dark house. "I don't think he's even home."

"Doesn't matter. There's a key hidden under the mailbox next to the door." He slid out of the truck, walked around to the passenger side, and opened her door.

"How do you know that? Brett never told me about a hidden key."

Logan grinned. "That's because he was afraid you would let yourself in when he had company...of the female variety." When she started to climb out of the truck, he said, "Here, give me your hand."

"I can do it." But her heel caught on the curb and she tripped, landing in the grass. She rolled over onto her back and laughed. "Oops. Maybe I can't."

He reached for her and helped her back to her feet and then kicked the truck door closed. "You okay to walk or do you want me to carry you?"

Her eyes were trained on the long sidewalk leading up to Brett's front door. "Well, I am pretty drunk. Maybe you should carry me."

He had a feeling she would say that. When she was younger, Brett used to carry her around in his arms like a doll. But he wasn't Brett. "Okay," Logan said, grinning. He leaned forward and tossed her over his right shoulder, hanging her upside down over his back.

She squealed. "That's not how I thought you were going to carry me."

"I know." Logan started for the house.

Her hand slapped him on the ass. "Jerk."

"You might want to think twice before doing that again," he warned, rubbing his free hand over her lovely rear and giving it a light tap. "You're vulnerable at the moment, princess."

She slapped him again, a little harder this time. "That's for calling me princess."

Though he couldn't see her face, he glanced over his left shoulder. "Okay, now you're asking for it. When we get inside, it's going to be *my* turn." After using the secret key to let them in, Logan flipped on the lights, kicked the front door closed, and carried her straight to the guest room. He set her down by the bed, sank onto the edge, and pulled her across his lap.

Valerie squirmed under him. "What the hell are you doing?"

"I'm bending you over my knee, which is something I've wanted to do for a very long time."

She laughed and glanced back at him. "You're not going to hit me."

"No, I'm going to spank you. There's a difference."

Her eyelashes lowered, and her breath quickened. Apparently she liked the idea of him smacking her on the ass as much as he did. Then again, it was on her to-do list.

"Okay, but if you're going to do it, then you're going to have to do it the right way." She reached back and fumbled with her dress. Within seconds, she had her skirt up over her back, baring the smooth roundness of her ass cheeks and the lacy white thong between them.

Christ. Logan closed his eyes and sucked in a large breath.

He was taking this whole thing way too far, and although he knew it, he couldn't seem to stop himself from doing so. Valerie had such a vibrant, sexy personality that it made him want to throw caution to the wind and play with her. Literally.

But she was also drunk. "We shouldn't be doing this."

"Who's stopping us?"

His eyes met hers. "I am."

"Exactly. So just shut up and spank me already." She giggled. "You know you want to."

No, what he wanted to do was sink his teeth into that tight flesh while his fingers slipped between those glorious thighs. But he'd settle for spanking her because, with her beautiful, bare ass right in front of him, the temptation was just too much to resist. "Tell me the truth. Do you want me to spank you?"

"Yes, how many times do you want me to say—"

His hand came down on her backside with a quick slap, and she jumped a little. "Too hard?" he asked, though he knew he'd barely touched her.

"Hmm, actually I'm thinking you can do better than that. Try again."

He pulled his hand back and slapped it down with a bit more force than the last time. Her breath hitched a little and then she hummed appreciatively. "Again," she murmured, her tone sultry.

A smile lifted his cheeks, and his hand made a couple of slow circles over the round curve of her cheek, as if winding up for the pitch. Then he smacked her on the ass even harder this time, leaving behind a subtle sting in his palm from the effort. A sharp gasp flew from her lips, and a red hand print appeared almost instantly.

He rubbed his fingers over the marred skin and frowned. "Okay, that's enough. I don't like leaving marks on you. It takes all the fun out of it for me."

She rolled and lifted herself up, curling into his lap. "Mmm, but it felt so good on my end," she purred.

Logan grinned at the unintended pun. Yeah, maybe, but he noticed she wasn't asking him to do it again. "I guess I can see the lure of it and get why people do it. But your ass is too damn cute to blemish it with such an ugly handprint. I can think of better things to do to your flesh that would be much more pleasurable for the both of us."

Her eyes lifted to his, challenging him. "Show me."

God, he wanted to. Especially since he already knew how good she felt in his arms. This time the urge was definitely harder to tamp down. But there were so many reasons they shouldn't—*no, couldn't*—do this. One being that she was drunk and probably didn't even know what the hell she was saying.

Damn it. Someone had to be the responsible one here. "I already told you we can't, Valerie."

In a huff, she crawled off his lap, pushed her skirt down over her rear, and faced him with her hands on her hips. "Was that before or after you played with my ass?"

He swallowed. "Look, I wasn't trying to lead you on, if that's what you're thinking. We took it too far. I didn't mean for any of this to happen. It just... did."

"Whatever." Without any warning, Valerie slid her arms out of her dress and shoved it down her body.

Logan blinked rapidly.

Beautiful, full breasts stared him in the face as she shimmied out of her tight dress by rocking those magnificently round hips back and forth. Hips that begged for his hands to grab a hold of them and pull her to him. When the thin material fell to the floor, it left her standing there in front of him wearing only her white G-string.

Logan's mouth watered. Just one. One fucking tug. That was all it would take for him to have those off of her too. His balls tightened. "W-what the hell are you doing?"

"I'm getting ready for bed." She turned and opened a drawer on the dresser and pulled out a supersized T-shirt that look like one of Brett's old football shirts, then dropped it over her head.

Thank God.

Valerie crawled onto the bed, slid under the tan-colored sheets and blanket, and turned her head away from him. "You can go now. I'll be fine without you."

Logan had a feeling she wasn't just talking about tonight. "No. I'm not leaving you yet. You're stuck with me at least until your brother gets home." He moved to sit on the edge of the bed next to her, and she began to shift away from him. Logan stilled her with his hand on her shoulder. "I'm sorry, okay? I'm not trying to hurt your feelings, piss you off, make you feel bad, or whatever else it is that I'm doing."

"It's fine. I just... Never mind." She glanced away.

Her long, wavy blond hair cascaded softly around her face. He tucked a lock behind her ear. "No, tell me. I'd rather we talk about it than for you to have hard feelings toward me."

She sighed and laid her head back on the pillow. "That's the thing, Logan. I've never had hard feelings for you... just feelings."

Crap. Logan sighed. "I'm sorry, okay?"

"For what?" she asked softly, her voice trembling.

"Everything. I didn't mean for any of this to happen." He placed his hand on hers and gave it a little squeeze.

She shook her head adamantly and moved her hand. "God. I don't need your pity, Logan. Nor do I want it."

"Good. Because that's not what I'm offering."

Valerie tilted her head toward him, her tongue darting out to lick her bottom lip. "Then what exactly are you offering me?"

His heart jackhammered into his ribs. Coming from her, words like that were dangerous. For both of them. She was everything he wanted, yet had no right to take. "Friendship, Valerie. It's the only thing I can give you."

"And if I don't want that?"

"Then that's your decision. But you deserve a guy who's all in and can give you what you want. I'm sorry I can't be that guy for you."

She paused thoughtfully then bit her lip. "It's because of Brett, isn't it?"

Valerie's brother had always handled her with kid gloves, treating her as if she were a rare, precious gemstone that might break in the wrong hands. But he'd only done what most big brothers would probably do. He slid his sister behind a glass barrier made up of trust and friendship.

Logan had always refused to go there, but the threat hadn't stopped all of Brett's friends in the past. In fact, the hands-off factor only succeeded in making Valerie more appealing, if that was even possible. Some guys had a tendency to want something they couldn't have. He should know. "No. That's not all of it."

"But he's part of it?"

Of course he wanted to keep his relationship with Brett on solid ground. Brett might be a meathead with the unsavory temperament of a pissed-off bull, but he was also a damn good friend. The kind who would follow his buddy to hell just to make sure he got there okay. Logan wasn't scared of Brett, but the guy wasn't someone he really wanted to piss off either. "Yes, he's part of it."

"Oh, that's just great. I can't believe you of all people are actually worried about my brother."

Logan rolled his eyes. "Not in the way that you think. I've sparred with Brett enough times over the years to know how evenly matched we are. It would be a fair fight."

Most people who got a good look at Brett's muscular frame and surly attitude walked in the opposite direction at a very fast pace. But Logan had never been afraid of him. Logan just understood the need to protect family.

"Then what's the problem?"

"Let's just drop this, Valerie. All you need to know is that I'm not the right guy for you."

"Even if you're the only one I want?"

He didn't want to encourage her, but he couldn't help but grin. "That alcohol is giving you loose lips."

"No. That's not it. No matter what happens or doesn't happen between us now or in the future, I want you to know how I feel. I've had a pretty permanent crush on you for years."

His eyebrow rose. "Permanent, huh?"

"Yeah. It's been around long enough that I don't think it's ever going to go away." She shrugged. "Guess you're just going to have to live with that knowledge."

He grinned. "You're so going to regret telling me all of this tomorrow."

"Something tells me you already knew anyway."

He nodded. "I had my suspicions," he said, though that was putting it mildly. He heard a vehicle pull into the driveway and lifted his head. "Sounds like Brett's home. I guess now that my relief is here, I should probably get out of here before Brett sees your dress on the floor and thinks I'm the one who put it there."

He stood, but Valerie's hand reached out and touched his arm, stopping him from moving away from her. "Thanks for coming to my rescue tonight. I guess that makes you my knight in shining armor."

"Yeah, maybe," he said, flashing her a quick grin. But everyone knew that the knight was the one who usually died alone in battle while the prince rode into the sunset with the girl. He leaned forward and pressed his lips to her forehead. "Good night, princess." Then he eased off the bed and headed to the bedroom door.

"Logan?"

He paused in the doorway. "Yeah?"

"Why do you call me princess?"

He hesitated to tell her the truth, but he doubted she would remember it tomorrow anyway. "Because you deserve someone better than me."

Chapter Ten

Valerie couldn't breathe.

She lifted her head and realized that she was lying on her stomach with her face stuffed into her pillow. Her head pounded mercilessly, and her throat felt gritty like she'd spent the night in the desert eating sand.

"About time you woke up," a piercing voice said. She glanced over and saw Brett lazing in a chair across the room with his legs stretched out in front of him...as if he'd been there all night. "Morning, sleepyhead. Glad to see you're alive and still kicking."

Jesus. Why was he talking so loud? She groaned and stuffed her face back into the pillow. "What time is it?" she asked, her words muffled by the fabric.

"It's two o'clock."

Valerie shot into a sitting position and gazed out the window, noting the bright gold light filtering through the curtains. "Two o'clock? As in the afternoon?"

"No, it's the middle of the night, and the sun decided to pay us a visit." He gave her a sardonic look and shook his head. "Wow, you're a quick one today. How much *did* you drink last night?"

"Oh, shut up. You know what I mean. I was supposed to work at the bakery this afternoon. I'm way late and pretty sure Leah is going to kill me."

He grinned. "She already called. When she saw that you weren't home, she got worried. I told her that your lazy ass wasn't coming in because you got hammered last night. She said she would cover your shift for you."

God, had he always had such an annoying voice? "I wasn't hammered. I was…tipsy."

"Uh-huh. Right. Tipsy with a side of hammered."

His voice grated on her nerves even more than his smug grin did. "Whatever. So what happened last night?"

"You don't remember?"

"I don't know…I think I do. Bits and pieces anyway."

Brett smirked. "Logan said he didn't think you would remember much."

"Logan? Why would he say that? I didn't work at the bar last night. How would he even—" No, wait. Logan had been there last night. That much she remembered. "He picked me up at Rusty's Bucket, didn't he?"

Brett nodded. "The waitress tried to get a hold of me, but I wasn't near my phone at the time. So they called Logan instead. I don't know how the hell they knew to call him."

Valerie shrugged as if she didn't know either, but she distinctly remembered mentioning Logan's name more than once to the waitress while they were commiserating over their nonexistent love lives. "Who knows? Maybe she heard that he was your friend or something. You know how small towns are."

"Probably. Either way I appreciate him helping me out like that. I'm sure he gets plenty of you at work as it is."

Yeah, Logan had gotten plenty of her at work all right. Just two nights ago...and not in the way her brother meant. Her body tingled at the thought. "Why? Did he say something to you?"

"No. I just know from personal experience how annoying little sisters can be." He punctuated the dig with a wide grin.

Valerie rolled her eyes. "Of course I frustrate the hell out of you. I'm supposed to. It's my job as a sister. But Logan's not my brother."

Brett shrugged one muscled shoulder. "Close enough."

Her stomach churned. "Um, no. Not really. I don't look at him like a brother...like at all. Never have and never will."

"Well, I don't know why not. Whenever the two of you are together, you're always bickering about something. You act just like a brother and sister already."

Oh God. Make him stop. Bile crept up her throat, but she swallowed it back down. Brett needed to stop saying things like that. She'd seen Logan's penis, for goodness' sakes. That automatically disqualified him as brother material in her book. Not that she could tell Brett any of that.

Now that she was fully awake, her synapses began firing off distant memories that hit her like a cannonball to the brain. She already knew Logan had picked her up from the bar, but what she hadn't recalled until just now was that he'd also tossed her over his shoulder like a caveman and then...spanked her?

For a second, she considered it had been a dream. But no. She had apparently committed to memory the way his large hand had come down on her backside with a sharp slap that had sent electricity zinging through her nerves and a wave of heat straight to her core. She doubted the hand print would still be visible, but judging by the memory of the pleasurable sting he'd inflicted, the mark had probably taken a few good hours to fade.

That intimate knowledge invoked wicked sensations and sent heat spiraling up her neck. She felt wild and crazy, maybe even a bit naughty. *Definitely not a princess.*

The second the thought passed through her mind, another memory from last night quickly followed. It was the last thing Logan had said to her before walking out the door. *You deserve someone better than me.* Valerie huffed out a hard breath. "Um, I need to get going. Could you give me a lift back to my car?"

"Sure. But I don't know why. Leah said you could take the day off since you're covering for her next week."

"Well, that's because she'll be on her honeymoon. But it doesn't matter. I still have to be at Bottoms Up by seven o'clock."

Brett glanced at the silver watch on his wrist. "You've got almost five hours. If I were you, I would go home and rest up before work. It's Friday, and the bar is probably going to be packed tonight."

"Yeah, I'll do that." *Not.*

Valerie didn't need to go home and rest. What she needed was to go see Logan . . . and tell him how wrong he was.

* * *

Logan tossed the stack of papers onto the kitchen counter.

Although he'd read over them at least ten times already, the words hadn't changed no matter how many passes he made. He still had only two weeks to come up with ten thousand dollars or his mother was going to lose her home for good.

He took in a deep breath, but it did little to help loosen the knot growing tighter in his stomach.

When he'd first learned about the foreclosure, he had his mother assign him power of attorney privileges so that he could act on her behalf. Then he immediately set up a meeting with the bank manager in order to ask for an extension on the deadline.

He'd hoped the business meeting would be productive, but it hadn't gone as planned. Not only did they decline his request for an extension, but they also notified him that his mother wouldn't qualify for any type of foreclosure relief programs, whether it be a loan balance reduction or refinancing.

Having been in denial about how dire her situation really was, his mother had done the worst thing you could possibly do in this scenario. She'd ignored the signs of foreclosure and dodged the lender's calls for six months, hoping they would go away on their own. And chances were good that they eventually would…but they were planning on taking her home with them.

According to the bank manager, Mr. Anderson, six months was actually twice the amount of time that a financial institution would normally give someone in default to bring their account current. Thank goodness

Granite was a small town and the man knew Logan's mother personally. Even said he liked her and that she was a sweet woman. But although he'd done all he could to delay the foreclosure as long as possible, the board of trustees were now forcing his hand and he had no choice but to follow through.

Logan couldn't really fault Mr. Anderson for not wanting to risk his own employment to help his mom out more than he already had. The man seemed genuinely concerned about his mother, and he'd been more than fair already. Besides, Logan couldn't help but think it was his own fault that his mother was in this desperate situation to begin with.

Sure, he hadn't known about her financial problems from the start. But that was only because he hadn't been there when she'd needed someone to rely on. And even though they'd talked on the phone regularly, her embarrassment over the whole situation had ensured her silence. That knowledge still felt like a punch in the gut.

But none of that was important now. The only thing that mattered was coming up with the money to get her mortgage reinstated.

When a knock sounded on the front door, Logan answered it and found Valerie standing on the other side wearing a light purple sundress and staring up at him with her big blue eyes. God, she looked amazing. "We need to talk."

"Now is not a good time."

"Well, tough shit."

She started inside, but he threw an arm up in front of her to block the entrance. "Look, I'm tired and cranky as hell. I really don't need this right now."

"Fine. Then we'll have our little conversation right here in the doorway. But either way, I'm not leaving."

Goddamn it. He sighed. "What do you want?"

"I want to talk to you about last night."

Figures. "What about it?"

"Well, for starters, I..." She stared at him for a moment and then frowned. "Why do you look like you haven't gotten any sleep?"

"Because I haven't, hence the part where I said I was tired and cranky."

After leaving Valerie in her brother's care last night, Logan had returned to the bar and worked well into the night to get all of his paperwork done. Then he'd gone home and crawled into bed, hoping to get at least a few hours of sleep. But sleep hadn't come. Instead, he'd spent a few hours in bed, tossing and turning, while letting guilt swallow him whole and contemplating just what a shitty friend he really was.

"How come? Is something wrong?"

Yeah, there was something wrong. If he didn't get her out of his head soon, he was going to go fucking insane...or possibly lose the best friend he'd ever had. "No, everything's fine. I was at the bar doing paperwork until early this morning."

"Oh, I see. Well, first off, I wanted to thank you again for—"

"Don't."

She cocked her head. "Don't what?"

"Don't thank me."

"Why not? Isn't that what you do when someone helps you out?"

"Yeah, well, your brother already thanked me for taking care of you last night when he should've been drop-kicking me in the dick and stomping my nuts into the ground."

Maybe then he would learn his lesson and stay the hell away from her.

"Um, I don't get it."

"Oh, come on, Valerie. How do you think Brett would've reacted if he had walked in moments before when I had you bent over my knee while smacking my hand across your bare bottom?"

Her very curvy, luscious bare bottom... Damn it.

"So that's why you're so pissy? You're feeling guilty?" When he didn't say anything, she shook her head. "I'm an adult. It's not up to Brett." Her piercing blue eyes never left him.

Okay, so she had a point. But still... "Yeah, well, you're his sister...and he's like a brother to me. So, like it or not, his opinion matters."

"No, this isn't about Brett. It's about us. Besides, he can't have an opinion on something he doesn't know about. I know you didn't tell him about us."

Logan rubbed a hand over his face and shook his head. "Damn it, Valerie. There is no us. The only reason I didn't tell him is because I didn't want to throw you under the bus to your brother. But we can't be a couple. You know as well as I do that your brother will never allow it, and I don't like keeping stuff from him."

"I'm not suggesting that we keep it from him forever." She shrugged. "I mean, who knows if this thing between us would even work. We could just try it out for a solid week and—"

"We can't do that," he said, though the desperate hope of having something with her, even temporarily, was starting to cripple his mind-set. "It's too risky."

"So what then? You'd rather just move on and pretend

like none of this happened? Hope that I eventually let go of this stupid crush I've had on you for years?"

Dismissing any thoughts of Valerie was impossible. He didn't want to forget her. Or the things she'd told him in her drunken stupor. Last night he'd gotten to see past her tough exterior down to her soft, vulnerable side, one that she didn't share often, and the things she'd said had meant a lot to him. *She* meant a lot to him... and always had.

Logan sighed. "No, goddamn it, that's not what I want."

"Then what is?"

His gaze locked on to hers, and a spark ignited in his gut. What the hell was wrong with him? This would never work. He'd been best friends with Brett since... well, forever. Maybe it was the heat of the moment. Or maybe it was a turning point in his life. Because even if it meant keeping their relationship a secret from her brother, Logan couldn't stay away from Valerie another minute.

The bottom line was that he wanted her. Had always wanted her. And this time, he couldn't stop himself from having her. "I want the same damn thing I've always wanted. You."

Chapter Eleven

Valerie couldn't believe what she was hearing.

For years, she'd longed for Logan to say those words to her but never thought he actually would. Now that he had, she had to wonder if they were doing the right thing. Which she knew was stupid. But she didn't want to keep her relationship with Logan a secret. From Brett or anyone else, for that matter. And she wasn't entirely sure Logan had thought it all through any more than she had when she suggested the stupid idea.

But on the plus side, she'd finally gotten Logan to let down his guard. Yeah, Brett was going to kill...well, both of them. But at least she would die a happy death. A slow smile spread across her lips. "So do I get to come in now?"

He moved aside, but the blast of heat from his eyes warned her to enter with caution. And she did. But apparently she wasn't cautious enough. The moment he closed the door behind them, he wrapped his strong arm around her waist and spun her toward him and then walked her back into the wall by the door. She came to a dead stop, his hands still loitering at her hips.

He stood perfectly still, as if he were cast out of molten rock like a dormant volcano with something sinister simmering just below the surface. She could almost feel the frustration in his fingertips, but with a seemingly determined spirit, he continued to keep himself in check.

Her stomach fluttered with anticipation, and her racing heart hammered against her rib cage so she sucked in a deep breath and released it slowly. Did he even know how he was affecting her? She licked her dry lips, and his piercing gaze lowered to her mouth. She watched as a wicked grin developed on his face. Oh yeah. He definitely knew.

His dark eyes grew with intensity, and his pupils dilated, but he still didn't move. Like he was giving her an out or a chance to reconsider. Maybe it was his way of telling her that, once this began, there would be no going back. But she didn't want to go back. Not to a time where Logan wouldn't be hers. She'd been there, done that, and she hadn't liked it one bit. So she blew out another breath and forced her body to relax.

Logan must've taken that as a sign of surrender. Because, without warning, his strong arms lifted her, locking her legs around his waist. She squeaked at the unexpected movement and clutched at his broad shoulders, but the sound came out muffled as his lips fiercely took hers with a kiss that was anything but gentle. Then he turned and carried her down the hallway toward what she hoped was his bedroom.

With each step, the solid bulge in his black athletic shorts rocked against the notch between her legs, sparking a fire in her core. Her body ached to feel more of him so she leveraged her hands on his shoulders and rubbed herself more firmly against him. The frenzied kiss instantly grew to frantic proportions, and his tongue invaded her mouth, penetrating deep.

When they got to the bedroom, Logan loosened his tight grip on her, and she slid down his ripped body until her feet touched the floor. In between kisses, he paused and whispered, "Please tell me you're wearing panties this time."

Though she wasn't sure why he'd asked such a thing, she grinned against his mouth. "I'm wearing panties this time."

A low hum fell from his lips as he pulled away from her, ignoring the grunt of protest bubbling from her throat. "Good. Now take them off."

"Why don't you?"

His face grew serious, and his ferocious eyes met hers. "Because it's one of my fantasies. You removing your panties while I watch."

With his words, the pulse between her legs grew stronger, and she arched one eyebrow. "Do you want me to take them off slowly or rip them from my body?"

His eyes glazed over, and he groaned under his breath. "Surprise me," he breathed out in a strained, husky voice that didn't sound anything like his own.

With his hard gaze focused intently on her, Valerie slid her hands slowly under her lavender dress. She grasped the band of her lacy white panties, feeling the thin material stretch between her fingers. Then she bent over slightly, wiggling her butt, as she lowered them slowly down her legs and let them drift to the floor.

Logan stepped forward and lifted her dress, tugging it over her head and discarding it onto the floor as well. Then he gently directed her backward until her rear landed on the mattress behind her. One more little shove and he had her on her back as he knelt down in front of her, wedging his head between her legs. His mouth trailed over her sensitive thighs, moving higher and higher until he reached a more intimate part of her and lightly kissed it.

"More," she murmured, needing to feel all of him on all of her.

She sucked in a quick breath as he flicked his tongue over her clit and worked two large fingers inside of her, scissoring them together. One warm hand closed over her breast, lightly stoking and stimulating before plucking firmly at her hardened nipple. She admired his amazing dexterity and loved how he slackened his touch just enough before applying more pressure just where she needed it most. As if he was learning her body and making it his.

His. She liked the sound of that.

Glancing down the length of her body, Valerie caught him staring back at her with blatant hunger in his piercing brown eyes. His hot mouth pressed more firmly over her mound, pleasuring her, possessing her, owning her. The erotic view took her breath away, and a deep, penetrating need roared to life inside of her.

Her head fell back, whipping from side to side, as

her fingers clutched tightly to the comforter beneath her. "Oh God," she moaned. "Yes, like that. Right there. Don't stop."

A furious storm grew inside of her. Her vision grew hazy as her heart thundered in her ears. Heated blood sloshed through her veins, and electricity crackled along her nerve endings before settling low and deep in her abdomen, growing into a hot ball of desperate energy that needed to be released.

Valerie cried out as the ball of lightning inside of her exploded, shattering her into a million pieces. Her thighs wrapped tightly around Logan's ears, restricting his movements, but he was apparently hell-bent on following her all the way to the end. With rough hands, he yanked her legs open and held her in place with one large hand on her stomach as he continued to assault her with wave after turbulent wave of pleasure.

Even after she'd ridden through the crests and her languid body was weakened to the point of sensitivity, Logan didn't stop. Hell, he didn't even slow down. She was limp and light-headed, and when she couldn't stand it any longer, she finally said, "Um, Logan. I know I said for you not to stop, but I didn't mean for you to take that literally."

She felt him smile against her. The sadistic jerk.

Logan drew his tongue over her one last time and made her shiver before rising to his feet and licking his glistening lips. "Mmm. But I like the way you taste."

Valerie grinned and sat up. "Yeah, but it's my turn now," she said, pushing his shorts down his legs and grasping the thick, gloriously hard cock twitching in front of her face.

ON THE PLUS SIDE 161

Before she could take him into her mouth, Logan placed his hand over hers. "Not this time, baby."

She poked out her bottom lip. "What? Why not?"

"Because there are other things I want to do to your sweet body right now that don't involve my dick in your mouth. We'll save that one for later."

Though his large hand stayed over the top of hers, he didn't try to stop her from gliding her fingers down his length with a strong, firm tug. "I could change your mind, you know."

"I don't doubt that you could," he said with a grin. "But right now, I just really need to be inside you. I want to fuck you for a while, and I can't do that if you put your mouth on me. So why don't you get on the bed and put that beautiful ass of yours in the air."

Her eyebrow rose a fraction of an inch. "Is that an order?"

"No, it's more of an impolite suggestion," he said with a smirk. "Now do it. And in case there's any confusion, *that's* an order."

Valerie giggled but climbed onto the bed and got into the requested position. Since he'd asked so nicely and all.

"Good. Now don't move," he told her.

"You're so . . . bossy. I kind of like it."

His soft chuckle drifted to her ears from behind her. "You don't know the half of it, sweetheart." His big hands rubbed over her backside, long fingers dipping between her cheeks. "God, your body is fucking amazing," he murmured appreciatively.

"Look who's talking," she replied, trying to stifle the moan gurgling in the back of her throat. "You're incredibly easy on the eyes." Actually, he was rugged, manly, and hot as hell. But whatever. Same thing.

He leaned off the side of the bed and pulled a condom out of the nightstand. A crinkling of foil sounded, assuring her that he was unwrapping it and sheathing himself. Moving in behind her, he grasped her hip with one hand and positioned himself at her entrance with the other. Slowly, he inched into her until his long, thick member was seated fully inside, and a strangled gasp flew from her lips.

"Too deep?" he asked, holding himself motionless behind her.

"Um, a little." She'd like to keep her cervix intact, thank you very much.

"Lean up and put your back against me," he told her, guiding her torso backward until they were both on their knees and she was kneeling in front of him with his length still firmly lodged inside her. "How's that? Better?"

"Mmm-hmm."

"Good," he said, his voice growing huskier by the second. "Because as sad as it is, this really isn't going to take long. You're too fucking much. I haven't even started moving yet, and I'm almost there."

Holding on to her hips, Logan rocked into her slowly with an unhurried glide, as if he were allowing her time to adjust to his thick size. Desire pooled low in her belly, and she rolled her hips backward, meeting each of his thrusts head on. With both of their heated bodies in motion, the tempo gradually increased as did their erratic breathing.

One of his hands slid around her front to her breast,

deliciously torturing her nipple with the pads of his fingers, while the other ran down between her legs to apply direct stimulation to her aching clit. As if it wasn't bad enough that every part of her was already on fire, her ears were burning from all the dirty, uncensored words that he continually whispered as he pumped himself in and out of her.

Adrenaline swamped her system, and her breath bottomed out. Although she'd planned to wait for him so they could fly over that orgasmic ledge together, she suddenly found her head arching back over his steady shoulder as her inner muscles clasped around him. The moment her body gripped on to his, he grunted and pounded harder into her with rough, vigorous strokes.

She barely remained upright, her thighs quivering from the effort. But Logan dug his fingers into her hips and held her in place. He slammed into her repeatedly, and she took the brunt of his lovemaking in stride, reveling in the way his cock throbbed hot inside of her since he was apparently in the zone and showed no signs of being close to finishing. *Christ. How long can a guy be almost there?*

After a few more minutes, Logan finally bit down on her right shoulder, held himself deep inside her, and released a guttural groan as his body jerked involuntarily. His hard chest heaved behind her as he gulped in large breaths, blowing them out against her neck and back. Once his breathing slowed a little, he carefully removed himself from her and fell onto the bed, pulling her down with him. Then he shifted her toward him, settling her onto his sweaty chest. "You okay, baby? I didn't hurt you, did I?"

Hurt? No. Ravaged? Oh, hell yeah. That was the only way to describe how she felt right now. "No, I'm fine. Now rest up. Because in a few minutes, we're doing all of this again."

* * *

Logan was going crazy.

He'd spent the past two nights at the bar with his eyes glued to Valerie's voluptuous body and his tongue hanging halfway out of his mouth like a panting dog with his favorite treat dangling in front of him. But when he glanced at her this time and spied Valerie wiggling her ass to the beat of the music, he realized there was no "going crazy" to it. He was already there.

Keeping his eyes off her was hard enough to do when she wasn't moving her body in ways that reminded him of them having sex. Did she really have to tease him like that? When Valerie's gaze caught his, she gave him an imperceptible nod toward the back room and a secretive little smile that forced him to take a deep breath and adjust the growing bulge in his pants. Damn her. He wished she would behave herself.

They'd already had so much sex in the past two days that he was surprised he could even still get it up. Before work. After work. A quickie in the backseat of his truck behind the bar because he couldn't wait long enough to get her back to his place and into his bed. And then there was his office. The stuff they'd done together in there was permanently burned and branded into the back of his mind.

But he knew the risks they were taking by being together like that. And what he could lose in the process. Yet now that he had her, he couldn't fathom the idea of letting her go. Even if it would be in her best interest. Guess he was more of a selfish bastard than he'd thought.

Valerie leaned over and said something to James that had him nodding in response. Then she grabbed the keys to the storeroom and strutted toward the swinging doors with a feral gleam in her catlike eyes and a lovely sway in those feminine hips. With both hands on the door, she paused long enough to throw a seductive, come-hither glance over her shoulder at Logan, and then she pushed her way through them.

And as pathetic as it was, Logan's dick practically dragged him through that door after her. He barely made it into the storeroom before she slammed the door shut behind him and pounced on him like an attacking, deranged panther. She pawed at his shirt and pants, trying to rip them off his body, as her claws raked against his skin and her teeth sank into his bottom lip.

For a second, he almost considered not stopping her, but then he remembered why he'd followed her in there to begin with...and it hadn't been for this. Okay, so maybe that was a lie. His dick had definitely planned for this. But he really needed to put a stop to all of it before they got caught together. It was too big a risk.

So Logan did the only thing he could. He grabbed her by the scruff of her neck and gently held her away from him so the little sex kitten couldn't scratch or bite him anymore...though he loved it when she did both. "Sweetheart, you have to stop. We can't keep doing this at work. We're going to get caught."

Valerie batted her eyelashes innocently. "Well, it's not

like I forced you to follow me in here. You did that all on your own."

"True. But I didn't come in here for—" He noticed the hardened nipples poking through her top. "Are you cold or something?"

Her mouth curved into a wicked grin, and she pushed out her chest. "Right now I would say I'm the exact opposite of cold."

His cock twitched, and he groaned under his breath. "Baby, you're killing me here."

She let out a hearty laugh. "What's wrong? No self-control?"

"You know damn well that went out the window when you showed up at my house on Friday afternoon." He released her and took a step back. Ya know, just in case.

"Poor baby," she said, smirking. "Am I overwhelming you already?"

"God, yes." He ran his trembling fingers through his hair and blew out a deep breath. "You're doing shit to my brain and making it hard as hell to concentrate. Now what was I saying again?"

She rolled her eyes. "I believe you were chastising me about my insatiable need to have you inside me."

"Oh yeah. That." He paced toward the back of the room, putting more distance between them. "So as I was saying," he began, turning to face her. Her gaze had apparently lowered but quickly darted back up to meet his. "Damn it, Val. Did you just check out my ass?"

"Um, no."

"You did, you liar."

She grinned. "Well, if you don't want me to look at

your ass, then don't point it in my direction. By the way, it's a great ass. Even better when there aren't jeans covering it."

"Valerie." His voice held a stern warning.

"Okay, fine. I'll stop trying to lure you into the storeroom. But I'm not promising anything else. Any time we *aren't* at work, all bets are off. Just like my clothes will be."

Yeah. He figured that much. And he was in complete agreement. "Fair enough."

"Well, since you didn't come back here to ravish me like I had hoped, then tell me, what are you doing in here?"

"Two reasons," he replied. "One, I wanted to thank you for working with Derek and showing him some of your moves. He's having fun with it, and I've seen a huge improvement in his speed and performance. I think you actually lit a fire under him."

She waved him off. "Oh, that? I didn't do much. He really wanted to learn so he's been practicing the moves I showed him at home. He's getting pretty good at some of them too."

"I still appreciate it. This weekend ran a lot smoother because of it. By next week, I should have all the money I need."

"Money you need for what?" she asked.

Shit. Why had he said that? "Uh, nothing. I'm just glad we're all making money, that's all. I hear the bar staff and waitresses have been bringing in several hundred dollars in tips per night. That's great. Exactly what I was hoping for."

She gazed at him warily, as if she sensed that he wasn't

telling her something. But he couldn't tell her about the foreclosure on his mom's house. The information was private, and his mother had gone to great lengths to keep everyone in town from finding out about the financial situation she was in. Including Logan.

If he hadn't seen the foreclosure document sitting on his mother's kitchen table when he'd paid her a visit, he probably never would've known what kind of mess she was in. Well, at least not until her house had been taken away from her. Then everyone would've known.

To keep Valerie from inquiring further, Logan quickly changed the subject. "The second thing I came in here for is to ask you a question. When is your next day off from the bakery?"

"Um, tomorrow. Why?"

"Let's do something together." Her sultry eyes lit up with ideas before he could even finish. "I mean something else. Like go out."

Her brows furrowed. "Why can't we just hang out at your place?"

"Because I want to take you out."

"Okay. So where do you want to go?"

He shrugged. "We could go to the movies."

"On a Monday?"

"Yeah, why not? Brett will be at work so we don't have to worry about running into him. And since it's dark in the theater, no one will see us together. It's actually perfect."

"Okay, so what are we going to see?"

"Well, I don't know about you, but I'm going to see all the erotic faces you pull as I give you one hell of an orgasm with my fingers."

Her mouth fell open. "Uh, Logan, I don't think—"

"Exactly. Don't think." He leaned in and gave her a quick kiss before heading to the door. When he reached it, he turned back and winked. "And don't forget to wear a dress."

Chapter Twelve

As they headed inside the movie theater the next day, Valerie gave Logan a strange look. "I don't know why you're bringing in a jacket. It's like ninety degrees outside today."

"Yeah, but everyone knows it gets cold in the movie theater. Besides, you're wearing a skirt. You can drape it over your legs to keep them warm." Then he gave her a sexy little smirk and lifted one eyebrow. "Don't you think?"

She gave him a *yeah, right* look. "I know where you're going with this, but I already told you that we're not doing *that* in here," she said, crossing her arms. "I mean it, Logan."

But he continued to grin as he walked up to the counter and stood in line to buy their movie tickets. Valerie watched a young girl stuff popcorn into a big bucket for one guy and then hand another woman a couple of drinks.

The theater wasn't packed or anything, but there were several people milling about the oversized room and a couple of kids playing in the small arcade located by the restrooms.

The moment Logan got the tickets, he motioned for Valerie to follow him down the dimly lit corridor to find the theater they were in. And he was still smiling like crazy. Damn, she had a bad feeling about this. But that didn't stop her from following him anyway. Part of her was fascinated by the idea of what he wanted to do while the other part of her cringed at the possibility of getting caught.

The darkened theater wasn't at all crowded, but there were several groups of people all sitting near each other in the center of the room, separated by a couple of rows or even a few chairs. Valerie breathed a sigh of relief when Logan found them seats at the edge of the far aisle, probably figuring no one would sit anywhere near them.

But she still wasn't doing what he'd planned. Nope. Not going to happen.

As they sat down, Logan slid his arm around her shoulders and whispered, "You nervous?"

She smiled. "Not at all, I'm sure you chose a great movie." Then she stared ahead at the screen. "Which one is it?"

"I have no idea. I just picked one out randomly," he said quietly with a soft chuckle. "You know damn well that we're not here to watch a movie."

"Really, Logan? Here?"

He nodded. "Oh yeah. Definitely here."

"We shouldn't. Somebody might see us."

"Yeah, that's what makes this all the more exciting." He lifted the armrest and laid the jacket over her legs, sliding his hand on her bare thigh beneath it.

He wasn't touching her in a sexual manner...yet, but she had a feeling that would be changing very soon. She could feel the sexual tension vibrating off of him, and it only had her heart beating faster.

Logan looked like a tiger lying in wait, which made her the defenseless, unsuspecting prey about to get eaten. *Um, no. Definitely not eaten. We sure as hell aren't doing that in here.* God, she really needed to calm down. Her nerves were firing warning shots to her brain while her stomach twisted in anticipation.

Finally, the lights dimmed, the room went mostly dark, and the previews began playing. But Logan sat there staring straight ahead. Had he been messing with her the whole time? She almost hoped the answer to that question was a resounding yes, but the moment the featured movie began to play, a slow grin lit up his face.

Logan leaned toward her, his eyes still focused on the screen in front of them. "Open those beautiful legs for me, baby."

The moment he spoke, Valerie lost all muscle function throughout her entire body. "I...uh, can't."

He sat up straighter. "The hell you can't. We're doing this. Right here, right now. It's on your list. That means it's happening."

"That's what I meant. But Logan, about that list—" His hand moved higher on her thigh, and she about fainted.

"Shhh! No talking. We're in a movie theater." His fingertips slipped under her satin panties and began making circular motions around her clit. Her breath caught in her throat. "Just sit back and enjoy the show," he murmured, his tone rough as gravel and sexy as all get-out.

A soft gasping sound left her throat, but she tried to stifle it.

His fingers pressed a little harder, moving a little faster over the slick bud. "You like?"

The man was touching her between her legs. What the hell was there not to like? "Mmm-hmm."

Logan swirled a finger in her wetness then drove it inside of her. First one, then another. He pumped them in and out of her with a quick pace while grinding his palm against her mound, letting the friction drive her slowly insane. Her erratic breath panted out faster, and a frenzy of sensations welled up inside of her. Hot desire coiled inside her as frantic need spiked low in her abdomen.

Within minutes, she was on the edge of insanity, moaning so loud that she had to turn her face into his shoulder. It only made him grin more. Exquisite pleasure raced through her veins, and she quietly begged for him to let her come.

Her body convulsed twice in her chair before she managed to brace herself against the other armrest, holding herself still. God, she hoped no one saw that. Otherwise, they might think she was having a seizure and come over to offer their assistance or call an ambulance. The last thing Logan needed was help in getting her off. He was doing a fine job of that all on his own.

Unable to hold back any longer, she bit into his arm to keep from screaming out his name. His fingers slowed, but he held them deep inside her. Her heart pounded in her ears as she rode out the long, drawn-out wave until the tremors subsided. Then Logan slid his fingers from her.

"I have to taste you. I can't wait," he said, bringing them to his mouth and licking the wetness from them.

Holy hell. She practically came again right then and there.

"Feeling a bit more relaxed?" Logan asked, grinning from ear to ear.

"Yes," she breathed out, and then ran her hand over the hard ridge in the front of his jeans, pushing her fingers against the head of his swollen cock. "So now it's my turn, right?"

He grasped her wrist and stilled her hand. "Uh-uh. No way. Don't start something in here that you can't or won't be able to finish."

She tilted her head at the challenge. "Oh, I can finish it. Let go of my hand and see for yourself."

Apparently, he had less scruples than she did because he immediately released her and linked both of his hands behind his head with a grin. "Go for it."

So she did.

Valerie unbuttoned his pants and started to pull the zipper down slowly to minimize the sound. But it didn't work. Actually, that never worked in a movie theater. For some strange reason, the smallest sounds were always amplified by a billion. Like when you're watching a movie while trying to get the last few M&M's out of the bottom of the bag, but it sounded more like you were playing Chinese checkers and accidentally bumped the entire board.

So Valerie did the only thing she could do in a situation like this. She fake-coughed to cover the sound and quickly unzipped his jeans the rest of the way at the same time.

Logan chuckled under his breath. "Nice move, slick."

"You haven't seen anything yet," she said, wrapping her fingers tightly around him.

He tensed and hissed out a slow breath. Leaning toward her, he whispered, "You're driving me insane already. Just the thought of you giving me a hand job in here has me so close to coming. Consider that the only warning you're going to get."

Valerie smiled, and her tongue darted out, wetting her lips. "Who said anything about a hand job?"

She ducked her head under the jacket and dropped her lips over him, sliding them all the way to the base of his hard cock. His thigh muscles tightened beneath her as he kicked his long legs out and locked them underneath the seat in front of him. He took a deep breath, his stomach muscles hardening against her shoulder, as she dragged her lips over him again.

After a few minutes, one big hand snaked under the jacket and fisted in her hair, stilling her lips on him. She thought for sure he was about to come in her mouth. But then he said, "Oh, don't worry. She's okay. My girlfriend felt a little sick, that's all, so I told her to take a nap in my lap while I finished the movie. Didn't want to miss it."

Oh my God! He's talking to someone?

A sweet-sounding woman's voice filtered through the jacket. "I don't blame you, dear. I get the senior discount, but I don't like to waste money like that either. I don't normally even step out to grab a drink during the movie, but my granddaughter isn't here today, and my ulcer is acting up."

A grandma? He's talking to a fucking grandma? Seriously? While I'm sucking his...

Valerie scraped her teeth lightly against him, hoping it

would hurry him along. But he just gripped her hair tighter and kept on talking. "I just love Bruce Willis, don't you?"

"Oh yes. He's one of my favorite actors. And you know who else I really like?" the lady asked him, yammering on. "Oh, what's his name? He played in that movie as a bank robber. Or was he the policeman? Maybe he was the teller. My memory isn't what it used to be."

"Hmm. I'm not sure I know which actor you're talking about," Logan said. "Can you describe him for me?"

Valerie could almost hear the smile in his voice. He was obviously doing this on purpose, the jerk. But he wasn't the only one who could toy with someone. With the tight grip he had on her hair, she couldn't move her head. But she didn't need to move her head in order to torture him.

Squeezing her lips tighter around him, she rolled her tongue over his length. His cock jerked in her mouth and became even harder, thicker, longer. He grunted softly, his body stiffening as he told the woman, "Well, it was nice talking to you. Enjoy the rest of the movie."

"You do the same, dear."

Valerie increased the firm suction, and he released a small groan that he covered with a fake cough. "Oh, trust me, I'm enjoying the hell out of it," he said, his gravelly voice deepening.

"And I hope your girlfriend feels better soon."

"Thanks, I'm sure . . . she . . . will."

She knew the moment the old woman walked away because Logan released his death grip on her hair. "Okay, that's it. I'm changing my mind about the spanking stuff," he whispered. "You obviously still need one."

Valerie giggled beneath the jacket. "Shhh! We're in a

movie theater. Sit back and enjoy the show," she said, then took him into her mouth once more.

*   *   *

The next day, Logan waltzed into the garage and knocked on the hood of the shiny silver Mustang. "Anyone home?"

"Is that you, Logan?" a voice echoed from underneath the car.

"Yeah, it's me."

"Good," Brett said. "Hand me that ratchet in the top drawer of my black rolling toolbox."

Logan stepped over to the giant toolbox on wheels and riffled through the top drawer. "Is it the one with the blue grip handle?"

"Yep, that's the one. Pass it down here to me." Brett's grimy hand slid out from beneath the car. Black grease coated the underside of his nails and a fresh, bloody scrape decorated his knuckles.

Logan handed the tool over, which quickly disappeared under the car before a ratcheting sound drifted to his ears. "What happened to your hand?"

"It slipped off this fucking wrench I was using to crank on this bolt and hit the fucking exhaust pipe, the cocksucker."

Logan grinned. Guess Brett was still a little pissed about the whole thing.

Logan glanced back down at the two limbs sticking out from beneath the car, noting the oil stains covering the dirty overalls. "By the way, nice legs." The greasy hand appeared again, this time with only one middle finger sticking straight up, which made Logan chuckle.

Seconds later, Brett wheeled out from under the low-profile car, his back cushioned by a red vinyl-covered creeper. Dirt and filth smudged his face, and rusty metal flakes littered his hair. He held out a hand, as if he wanted help up.

Logan glanced at the grungy palm. "Um, you're kidding, right?"

"You pansy," Brett said with a chuckle as he lifted himself off the ground. "Afraid of getting a little dirty?"

"Not usually, but I have to be at the bar soon, and I don't want to go home and take another shower." Especially since there wasn't any hot water left. Not after he'd spent two hours in there with Valerie before dropping her off at home and heading to the garage where Brett worked.

He wasn't even sure why he'd come. Just felt like hanging out with his buddy without feeling guilty about sleeping with the guy's sister.

Brett walked toward the dirty shop sink and pumped some pink cleanser on his hands from a nearby container. He rubbed them together, forming a dark lather, and scrubbed his grungy fingers with a small bristle brush to help remove the grease embedded under his nails. Then he rinsed his hands off and dried them on a red shop towel hanging from a screw sticking out of the wall. "What are you doing here anyway?"

Hell if Logan knew. "Just stopped by to see how you were doing. We haven't talked much lately."

"I've been working a lot of overtime lately. My boss has me rebuilding a transmission in his cousin's race car. What have you been doing all week?"

Your sister. Logan sighed, feeling the guilt creeping back in. "Not much. Just working."

A red truck pulled into the lot and parked in front of the open garage door, grabbing both of their attention. Two men were inside the cab, but only Sam climbed out. "Hey, guys. How's it going?" He stepped around the front fender and shook each of their hands.

"Hey, Sam," Brett said. "That fuel pump still giving you problems? If I remember right, it should still be under warranty."

"Nope. Ever since you changed out the filter, the truck's been running fine. If it starts acting up again, I'll let you know."

"Sounds good. So what brings you out here then?"

"Leah asked me to stop by on my way home and let you know that the wedding has been moved up to this Saturday. Same place, same time. She tried to call, but she said the shop phone rings and rings and no one ever answers it."

Brett leaned his hip against a nearby counter and grinned. "I was under a car all afternoon, and my hands were dirty."

Sam nodded. "Well, we hope you can still make it to the wedding on such short notice." Then he glanced in Logan's direction. "And I know we don't know each other well, Logan, but you're welcome to join us. It's a two-hour drive down to the coast, but I know it would mean a lot to Leah if you could both come."

"I'm not sure that I can," Logan said. "Since Valerie is the maid of honor, she'll need to be off from the bar that night, which only leaves me with two bartenders to cover the shift. They might need a hand."

"Well, the beach wedding starts at four o'clock, and the reception will follow directly after. Even if you stayed for only a few hours, you could make it back here by ten o'clock at the latest."

"This coming Saturday?"

"Yep. I'll have Leah send an invitation over to the bar with Valerie so that you have the address. We'd love to have you, but we'll understand if you can't make it."

"Sounds good," Logan told him. "Thanks for the invite."

"No problem," Sam replied, shaking hands with both of them again. "I've got to run, but I hope to see you guys on Saturday." He slid back into his truck, but as he pulled away, the other man in the passenger seat grinned at them out the passenger window. Then he gave them a little wave.

Brett glared after the truck. "I hate that bastard."

"Sam?"

"No, not him. Sam's one of the good guys. Besides you, he's the only other guy who doesn't look at my sister like he wants to rip her clothes off like some kind of pervert."

No, Logan didn't look at her like that. He just did it.

Logan shook his head to clear the image from his mind. "Who were you talking about then?"

"Did you see that other guy in Sam's truck?"

"Yeah."

"Well, that's Max. He apparently works for Sam as an electrician or something. But the night of your grand opening, I came close to punching the guy out."

Logan's body went rigid. "Why?"

"Because my sister was letting him put his hands on her."

First Paul, then Max? Jesus. How many guys did Valerie flirt with that night?

Brett shook his head. "Since I've been working so much overtime, I considered not going to the wedding at all. But then I found out that Max is the best man. Now I'm just going to make sure that dumbass keeps his damn hands to himself."

"Yeah, no kidding." *That makes two of us.*

Chapter Thirteen

Valerie stuck her finger in her mouth and sucked off the chocolate as a pair of emerald eyes narrowed at her. "What?" she asked.

Leah shook her head and went back to smoothing buttercream around the sides of her cake. "Please tell me you don't lick your fingers when you're making desserts for my customers."

"Depends on what I'm making," Valerie said, grinning as Leah clutched at her heart. "Oh, calm down. I'm just kidding."

"God, you better be. That's gross." Then she grinned and glanced back over at the square groom's cake sitting in front of Valerie. "Not that Sam would care. It's chocolate. He would eat it off the floor if I let him."

Valerie set aside the bowl of ganache she'd just warmed and then pulled out a wire rack and set it on top of a deep, silver baking pan. "Are you sure you don't want me to work on your wedding cake instead of his groom's cake? I know you're way better at the decorating than I am, but I feel bad that you're having to make your own cake. Maybe we should have ordered one from another bakery or something."

"Hush your mouth, you traitor," Leah said, outraged at the very suggestion of getting a cake from someone else's bakery. "Besides, I don't mind making my own cake. Since my mom took over most of the wedding planning, it's the only thing I have control over at the moment."

Lifting the square chocolate cake with two hands, Valerie set it over the wire rack. "Is that why you decided to up the wedding date?"

"Basically," Leah told her, running the metal elbow spatula flat over the top of the white cake to remove any air bubbles in the frosting. "My mother has been driving me insane with all these last-minute details so Sam and I agreed that the quicker we got through with the wedding, the better off we both would be." She shrugged. "Plus, I think he likes the idea of eating lots of cake and then having a bunch of sex this week rather than next week."

Valerie rolled her eyes. "Figures. Such a male way of looking at a wedding." She noticed another spot of chocolate on her pinkie and stuck it into her mouth, sucking it off. "So everything else is done? You're ready for this wedding to happen?"

"I am, but I'm not sure my body is." Leah sighed. "I really wanted to lose a few pounds before I walked down the aisle."

"Aw, honey. Sam loves you. If he was here right now, he'd have his eyes glued to your backside like he does every time I'm around him. He doesn't care about those few pounds that you're so determined to shed."

"I know, but every bride wants to feel beautiful on her wedding day."

"Leah, you *are* beautiful—inside and out. Sam loves you just as you are. And you know damn well he would tell you that himself."

"Actually, he already has. And of course I believe him. He makes me feel beautiful all the time. It's just my stupid insecurities bubbling back to the surface on occasion. It's hard to break a bad habit that I've had all my life." She gestured to Valerie with her frosting-covered spatula. "If only I could be more like you. You're always so confident and carefree when it comes to your size. You own it rather than letting it own you. Unfortunately, we're just not all that way."

"You're improving, Leah. Don't discount that. It just takes time to get there, that's all. If I had a mother who was picking on me about my weight my entire life, I'd be just as neurotic as you are." Valerie grinned to show that she was teasing.

"Gee, thanks," Leah said, laughing. "By the way, I meant to tell you that I appreciate you covering my days next week on such short notice. We've rented this cute little A-frame bungalow on the beach for a few nights. But if you need anything, I'll have my cell phone with me. Don't hesitate to call. I can be back here in two hours flat, if necessary."

Valerie lifted the bowl of warm ganache and began pouring it over Sam's cake, letting the shiny melted chocolate coat the top and drip the sides. "Leah, I'm not calling you during your honeymoon."

"But if you need to—"

"I won't. You and Sam enjoy your time away and don't worry about a thing. Max has Sam covered at the construction site, and my job is to cover you at the bakery. Let me do my job."

Leah smiled and slapped more of the white frosting on the sides of the large round cake. "Speaking of jobs, how is it going at the bar? You seem to really love working there."

Valerie righted the bowl of ganache and ran her finger along the edge to catch the drip then slipped it into her mouth with a grin. "I do. It's the best job I've ever..." Her words trailed off, and she gazed over at her friend, who had arched one brow. Well, shit. "I'm sorry. I didn't mean anything—"

"It's okay, Val," Leah said, giggling. "Did you think I didn't notice how much you were enjoying your new job? Your face positively lights up when you're behind that bar and entertaining the crowd. Just like I'm sure mine does when I'm working here."

But guilt still weighed heavily in Valerie's stomach. "Yeah, but that doesn't mean I don't enjoy being here too. You know I do, right?"

"Of course. But just because the bakery is *my* dream job doesn't mean that it has to be yours too. I've actually been thinking about hiring someone to replace you."

Valerie blinked and dropped the metal mixing bowl to the counter with a clatter. "What? You're firing me?"

"No, silly. But I can see where your heart lies...and it's not in frosting cakes and playing with pastry dough."

She shook her head. "You don't have to hire someone

else, Leah. I wasn't going to quit on you, if that's what you were thinking. I'd never do that. Especially to my best friend."

"So you're going to force me into firing you then?"

Valerie's eyes widened. "B-but you just said—"

"Oh, honey," she said, setting her frosting utensil down, "I just want you to be happy no matter where you work. If you truly want to continue working here, of course I'd love to keep you on. But if you prefer to work at the bar full-time, then I'm not going to stand in the way of that. And I don't want you to feel guilty about it either. It won't affect our friendship one way or another, I promise."

"Well, I don't know that Logan would even consider keeping me on full-time. He's probably still planning on replacing me when he finds another competent bartender."

"It's already been two weeks, and he hasn't done it yet."

"Yeah, but... well, something happened recently that might interfere with our working relationship. I'm not sure what's going to happen at this point."

Leah locked eyes with her. "Oh my God. He finally noticed you!"

"Um, well, yeah, but it's more than that."

She squealed. "You kissed him?"

"No, I mean a lot more than that." Valerie wound her hand in the air, trying to get Leah to continue her train of thought. "Keep going, you're almost there."

Leah's brows furrowed in thought, and her forehead wrinkled a little. "Um, he kissed you back?"

Valerie sighed. This was taking way too damn long. At

this rate, the girl would never figure it out. "I had sex with Logan."

"Oh." She paused for a moment "I guess I didn't jump far enough ahead."

"No kidding."

"When did this happen?"

"Um, I think the better question is when has it *not* happened. I've been sleeping with him on a regular basis since last week."

Leah's eyes narrowed. "And you're just now telling me? What kind of friend are you? You're lucky it's too late for me to find another maid of honor. You don't deserve the title, you little...secret keeper."

Valerie laughed at the empty threat. "I wasn't hiding anything from you. At least not on purpose. You've been busy dealing with your mom, and I haven't gotten you alone long enough to tell you anything. Until now, that is."

Leah pulled out a couple of dowel rods to slide inside her wedding cake to support the top layer. "True. And we are working hours opposite of each other. But how are you even doing it?"

"Doing what?"

"Him. Logan."

Jeez. Was she wanting a blow-by-blow description of their sexual activities? Valerie shook her head. "I don't think I know what you mean."

"You've been holding down two jobs for a couple of weeks now, helping me with wedding stuff constantly, and if I know you as well as I think I do, I'm sure you've been avoiding your brother for the past week. So how is it possible you still have any energy left? You're bound to be tired. Do you just lay there and let Logan have his way with you?"

Valerie laughed. "Are you kidding? I've waited way too long to get his attention to just lie there during sex. I climb that man like a tree."

"You hussy," Leah said, a playful gleam flashing in her eyes. "You're terrible."

"I'm certain Logan would completely disagree with that statement." Valerie winked. "He seems to be enjoying himself...um, especially since he found your list."

Leah squinted at her. "What list?"

"The one you made me write at the bar. You know, all the sexual things I never wanted to do."

Leah giggled. "He read it? Oh God. What did he say?"

"Not much seeing how he thinks that it was a list of my sexual fantasies."

Leah bent over at the waist and laughed until her face turned red. "Oh man! I would love to have seen his face. Did you correct him?"

"Uh, not exactly. As weird as it sounds, when he got his hands on that list, it set things in motion for us."

"How so?"

Biting her bottom lip, she hesitated.

"Valerie?"

She sighed. "Okay, fine. I was never good at keeping stuff from you so you'll just find out later anyway." She blew out a quick breath. "Logan saw the napkin and got pissed because he thought I was going to do all the things we listed with God knows who. And from what I gathered since then, he's trying to make sure I do all of them...with him."

Leah's body stiffened. "He wants you to have an orgy?"

"No. I mean I hope not. That's definitely not happening. But he's been ticking items off that list ever since last week."

"Which ones?"

Valerie didn't blush often, but her cheeks filled with heat. "Semi-public sex, dirty talking, and we went to the movies the other day."

Leah raised one curious brow. "What movie did you see?"

"I have no idea. We were...busy at the time."

"Oh my God. I didn't know you were so kinky."

Valerie groaned and slid a hand over her face. "Apparently, I didn't either. And honestly, those were all pretty tame compared to the rest of the list."

"So what's next on the agenda?"

"I have no idea. In fact, I'm almost certain I don't want to know."

Leah grinned. "You're probably lucky you didn't put a gangbang on that list. I thought of that one after you walked off that night."

"Jesus. Okay, so what should I do?"

"Tell him the truth about the list. And do it fast before he starts inviting a few friends to one of your private parties."

Valerie shook her head. "Logan wouldn't do that."

"You sure?"

Damn it. No, she wasn't entirely sure. He'd been shocking her left and right with all the crazy shit he had talked her into doing. "No. But I hope not because *I* would never do that. I don't want anyone but him. I've never felt this way about anyone before. I...I think I'm falling hard for him."

Leah smiled. "You fell hard for him years ago. Or did you forget about that?"

"Yeah, but that was more of a teenage crush. This is...I don't know, something different."

"So what about Brett? Does he know?"

"God no."

"Are you going to tell him?"

Valerie shrugged. "I mean, yeah. I guess we have to at some point. But I don't want to ruin anything by doing it right now. Besides, Logan said Sam invited him to the wedding, and my brother is going to be there. I don't want any, uh, awkwardness on your wedding day."

Leah wiped her hands off on a clean rag as she stepped over to Valerie and gave her a woeful look. "You mean fighting, right? Because you know that it's probably going to come to blows between Logan and Brett. I can't imagine your brother being okay with anyone sleeping with his sister, especially his best friend."

"I don't want to ruin their relationship. But I'm not willing to let Brett screw up whatever this is between Logan and me either. I know when he finds out that he'll be upset with Logan...and probably me too. But I can't base who I fall for on whether or not my brother is happy about it. This is my happiness we're talking about."

"Are you happy?"

Valerie nodded. "Honestly, I've never been happier in my life."

"Good. I'm glad to hear that. You deserve to be happy."

Leah glanced down at the warm ganache in front of them, and her brows knitted together. "In fact, we both do. Screw the stupid diet," she said, swiping her finger around the lip of the bowl to catch the drip running down the side. "It's too late to order the dress in a bigger size, but I can always buy some Spanx." Leah plopped her chocolate-coated finger into her mouth and groaned in pure bliss.

Valerie smiled. After spending the last week in Logan's bed, she knew that feeling well.

* * *

God, Logan couldn't get enough of her.

His mouth took hers again as his hands slid under Valerie's top and closed over her nicely rounded breasts. He ground his pelvis against hers, letting her feel his hard length as soft mews fell from her lips. She ran her fingers through his hair and arched her neck, exposing the delicate skin that he traced with his tongue until he ended up at her collarbone.

"Brett," she gasped out.

Did she just call me by her brother's name? He lifted his head. "Excuse me?"

"My brother," she said, panic flashing through her eyes. "He's here. He just passed by the window."

Logan released her immediately and backed away just as a knock sounded on the door. Damn it. He quickly untucked his shirt to help cover the bulging evidence of his arousal and blew out a calming breath. He waited for Valerie to straighten her clothes and then said, "Come in."

Brett poked his head through the door. "Hey, I wanted

to see if you—" His words froze on his tongue as he spotted his sister standing in Logan's living room. "Oh. I didn't know you were here, Val. Where's your car?"

"It's, um . . . at the bakery. Leah needed to borrow it for a little while."

Her brother grimaced. "Why? Did something happen to hers? Does she need me to take a look at it?"

Valerie shook her head adamantly. "No, it's fine. It just . . . had a flat tire, that's all. Sam's already fixing it, but she had some deliveries to make that needed to go out by a certain time so I gave her the keys to mine. It's all taken care of, don't worry."

But he still looked concerned. "So then what are you doing here?"

When Valerie hesitated with an answer and bit her lip, Logan jumped in to take the heat off of her. "I needed Valerie's help in figuring out a problem with the beer order I placed last week."

"But isn't it her day off from the bar? Don't tell me you're taking advantage of my sister, asshole." Brett offered him a playful grin.

But the comment still had Logan cringing inwardly. And judging by the way Valerie's face paled, she had done the same. And that pissed him off. Logan clenched his jaw. "You don't have to worry about her. If she wants, I'll pay her for her time. I'm more than happy to compensate her."

Brett seemed content with that answer and turned his attention back to Valerie once again. "So how did you get over here? Did Leah drop you off or something?"

"I picked her up," Logan said, cutting in again and not giving Valerie a chance to answer.

Brett seemed surprised by it but gazed back at her again. "Okay, so do you need me to wait and give you a lift home?"

"No. I'll be taking her home too." Logan hadn't meant for the words to come out so firm. Final even. As if the subject was no longer up for discussion. But he was doing the one thing he never thought he'd have to do. He was protecting Valerie from her own brother.

Brett's sharp, suspicious glare landed directly on Logan, but before he could say anything, Valerie spoke up. "What Logan means is that it's going to take us a while to figure out this whole mess. So there's no point in you waiting around for me."

"You sure?" Brett asked her warily.

Damn it. Would he just leave her alone already? When the hell had Brett become so involved with his sister's affairs? *Oh, yeah. Always.* But somehow, in the past, it had never irritated and frustrated Logan nearly as much as it did in this moment.

Valerie nodded. "Yes, it's fine. Logan will make sure I get home okay."

"All right," Brett said, heading to the door. "Well, I only stopped by to see if Logan wanted to go bowling. But since y'all are busy with work stuff, we can do it another day."

"Sounds good," Logan replied.

Even after Brett left, Logan stood there quietly, suffocating in a cloud of guilt. He tried to organize his thoughts and feelings and ignore the nagging voice inside his head telling him that what he had going on with Valerie was a mistake.

But he couldn't. Because it was true.

"I guess I'll have to ask Leah and Sam to cover for me in case Brett asks them about the flat tire at the wedding." When he didn't say anything, she said, "Logan?"

He released a heavy breath. "What the fuck are we doing, Val?"

"What do you mean?"

"You know what I mean. This," he said, motioning to the two of them. "This thing we're doing. We both know this can only end badly."

She walked over to him and put her hand on his chest. "It doesn't have to. If we get caught—"

"Damn it, Valerie. It's not *if* we get caught, it's *when*. Because he's eventually going to find out about our…extracurricular activities. And then what?"

"He'll get over it. After all is said and done, it might take him some time, but you can talk to Brett and—"

"And tell him what? 'I slept with your sister. My bad.' Do you really think that's going to make everything okay?"

The look she gave him could've cracked glass. "Is that all this is to you? A booty call? Because I actually thought it was something different." Hurt registered in her eyes, and she turned away from him.

He grabbed her shoulders and turned her back. "I'm sorry. That's not at all what I meant. Of course this isn't just a booty call. I care about you," he said, threading a loose strand of her blond hair behind her ear. "But that isn't the way it's going to come across to your brother. You heard what he just said. No matter what really happens between us, he's going to assume

I took advantage of you. Especially now that you're working for me."

"I don't care what he thinks." Valerie fisted her hands on her hips and lifted her stubborn chin. "Do you want me or not, Logan?"

"You know I do."

Her arms slid around his neck. "Then tell me."

Logan wrapped his arms around her and ran his hands up her back, pulling her closer to him. He bent his head until his forehead touched hers. "I hate myself for wanting you so much."

She gazed at him lovingly and smoothed her soft hand over his cheek. "I know you don't believe this, but we're not doing anything wrong."

He didn't say anything. Just leaned down and brushed a tender, chaste kiss across her mouth as he held her tighter. Her lips parted slightly, and she sighed under her breath. Hooded blue eyes rose to his as a subtle, underlying tension began to form between them.

Logan knew that look. It was the same unspoken proposition she'd given to him years ago, but she'd been only a teenager then. A kid, really. He was fairly certain that, at the time, she'd been untouched and hadn't had a clue what she was offering him...or how much he'd wanted to take advantage of her naiveté.

But he hadn't laid a finger on her. Not because he was a nice guy, a gentleman, or even a saint. *Though any guy who managed to ignore an offer like that from Valerie Carmichael damn sure deserved a title worthy of sainthood.*

Plain and simple, he'd done so out of loyalty. Logan

sighed. "You know your brother is going to hate me for betraying our friendship."

"Are you saying we're not doing this?" she whispered, her gaze still connected to his.

He buried his face into her neck. "No. It's too late to go back. I can't stop touching you. Ever."

Chapter Fourteen

Valerie's eyes fluttered opened.

Her head rested in the crook of Logan's arm as he lay behind her, softly snoring in her ear. His big, warm body outlined hers, spooning her from head to toe. She loved the feeling of waking up next to him, but the room had grown dim, and one glance at the window confirmed her suspicion. Darkness was falling fast.

She rubbed her fingers over the heavy arm he'd draped over her waist. "Logan, you need to get up."

He released a low groan. "Again? Already?"

She giggled. "Well, I wasn't really talking about that, and although I'd love to extend playtime..." She shifted her body, turning in his arms to face him. "Don't you have to go to work?"

One of his eyes crept open. "I called James earlier and told him I'd be in late tonight. So I've got some time before I need to be there," he said, opening the other eye. He stretched and yawned. "Thursday nights are always slow anyway."

"James really takes care of the bar. I bet he would make a great head bartender."

He smiled. "I know. I already offered him the position and gave him a raise. He definitely earned it. I'm going to announce it tomorrow when the whole staff is there."

"Well, he's a much better choice than Paul ever was."

At the mention of Paul's name, Logan's forehead creased. "Did you date him or something?"

"Who, Paul? God, no. I would never let that slime touch me."

Logan squinted at her. "But in the hallway—"

"That wasn't what it looked like."

"So you were just trying to make me jealous? Because if so, it worked."

She gazed up at him, hoping he could see the sincerity in her eyes. "I wasn't flirting with Paul that night. You misunderstood the whole situation."

Confusion swam in his eyes. "Then what was that all about?"

Valerie sighed. "I only went back there to ask Brett to take me home. But I caught Paul pocketing the cash Brett gave him for the T-shirt."

Logan blinked. "He was stealing from me?"

"Yes. And I got the feeling that it wasn't the first time that he'd done so. But when Paul realized I'd caught him and that I'd planned to tell you what he was doing, he cornered me against the wall and threatened me."

Logan shot into a sitting position, his muscles tense. "What? Why didn't you tell me? I thought—"

"I know exactly what you thought. And I was going to tell you the truth. But you were so mad, and well, Paul quit on you and walked out so it didn't really matter anymore. The problem took care of itself."

His body was practically vibrating with anger. "The fuck it did. No one threatens you and gets away with it. Especially that bastard." He started to crawl out of bed.

She latched on to his arm. "Where are you going?"

Loaded with rage, his fierce eyes met hers. "To kill Paul. I know where he lives."

Valerie shook her head. "No, please don't. He didn't hurt me. He was only trying to scare me, that's all."

"That's a death sentence in itself, if you ask me. No one is going to scare my woman and live to tell about it. No one."

Though the words lashed out of him in anger, Valerie couldn't help but grin. "Your woman, huh?" Yeah, she liked the sound of that. "So you're staking a claim on me?"

"Baby, I've had a claim on you for years. It was just that neither of us knew it at the time. Now move your hands. I've got somewhere I need to be."

"No."

"Valerie."

"Please, I'm begging you not to do this. The last thing I need is for you to end up in jail. Promise me that you'll let this go."

He stayed motionless and didn't respond.

"Logan, I'm serious. Besides, Paul didn't leave there unscathed. I crushed his nuts so hard in my hand, I'm sure they hurt for a week straight. Now promise me."

He flopped back on the bed with a loud groan. "Fine.

I promise I'll let this go…for now. But if I ever see Paul anywhere near you again, he's going to have a lot more to worry about than just his balls."

She was glad he agreed, but she wasn't stupid. He had other ways to get to Paul and make him pay. "And you can't say anything about this to Brett either."

Logan grinned maliciously. "You know me too well."

Valerie leaned into his chest and sighed. "Well, I don't know everything about you. Like you never told me why you wanted to open a bar in the first place."

"I guess I thought it would be nice to have one place I couldn't get kicked out of," he said with a chuckle.

"Come on, I'm being serious."

"So am I. Do you know how many bars Brett and I were thrown out of when we were younger? We were always getting into some kind of trouble."

She shook her head. "You weren't all that bad. Just mischievous perhaps."

"No, it was more than that." Logan hesitated but then finally said, "I was getting into a lot more trouble than anyone knew. And I was dragging your brother down with me."

"Are you kidding me? I can't imagine anyone having to drag Brett into anything. He lives for trouble."

"You apparently don't know your brother as well as you think you do. He's not the troublemaker everyone thinks he is. I mean, sure, the guy can be a real asshole and has his moments, but if it wasn't for him, I would've spent a hell of a lot more time in jail than I did."

Valerie didn't know what he was talking about. Granite was a small enough town that she would've heard if he'd been arrested. "You were in jail? When?"

"Do you remember that trip your brother and I took down to South Padre?" She nodded so he continued. "Well, one night we found this little pool hall in a bad part of town. Brett warned me not to do it, but I hustled this big guy at a game of pool. He and his two friends jumped us in the parking lot, and one of them had a knife."

She gasped, the sharp intake of breath making her light-headed. "Oh my God. Did anyone get hurt?"

"No, thank God. The moment the guy lunged for me, Brett jumped on him and knocked the blade out of his hand. Someone called the cops, and they took all five of us to jail. But if your brother hadn't been there to save my ass that night, I probably wouldn't be here now."

"I never knew about that."

"No one does. We were released by the judge the next day on our own recognizance and made it back in time for your graduation. I've never told anyone that story before. And as far as I know, Brett hasn't either."

"Then why tell me now?"

"Because I wanted you to know the kind of guy your brother really is. Yes, he can be a real jerk at times, but that doesn't mean he's not a stand-up guy. I wasn't a good influence on him. That's part of the reason I decided to leave town."

"And the other part?"

"Was because of you."

Her eyes widened. "Me?"

"Yeah, you." He paused, breathing out a sigh. "When you were younger, you would flirt with me constantly behind your brother's back, and it was cute. I ignored it though because you were just a kid. Then you turned seventeen. Your body filled out in ways that were harder to ignore, and your messages became a hell of a lot less subtle. But I was twenty-one."

Valerie grinned. "Practically an old pervert."

Logan barked out a laugh. "Yeah, basically. You were so young and innocent compared to me. I just wanted to keep you that way. But if I had stayed..."

The rough timbre of his voice swept over her skin, lighting it on fire. "I wouldn't have been so young and innocent anymore?"

"No, you would have still been young," he said, locking eyes with her. "Just no longer innocent."

Something hot pulsed between her legs. "Would that have been so bad? I wish that I had lost my virginity to you."

He shook his head. "No, you really don't. I'm not known for being all that gentle, and although I would've tried my best not to, I probably would've ended up hurting you."

"You wouldn't have," she assured him.

"Well, I wasn't about to take that chance. Especially with you. You deserve someone better than me."

Valerie sat up and looked him directly in the eye. "Why do you keep saying that? It's not true."

"It *is* true."

"You're wrong." She eyed him suspiciously. "Is that why you call me princess? Because you've put me up on some kind of pedestal?"

"No, I do it to remind myself that you're out of my league and that I'm not good enough for you."

"Logan."

"Don't tell me it's not true. I'm too much like my father, and that bastard never deserved my mother either."

It was common knowledge that Logan's father was an addicted gambler who spent more time in the casinos than he did at home with his wife. And their marriage had suffered greatly for it. They'd split up six months ago. "Is your dad back in town?"

Anger twisted his features as his hand clenched into a ball on the sheets. "No. And he better not show his face around here after what he did to my mom."

"Your mother? Does this have something to do with how strange she was acting the other day in the bakery? Is she okay?"

"She will be. I'm going to make sure of it. But if I ever see that man again, I don't know that I'm going to be able to control myself."

"What did he do?"

Logan sighed. "I'm sure you already know that he has gambling problems. That's been going on for years."

"Yes. Well, I mean, I've heard rumors."

"They're true," he said with a nod. "My mom and dad have both always worked, but he had a hard time keeping a job because of all the gambling binges he went on. So Mom kept a separate bank account from him so that he couldn't blow every last dollar they had. My mom's always been a saver rather than a spender, and she'd built a sizable nest egg that she'd hoped to retire on."

Valerie cringed. "Don't tell me your dad—"

"Yep, it's exactly what you're thinking. Not only did he max out every credit card they owned, but he committed check fraud by forging her signature and cleaning out her bank account before disappearing from town. He left her flat broke and with a ton of bills to pay. That was six months ago."

"Oh no," Valerie said, covering her mouth. "I'm so sorry to hear that. Now it makes perfect sense why she got so upset when she didn't have money on her the other day. I had no idea. I knew they'd split up, and I assumed it was because of the gambling stuff. But I had no clue it was over something like that. Your mom is the kindest, sweetest lady I know. I hate that he did that to her."

"You and me both. But that's not even all of it." He wasn't going to tell her about the foreclosure, but if he didn't come up with the rest of the money this week, it would be common knowledge all over town anyway.

"God, there's more?"

"Yeah. She hasn't been able to pay her mortgage for nearly six months so the bank is trying to foreclose on her house. If I don't come up with ten thousand dollars by next week, she's going to lose her home. It's the only damn thing she has left."

"That's not true. She has you."

His brows pulled down over his eyes. "Yeah, but I'd been telling her to leave my dad's sorry ass for years, and she never did. So when everything happened, she was too embarrassed to even come to me and ask me for help. And since I wasn't living here at the time, I had no way of knowing about any of it."

"So how did you find out?"

"After I moved back, I went to visit her one day and spotted the foreclosure notice sitting on her kitchen table. She hadn't realized that she left it there."

"Okay, wait, you lost me. If you didn't know about any of this until you got here, then why did you suddenly decide to move back to town?"

"It actually wasn't as sudden as you think. The day my

mom called me and told me that she and my father had split up, I'd planned on coming home. But at the time, I was making decent money at the bar I managed in Houston and couldn't just pick up and leave. My apartment lease wasn't up for another several months. So I used that time to save enough money to start up my own bar business."

"That was probably a smart move."

"I thought so too at first. But now that I know what my mom's been going through for the past six months, I wish I had come home right away. I could've fixed things for her a lot sooner and kept her from getting into this predicament. If she loses her house, it's going to be all my fault."

Valerie shook her head furiously. "You can't seriously believe that. How were you supposed to know your mom was going through something so horrible if she didn't tell you about it?"

Logan cocked his head. "You don't get it, do you? I left... way before my father ever did."

"So what? You were an adult, and you had your reasons. I'm sure your mom understood."

"Understood what? How her only son abandoned her and refused to come back home for a visit because she wouldn't leave the piece of shit she was married to?" Hurt and anger flashed through his eyes. "You said it yourself the first night I saw you, Valerie. I didn't come back. Not once."

She licked her lips and lowered her head. "I'm sorry. I shouldn't have said that. If I had known about all of this, I wouldn't have been so quick to judge. What I said, it wasn't right."

He shrugged. "You were just being honest. Though it stung a little at the time, you had every right to say it. That's one of the things I love about you. How honest you are with me. If I'm acting like a jackass, you're the first one to let me know it."

Guilt coursed through her. She hadn't been honest with him. Not completely. Otherwise, she would've told him the truth about not having the certificate that she needed to work at the bar. "I'm not all that honest," she said.

He flipped her over, pinning her beneath his weight. "Oh, so you've been keeping things from me, have you?"

She bit her lip as panic flashed through her. "Well, I, um..."

"Is this your way of saying I'm a bigger jackass than you've let on?"

He grinned to show her that he was playing, and she breathed a sigh of relief. God. If he ever found out that she lied to him, he was never going to trust her again.

If anything, that made *her* the jackass.

* * *

Valerie blew out a slow breath and glanced around the big white tent while waiting for the ceremony to begin.

"Your best man escort is here," Max said, stepping up beside her in a gray tailored three-piece tux.

She smiled at him. "And what a handsome one he is."

"You don't look so bad yourself. You nervous, Val?"

"Are you kidding me? I love this kind of stuff. I could do this all day, every day." She smoothed her hands down her sides. "I look hot as hell in this dress."

"I wouldn't exactly disagree with that statement," he

said, sporting a grin. "But then why do you keep looking around like you're searching for an escape hatch?"

A laugh fell from her lips. "I'm not. I'm actually checking to make sure all the exits are blocked off." She shook her head furiously. "Leah isn't like me. She hates to be the center of attention, and if I know her, she's going to take one look at all those people out there and probably get ready to bolt. Sam might have to come down here and drag her down the aisle caveman-style."

"Don't think for one second that he won't," he said seriously. "He's crazy about the girl."

"Wait until he sees her in her wedding dress. She looks amazing."

Leah's mother shuffled past them, clapping her hands to get their attention. "Places, everyone. We're about to start."

"You ready to do this?" Max asked, offering his arm.

"Absolutely."

Valerie laced her arm through his and allowed him to lead her over to the open doorway of the wedding tent. The sandy aisle in front of them led down between two large groups of people sitting on either side.

"What happened to Leah having a small, intimate wedding?" he asked. "There's probably over a hundred people out there."

Valerie nodded. "Leah's mom had her way with the guest list."

"Figures."

The moment the music started, everyone's necks twisted in their direction. As they started to walk toward the crowd, her eyes immediately fell on Brett and Logan, who were sitting near the back. Brett smiled warmly at her, but Logan's heated gaze blazed a trail over her that had her breath catching in her throat. Hot desire burned from his eyes, and he gazed at the dress as if he was thinking about ripping it off of her. Thankfully, he'd sat on the far side of her brother, which meant Brett hadn't noticed a thing.

Unfortunately, she couldn't say the same about Max. He kept a smile plastered on his face, but through clamped teeth, he said, "So you got something going on with your boss, huh?"

Caught off guard, Valerie stumbled. Max quickly wrapped his arm around her and held her up until she steadied herself. She smiled meekly at the guests and then leaned into Max as she clenched her teeth together and whispered, "No, of course not. Why would you even think that?"

He gave her a big, cheesy grin. "Well, at first it was because your boss looked at you like he wanted to bend you over the nearest sand dune." Max chuckled softly. "But now it's because he's looking at me like he wants to bury me beneath one."

Valerie glanced over at Logan, who was scowling in their direction. She waited until they passed by him and got to the front of the aisle and whispered, "It's, um, not what you think, Max."

At the front near the arch, they were supposed to part ways, but Max held her arm to keep her from walking away. "I'm betting it's exactly what I think," he said. "In fact, I can prove it." He leaned over and kissed her at the corner of her mouth before lifting his head toward Logan, chuckling, and then walking to Sam's side.

As she took her place, her gaze shot over the backs of

people's heads to land on the one pair of eyes she knew would be glued on her. Logan's face was red, his nostrils flared, and his eyes were damn near feral-looking. Great. He looked pissed.

Thanks a lot, Max.

Valerie held her composure throughout most of the ceremony, but the moment Sam took Leah into his arms and kissed her, she completely lost it. Tears of joy dripped down her face, and the minute the wedding party made it back to the tent, she immediately wrapped her arms around both of them.

She was so happy for them that tears still clung to her lashes even after they'd arrived at the Water Gardens for the reception. Leah and Sam excused themselves to greet the other guests, leaving Max and Valerie standing near the buffet table as the fading sun set behind them.

Guests milled about the large outdoor patio overlooking the dancing water feature. Color-changing lights flickered as water rose out of each of the small fountains in a sensual rhythm that followed a slow tune playing in the background. Twinkling white lights hung from the trees near the dance floor, and white roses made up the centerpiece on each of the crisp linen tables. Everything was perfect.

She glanced up at Max and sighed. Well, almost perfect.

If she had it her way, it would be Logan standing by her side, sharing in the romantic evening and taking in the gorgeous surroundings with her. Not Max. But with her brother nearby, she knew that wasn't going to happen anytime soon. In fact, she'd probably be lucky if she even got a chance to speak with Logan at all this evening.

After the searing look he'd given her at the wedding ceremony, the only thing keeping her sane was the anticipation of Logan peeling her out of this dress by morning. At least that was what she hoped he was planning on doing.

"So are you going to tell me what's going on with you and loverboss?" Max asked, grinning.

Loverboss? Valerie giggled. "I told you already. There's nothing going on between us. He's just my employer... and my brother's best friend."

"Bullshit," Max said while coughing into his hand. "Leah's your employer too, but she doesn't look at you like she wants to put her hand up your skirt to see if you're wearing panties."

Valerie laughed and shook her head. "Why do you care anyway? It's not like you even know Logan. Surely with all the single ladies here tonight you can find something better to do than stand here and harass me."

He slung his arm around her shoulders and kissed her on the temple. "But harassing you is entertaining as hell. Especially when it causes such a reaction among other male members at this shindig."

Max shifted their bodies so that Valerie faced the bar, where Logan and Brett were sitting. Both men were staring in her direction, and neither of them looked happy.

"Are you trying to get someone to kick your ass tonight?" she asked him. "Because if so, I'd be more than happy to do it myself."

He grinned wide, showing off his pearly whites. "There will be no fighting tonight, I promise. Just some good, clean fun."

"Max."

"Oh, calm down. I'm not going to do anything. Just hang out with you awhile and make your boyfriend a little jealous. You'll thank me later. It will probably be the best sex of your life."

Chapter Fifteen

Logan wanted to break the guy's fingers.

It was bad enough that he'd had to watch Valerie walk down the aisle with her arm looped through Max's during the opening ceremony. Then the bastard had to go and wrap his arm around her before practically kissing her on the mouth. And now that they were at the reception, the asshole still hadn't stopped touching her. Every time Logan glanced up, there was a hand lingering on her back, an arm sliding around her waist, or lips whispering near her ear.

And there wasn't a damn thing he could do about it.

"If that fucker doesn't get his hands off her, I'm going to forget my promise to Valerie about behaving myself tonight," Brett said, leaning against the bar.

Logan wanted to agree, but someone needed to be the voice of reason. "It's fine. They're friends, aren't they? He's just being...uh, friendly." A little too friendly, if you asked him.

Valerie's pale pink dress complemented her figure, but it was her impressive cleavage that stole the show. And apparently Max thought so too, since his eyes kept gravitating back to her chest. But it wasn't until Valerie gazed up at Max, an infectious smile flirting on her lips, that Logan groaned under his breath in agony and glanced away to keep from being too obvious.

Damn it. He hated this.

Beauty surrounded them in every direction, yet the only thing Logan was happy to stare at was her. And he wasn't even allowed to do that for very long without tipping off Brett to something going on between Valerie and him. He turned back to the open bar and motioned to the bartender. "Two shots of whiskey, please."

Brett shook his head. "You already know I'm not drinking. I'm the designated driver, remember?"

"Yep. Both of them are for me."

"You already had two beers."

"You keeping count?"

His friend grinned. "No, but I couldn't help but notice that now you're moving on to the harder stuff. What's bothering you tonight?"

Logan grimaced. "Nothing." Everything. The bartender slid two shots of whiskey toward him, and he immediately lifted one to his lips and knocked it back.

Since Brett had driven him to the event, it was safe enough for Logan to have a drink or two. Okay, four. Whatever. But he was pretty sure he would need each of them in his system for the ride home.

As maid of honor, Valerie had ridden with Leah earlier in the day to help her get ready before the wedding. But since Leah and Sam were staying the weekend at the beach for their honeymoon, Valerie was planning to ride back home with Brett and Logan. The three of them stuck in a car together for two hours straight? Yeah, that was bound to be the most awkward road trip ever.

He glanced back over in time to catch Max playing with her hair. God. Did he really have to keep putting his hands on her? That kind of crap definitely wasn't helping his attitude tonight.

"Excuse me," a feminine voice rang out, snaring their attention.

A pretty, young brunette stood next to Logan, twirling a strand of her long hair around her pinkie. She licked her pouty lips as her gaze flitted over his face. "Hi, I'm Amy. Is this seat taken?" she asked, gesturing to the one next to him.

He glanced down at the empty chair. "Yeah, it is. Sorry."

The woman blinked in surprise and then walked away with a scowl on her face, clearly disappointed with the entire exchange.

Brett punched Logan in the arm. "Dude! What the hell did you do that for? That Amy chick was hot. And she was flirting with you."

Logan shrugged. "I guess I'm not in the mood for company right now."

"But Amy was—"

"Damn it, Brett, if you like the girl so much, then go pester her and leave me the hell alone."

Brett's lips collapsed into a frown. "Christ. You're a grumpy ass tonight. You going to tell me what the fuck's got you wound up so tight, or do I need to punch the shit out of you?"

With a *yeah, right* gaze leveled at his friend, Logan said, "Any time you want to give it a go, you just let me know."

Brett shrugged. "Wouldn't be the first time I had to kick your ass."

"You mean it wouldn't be the first time you *tried*."

His buddy shook his head. "Man, you really are in a shit mood tonight. Lighten up already."

Logan smirked. "Like you have any room to talk?"

"Yeah, well, that's different. You're not the one who's been sitting here watching some guy paw at your sister all night."

No. Logan was only watching the asshole put his hands all over his fucking girlfriend. Way worse, if you asked him.

Brett gestured across the way, and they watched help-lessly as Max led Valerie out onto the dance floor, his large hand falling so low on her back that Logan held his breath and counted to ten to keep from marching out there and breaking the guy's fingers.

"If I go out there and say anything, Valerie's gonna be pissed," Brett said, nudging a sharp elbow into Logan's side. "So you do it."

"Do what?"

He nodded toward his sister. "Go cut in or something and get her away from that dickhead for me. I'll owe you one later."

Logan shook his head slowly. He couldn't do that. Especially just because her brother had asked him to. Valerie wouldn't appreciate it, and he would only end up looking like a jealous prick to her and probably everyone around them.

Then he saw Max dip her and graze his lips over her neck.

Logan lifted the crystal of whiskey to his lips and tossed it back. "Done," he said, then headed toward the dance floor to get his woman out of another man's arms... before Logan happily broke both of them for him.

As he reached them, he tapped Max on the shoulder. Probably a little harder than he meant to. "Mind if I cut in?"

They stopped dancing, and Max grinned at him. "Actually, I do."

A red haze dropped over Logan's eyes. "Well, I wasn't asking you," he ground out. "I was talking to her."

Valerie's eyes widened at his caustic tone, and she glanced around frantically, as if she was checking to see where Brett was. "Um, Logan, I don't think we should—"

"Damn it, Valerie," he interrupted, holding out a hand to her. "Now."

She blinked but didn't move.

Logan reached for her, but Max thrust his arm up to block the motion, which only succeeded in pissing Logan off more. He shoved Max away from her. "Back off," he growled. "I wasn't going to hurt her. Besides, you really don't want to go there with me."

But Max apparently had no qualms going there with him because he came right back and got into his face. "I don't care what you were planning to do with her. You reach for her like that again, and we'll go there... and anywhere else you want."

Swift, hot anger coursed through Logan, and he clenched his fists to keep from throwing a punch. "You might want to get out of my face."

A grin tipped Max's mouth. "Make me."

Make me? What? Were they suddenly in junior high? What the hell was this *make me* shit?

"Last warning," Logan sneered.

Valerie shoved her arms between them and pushed them away from each other, both of them allowing her to squeeze in between. "Stop it. You two are causing a scene at Leah and Sam's wedding reception. People are starting to look."

"So let them look," Logan said.

She gazed up at him. "Damn it, Logan. Knock it off already. Brett's watching."

He grinned. "So? Who do you think sent me over here to begin with?" He hadn't planned on telling her that, but she was obviously worried that her brother would realize something was going on between them.

"Oh, really?" Her eyes narrowed. "Max, thank you for the dance. But I need to speak to Logan in private."

"You sure?" he asked.

"Yes," she said, a tiny smile lifting her cheek. "I'll be fine. Thank you for your concern."

"Okay. But you know where to find me if you need anything. And I *do* mean anything." He winked and then bent his head and gave her a quick peck on the cheek before sauntering away with laughter in his wake. *Fucking prick.*

For a second, Valerie looked flustered, and that only made Logan want to go after Max and rip his head off. But he didn't want to ruin Sam and Leah's wedding reception. So instead, he tossed Valerie over his shoulder and marched off in the opposite direction.

* * *

Valerie couldn't believe it.

Not only had Logan thrown her over his shoulder—
again—but he'd done so right in front of her own brother.
Did he have a death wish or something?

"Put me down right now, Logan. What the hell are you
doing?"

"I'll put you down when I'm good and ready," he
replied, rounding another bend and marching a good distance away from the reception.

When he finally came to a stop in a dimly lit area and
set her on her feet, she swayed. She'd hung upside so
long that all the blood had rushed to her head, making
her light-headed. He held on to her as they waited for her
equilibrium to balance out, and then she gazed up at him,
locking her eyes to his.

He focused completely on her but didn't say anything.

"Well?"

"Well, what?" he asked.

"You tell me. You're the one who dragged me out of
there like a Neanderthal."

Logan grinned. "I have every right to haul you over my
shoulder and take off with you. Especially when you're
letting another man flirt with you."

She rolled her eyes. "I wasn't *letting* Max flirt with
me."

"You damn sure weren't stopping him."

"I didn't need to. He never got out of line."

His eyes narrowed, and a strangled sound came out
of his throat. "I think that depends on whose perspective
you're looking at it from. Where I was sitting, he crossed

the line the moment he got anywhere near you. That's why I came over."

"I thought you came over because my brother asked you to."

"That too," he said, nodding. "But if you thought that was the only reason, then you obviously have no clue what you've gotten yourself into with me. When it comes to my girlfriend, I don't play well with others, and I sure as fuck don't share."

She couldn't help but grin. "I guess that means we're scratching the orgy off the list."

His hard gaze leveled on her. "If you want a dick smorgasbord, I'll take you to a sex toy shop and buy you as many as you want. But that's the only kind of orgy you're getting anywhere near."

Thank God. But she wasn't going to tell him that. "Hmm. I think I'm willing to compromise on that."

"Valerie."

She giggled. "Okay, so no orgies. I agree."

"Didn't matter whether you agreed or not. It wasn't going to happen."

"Okay, now you're starting to act just like my brother. Controlling much?"

Logan's mouth curved. "Oh, baby, there's no way I'm as controlling as Brett. Max is still alive, isn't he?" Logan stepped into her personal space, and the hard bulge in his pants rubbed against her abdomen. "Besides, does this feel very brotherly to you?"

Valerie swallowed. "Um, not exactly," she said, flashing him a sly grin. "It feels more like something to look forward to later tonight."

Logan winked. "It's all yours."

"Good. Because I don't share either."

He bent his head and let his mouth linger near hers as he whispered, "Perfect. Because I don't want anyone but you."

Her heart squeezed painfully tight in her chest, and she licked her lips in anticipation as she waited for him to close the distance and kiss her fiercely. But he didn't. Instead, he just stared at her, his dark eyes overflowing with tension. In those few seconds, his body radiated more heat than she'd ever known, and she shuddered as a sharp spasm of desire rippled down her spine.

His lips parted in a slow smile.

In the past, every sexy encounter she'd ever had with Logan had been fast and hard and hot as hell. But this was nothing like those other times at all. Now there seemed to be a growing intimacy between them and a sexual awareness that went well below skin deep.

His hands moved to her neck, his thumbs stroking her jaw, and he tilted her face up to his. "I'm falling hard for you, princess. And I don't think I can stop myself."

"I don't want you to," she admitted, her stomach fluttering. "Go ahead and fall. I'll be waiting there to catch you."

Logan's mouth closed over hers, and, with heart-stopping tenderness, he kissed her slowly, deeply, and more thoroughly than ever before. Her lips softened under his as he focused only on her mouth, explored her depths, tasting every crevice, and feasting on her tongue for what seemed like days. And even though the kiss was tame in comparison to others they'd shared, there was no doubt that this one was the one to beat.

When he finally lifted his head from hers, he pulled

her closer and wrapped his arms around her, as if he never wanted to let her go. Endorphins flooded her bloodstream, and she snuggled into his chest, feeling his heart pulsing rhythmically under her hand. Damn this man. She'd secretly craved him for years but never thought he'd be hers.

Now she couldn't imagine her life without him.

Chapter Sixteen

Valerie hung out with Brett and Logan for the rest of the wedding reception, but the moment the newly married couple left the party, the three of them headed back to Granite. The two-hour drive wasn't nearly as painful as she'd imagined it, though her brother couldn't seem to wipe the stupid smirk off his face.

He kept bringing up how funny it was when Logan had thrown her over his shoulder and carried her away from Max. But if Brett had any idea of the things Logan had done to her while they were alone in the shadows, his smile would've surely evaporated hours ago.

They pulled into the bar's parking lot, all of them still dressed in their wedding attire. Valerie didn't mind. The pale pink dress she wore was flirty and feminine, and she was bound to get a lot of tips tonight because of it.

But as she stood outside the vehicle watching Logan remove his black jacket and tie, she realized that *he* might not be as keen on the idea of wearing a suit in the bar. "Do you want to run home and change your clothes?"

He rolled up the sleeves on his white dress shirt, displaying his spectacular, nicely toned forearms. "Nah. I'm fine like this."

Yeah, no kidding. She licked her lips and resisted the urge to fan herself.

Logan tossed the jacket and tie on the backseat, while Valerie considered shoving him in there, removing the rest of his clothes, and crawling on top of him.

But she didn't. Couldn't, actually.

It was Brett's truck, and her older brother was still sitting in the driver's seat staring at them through the open window. Since they'd both been drinking, Brett had refused to drop either of them off at home to get their own vehicles.

In Logan's case, that way of thinking made perfect sense. He wasn't slurring or falling down drunk or anything even close to that. But if him holding her hand in the dark cab of the truck while Brett drove them back was any indication, Logan definitely wasn't thinking with a clear mind.

Valerie was completely sober though. It had been nearly four hours since she'd drunk only half a glass of champagne during her maid of honor toast, and then immediately switched to sparkling water for the duration of the reception. Not only that, but she'd eaten plenty in the meantime, stuffing herself with mushroom pinwheels and shrimp canapés, as well as two pieces of wedding cake.

But she didn't blame Brett. It was always better to be safe than sorry.

"Thanks for the lift, Brett. If you don't want to come

back later, I'm sure James won't mind giving us a ride home after closing," Logan told him.

"It's okay. I'll be back in a bit to hang out for a while anyway. I just want to go home, get out of this monkey suit, and find something normal to eat. The wedding cake was the only thing edible at that damn reception."

Valerie giggled. It wasn't at all true, but leave it to the guy who lived off a diet of macaroni and cheese to snub his nose at gourmet appetizers. "Okay, then we'll see you in a bit."

She sashayed past the long line of customers waiting to get into the bar and headed inside with Logan on her heels. "So what are you going to be doing tonight, Mr. I Don't Drink on the Job?"

Logan grinned. "I'm going to go finish up a little bit of paperwork on my desk, and then I'm going to stand around the rest of the night looking pretty." As they reached the bar, he grasped her arm and pulled her toward him. "You sure you want to work tonight? I know it's been a long day for you. You can always go on home and get some rest."

She shook her head. "I don't mind. I like to stay busy. Besides, I thought I'd be spending the night with you tonight."

"I know. That's why I'm suggesting you go home and rest." His eyes gleamed with a predatory intensity. "I plan on keeping you *very* busy later."

Valerie nearly fainted from the heat wave that washed over her. "That sounds like a threat."

"It is."

"Good, then be prepared. And by that, I mean naked. Because the moment Brett drops me off at home, I'm jumping in my car and heading straight over." She started to move back behind the bar but paused and smiled at him. "And you might be interested in knowing that I'll be taking off one article of clothing at every stoplight between my place and yours."

An amused grin lit up his face. "Normally a comment like that would make me as hard as a rock. But this isn't a big town, baby. We're talking two stoplights max."

She lifted her shoulder casually. "Well, since I'm not wearing anything under this dress, I guess I'll only need one of them."

Logan groaned and pulled her around a thick support beam running from the floor to the ceiling, concealing them from most of the bar. Then he grasped her hand and placed it on the stiff ridge in his pants, grinding fully against her palm. "God. Do you see what you do to me?"

"Hmm. No, but I definitely feel it. If you'd like to show it to me, we could always take this to the storeroom and finish this discussion."

"Don't tempt me. I've drunk just enough tonight to impair my thinking. I might not be able to say no."

"Oh, well, in that case—"

"Valerie."

She rolled her eyes and laughed. "Okay, fine, you big baby. I won't make any more indecent proposals tonight."

"Thank you."

"Don't thank me yet. You don't know what's coming later."

His fingers dug into her waist, gripping her tightly. "Maybe not, but I know *who* is. And she's going to be screaming my name when she does."

"Oh, that poor girl," Valerie said with mock surprise,

lifting one eyebrow. "You plan on jackhammering her forehead into your headboard all night long?"

Logan shrugged. "Wouldn't be the first time."

"Mmm. If you keep talking like that, I'm going to forget my promise about not luring you into the storeroom."

"I'm starting to think I should let you," he said seriously. "So now would be a good time for you to turn around and walk your sweet ass behind that bar."

She sighed. "Okay, okay, but at least think about me while I'm gone."

"I always do."

As she walked away, Logan's hand reached out in a frisky move and patted her on the ass. She kept moving forward but glanced over her shoulder with a delirious grin and watched him head toward his office. When her gaze shifted forward again, her eyes landed directly on James, who was grinning like crazy. Apparently he'd witnessed the cheeky pat to her behind. Shit.

James nodded at her. "What's new, Val?"

"Um, that wasn't what it looked like."

He passed a beer to one of the customers. "Doesn't matter whether it was or not. You're an adult. What you do is not my business."

Valerie blinked. She'd never had a man tell her that before and wasn't sure how to respond. "No, I mean, it was innocent. Nothing is going on between Logan and me. Seriously."

"Still not my business," he replied.

"Yeah, I know. But I just didn't want you to think Logan and I were, uh...you know." *God, stop talking already, Val.*

James shook his head and then leaned on the counter

with one hand, a smirk tugging at the corner of his mouth. "Sweetheart, do you want some friendly advice?"

Obviously, he hadn't believed a word that had come out of her lying mouth. "Let me guess," she said with a sigh. "Learn to shut up while I'm behind?"

"No. Buy yourself a helmet. Because the way that boy was looking at you just now? You're bound to have one hell of a headache by morning."

Heat rose into her cheeks so quickly that it was as if someone had detonated a nuclear missile inside her body. She had never been the type of person to get easily embarrassed, but she and James had gotten close since she'd been working there, and it was a little awkward knowing that he overheard what Logan had said. *Jesus.* "You're not going to tell anyone, are you?"

James laughed. "Who is left to tell? Everyone who works here already knows."

Her jaw dropped to the floor. "What?"

"We all figured it out the day you started working here. You two think you're being slick, but Logan can't keep his eyes off you behind the bar any more than you can keep your hands off of him in the storeroom."

"Oh God."

A laugh rumbled out of him. "Look, if it's any consolation, I think you and Logan are great together. Just have fun and enjoy it."

"Um, thanks."

A customer hailed James from the end of the bar, and he went right back to work, as if the idea of Valerie fraternizing with their boss didn't bother him one bit. And maybe it didn't. But she'd have to check with the other employees to make sure no one was uncomfortable with her and . . .

Wait a minute. Valerie instantly recalled the night that the waitresses had made sexual remarks about Logan and then stared at her like they'd expected her to join in. But she hadn't done so. At the time, she'd been a little annoyed and had cringed at the things they were saying. Then she remembered that they laughed at the faces she'd made, and she couldn't stop the giggle that bubbled out of her now.

Those two little wenches. That night, they'd goaded her for a reaction to find out if their suspicions about Valerie and Logan were true. They actually hadn't been involved at the time, but the move on the waitresses' part was smart, if you asked her.

"Val, you working tonight or what?" James called out, throwing some bills into the tip bucket and serving another customer.

"What?" She glanced down the bar and noticed they were getting busier by the second. "Oh yeah. Sorry. I'm on it."

After an hour of spinning and flipping bottles, Valerie's arms felt like they were going to fall off. So she slowed things down by putting on a little show and entertaining the crowd with some good-natured but naughty fun.

Valerie had six women lined up side by side at the bar as she poured a mixture of Kahlúa and Baileys into six shot glasses and topped each with a spray of whipped cream. Then she slid one in front of each of them. "Okay, ladies," she hollered out. "You must keep your hands behind your back and use only your mouth to take the shot. This one's called a Blow Job."

The women giggled while the men in the room cheered and even sounded a few wolf whistles. All at once, the women lowered their heads and wrapped their lips around the shot glass before lifting back up and letting the liquid pour down their throats. Then they removed their shot glasses from their mouths and licked the whipped cream from their lips.

"I'll take one of those," a man's voice said, chuckling. "And I'm not referring to the drink."

Crap. She recognized that slimy voice.

Valerie's head snapped up to see Paul standing to her right on the opposite side of the counter. She immediately glanced around to make sure Logan was nowhere in sight. If he caught Paul in his bar, much less talking to her, he was going to flip his lid. She leaned on the counter and lowered her voice. "What the hell are you doing in here?"

Paul grinned. "What? Not happy to see me?"

"No. Now get out."

He shook his head. "Nope. I came in for a quick drink. I'll leave afterward."

"Well, I have the right to refuse service to anyone, including you." Valerie crossed her arms. "Go away or I'm going to have you thrown out."

"I'm a paying customer," he said, pulling out a ten-dollar bill. "You want to get rid of me, then give me a shot of tequila."

James stepped up beside her and glared at Paul. "Is there a problem here?"

She wanted to say yes, but knew that if she did, James would immediately alert Logan to a situation...and that was the last thing she wanted. So she shook her head and poured the shot of tequila, sliding it across the bar to Paul. "Nope. No problem."

James immediately moved on and went to help another customer.

Paul lifted the shot, swigged it back, and then smacked the glass back down on the bar. "How about one more?"

Valerie's eyes narrowed. "No. You had the only drink you're getting in here. Now get out before I have the doorman escort you to the nearest exit."

"Steve?" Paul laughed. "Who do you think let me in to begin with?"

"That's only because he doesn't know what you did the night you quit. But if I ask him to remove you from the premises, trust me when I say that he will."

"Why? Are you fucking him too? What happened to your boyfriend in the storeroom that night?"

Ignoring him, she rolled her eyes and reached for the empty shot glass.

Paul caught her hand in his, pulling her face close. "What's wrong? Don't like my dirty language?"

"The language isn't a problem for me, asshole. You're the problem. Now let go of me, or this time I'll rip your balls off and shove them down your fucking throat."

But it was too late. Only seconds after the words were spoken, a growl came from behind her, snaring her attention.

* * *

The moment Logan saw Paul's hands on Valerie, a growl had ripped from his throat that sounded more animal than human. Her head snapped to him, her face pale and her eyes wide. Anger lashed at his insides, and fire shot through his lungs. He moved swiftly, lunging over the bar like a pouncing tiger.

Paul released Valerie immediately, but that didn't stop Logan from pulling him away from her and shoving him back against the bar. People scattered out of the way, and a couple of women shrieked. The whole bar came to a standstill. The only sound was his own heavy breathing ringing in his ears, which drowned out the rock music blaring in the background.

"Logan, don't!" Valerie cried out.

But he wasn't about to let it go. Not this time.

He leaned into Paul's face, his fingers tightening onto the guy's shirt. "You're not welcome here. Get out of my fucking bar."

He shook his head. "Make me, asshole."

Great. Another idiot who had the fighting mentality of a thirteen-year-old. "You're a stupid bastard for coming back into my place. Not only were you stealing from me, but I hear you get off on threatening women."

Some females were covering their mouths in shock while the men in the back were peering around one another, trying to get a better view.

But Paul only laughed. "I didn't have to threaten her. That girl was all over me in the hallway. You saw it for yourself. She even had my balls in her hand." He glanced at Valerie. "Isn't that right, sweetheart?"

Logan threw Paul across the floor, and he rolled into a couple of chairs, knocking them over with a loud bang. "Don't talk to her. Don't even fucking look at her. In fact, if you ever come near her again, you won't be able to see or talk to anyone ever again."

Paul scrambled to his feet, his breathing rapid. "Ah, so

now I see how it is. You have something going with her, don't you?" He chuckled again. "Man, that bitch really likes to spread her legs."

The words barely made it past his lips before Logan grabbed Paul by his shirt collar, held him up against a support beam, and threw the first punch. Paul took a swing back at him, and his fist connected with Logan's jaw, snapping his head back a little. But the only thing it succeeded in doing was pissing him off even more.

Another hit from Logan split Paul's lip. Bright red blood poured out, trickling down onto Logan's white shirt. Paul tried to smash his hand into Logan's throat, but Logan managed to duck to the side just in the nick of time. Then he reared back and popped Paul again.

Valerie ran around the bar and grabbed his arm. "Logan, stop! That's enough. Someone's going to get hurt."

Logan gazed back at Paul, who was semi-limp and looking like he'd had about all he could take. His breaths wheezed out of him, and his lip was swelling something fierce. So Logan let him go. "Fine. Get the hell out of my bar and don't come back."

Paul dropped to his knees, gasping for a breath.

Logan turned toward Valerie, the relief evident on her face. He touched her cheek. "Are you okay?"

"Yes. Are you?"

"I'm fine."

But as they started to walk away, a hard arm wrapped around Logan's neck from behind, yanking his head back and cutting off his airway. The struggle knocked Valerie off her feet, and Logan shoved his body back into the one behind him to keep them both from landing on top of her.

Logan twisted around to face in the opposite direction

and then bent at the waist quickly to thrust the body behind him forward. Paul flew over his head and landed on
his back on a table in front of them. The table didn't hold
his weight though, and it broke, crashing to the ground.
Glass shattered in every direction, barely missing a couple of patrons who scrambled to get out of the way.

Logan turned to Valerie, who had risen to her feet.
"Are you all right?"

She nodded, but her hands were shaking. Then she
gazed over at Paul and blinked. "Logan," she whispered,
covering her mouth.

He turned back to Paul, and his eyes widened. The guy
was still lying on the floor flat on his back, his body lax,
but suddenly a red pool of blood had formed around him.

"Shit." Logan sprinted toward him and knelt down to
assess the damage. Not only was Paul knocked out cold,
but a huge chunk of glass from a broken beer bottle had
embedded itself into his side. "Valerie, call 911 and get
an ambulance here. Now."

Chapter Seventeen

Valerie fought the urge to gag.

She'd been waiting for over an hour for Logan to return from giving his statement to the police officer outside, but she hadn't been able to stand it any longer. As if staring at the red puddle on the floor hadn't been bad enough, dragging a wet mop through it and smearing it around only made it a whole lot worse. But she couldn't just sit there and do nothing. Not after a man nearly died in front of her.

Paul had bled profusely as they'd waited for the paramedics to arrive. Thankfully, when they got there, they'd managed to get him stabilized and transported him to the nearest hospital, where they said it was likely he would undergo emergency surgery to remove the glass from his side and repair the damage.

Since the fire marshal had cleared the place due to overcapacity, the bar had emptied out pretty fast. The police officers on the scene had briefly interviewed each of the staff members before allowing Logan to send them all home. All there was left to do was clean up the aftermath.

Demolished tables. Splintered chairs. Broken glass. All of which had been stained with Paul's blood. Though he was a jackass, Valerie prayed that he would be okay. No one deserved to die for having a shitty personality. Even him.

Valerie shoved the mop around again in a circle on the crimson-stained floor and then lifted it into the bucket. Blood dripped from the cotton strands, staining the water. Her throat went dry, and her hands shook. God. What if it had been Logan who'd gotten injured?

She barely heard the sound of the bar door opening, but seconds later, Logan's hands were taking the mop handle from her and guiding her toward a vinyl-covered stool at the bar. "I'll take care of it. I don't want you cleaning that up."

"I'm fine," she whispered, but her fingers wouldn't stop trembling so she sat down.

His hands rubbed at her shoulders from behind. "Are you sure? I hated being outside so long but they wouldn't let me come back in until they'd asked me the rest of their questions. I was worried about you though."

"I...I'm fine."

"You sure? Because it's all right if you're not. You just watched a man bleed out on the floor in front of you and almost die. It's okay to not be okay."

"No. Seriously. I—I'm fine." But her voice cracked, damn it.

"Valerie. You just said you were fine three times in a row. You're not fine."

A tear rolled down her cheek, and she dashed it away. "I'm trying to be, okay?"

Logan kissed the top of her head. "I know you are. But you can lean on me. That's what I'm here for. I'm sorry you had to witness all of that."

"You don't have to apologize. It wasn't like it was your fault."

"Well, I did punch him first. So yeah, it's basically on me. Especially since I was the one who threw him onto the table with all the glasses and beer bottles."

She turned around in her seat and gazed up at him. "No, you tried to put a stop to the fight when I asked you to. He came after you when you turned your back, and you were only protecting yourself."

"No, I wasn't. I was protecting you." He shrugged. "But it doesn't matter. I'm still the reason he's in the hospital."

"So the police think it's your fault that he—"

"No." He shook his head. "They didn't think it would be a problem. There are too many witnesses who saw Paul grab you first, and they've already told the cops that I was defending you. Yes, I punched first, but it's not like I purposely cut him with something. It was unfortunate that it ended the way it did."

She glanced back over at the mess. "What about all the damage?"

"The bar has insurance that will take care of all of that, as well as Paul's medical expenses."

"I'm sorry you had to close down early on a Saturday night. That revenue would've been a big help toward helping to get your mom's home out of foreclosure."

"Yeah, I know. But I have almost all of the money I

need. Even if we have fairly slow nights the rest of this week, I should still have enough to reinstate her mortgage by Friday. It'll be fine."

Valerie breathed a sigh of relief. She hated that his mom was going through such a hard time right now and hoped that everything worked out for her. Mrs. Mathis deserved to keep her home.

She stood and wrapped her arms around Logan's neck. "I'm so glad to hear that. I know it means a lot to you that you can help her."

"Well, it's about time I did something right in my life. I damn sure haven't done right by you."

Her brows furrowed. "What do you mean?"

"Look, I'm trying my damndest not to be anything like my dad. I know I don't deserve you, but I'm too much of a selfish bastard to let you go . . . just like him."

"I don't get why you keep saying that. Especially when it's not true."

Logan rolled his eyes. "It's true, Valerie. You do deserve someone better than me."

"Okay, then answer this question for me," she told him. "What is it that *you* deserve?"

Her question must've disarmed him because he blinked rapidly. "I . . . don't know."

"Then maybe I'm exactly what you deserve."

His fingers threaded into her hair, and he pulled her gently toward him. "You don't know how much I wish that were true."

"*I* know it's true. And if you can't believe that, then I'll believe it enough for the both of us."

The moment he traced his mouth over hers, warmth spread in her chest. Her hands traveled up his back, clutching him to her and feeling the muscles tighten beneath her fingertips. This was what she needed. To forget this horrible night and move on. And he had the power to do that for her. "I need you," she whispered between kisses.

He breathed out. "I know, baby. I want you too. We can go back to my place and—"

"No. Right now." She pulled back, her eyes meeting his. "I need you inside me, taking me, making me forget...everything."

"Here?"

She nodded. "Here."

Logan backed her against the bar and trapped her between his biceps. "You don't know how many times I thought about sitting you on top of this bar, spreading those legs, and having my way with you."

"Then show me what you want."

He bent his head and slid his tongue over her bottom lip. His large hand started at her knee and moved higher and higher until it was on her upper thigh and just about to strike gold. But a sound came from behind them and they broke apart, both of them spinning toward the door.

"What the hell do you think you're—" Brett stood there motionless, staring at them until realization dawned and rage surfaced in his eyes. "Oh my God. You're fucking my sister?"

* * *

Logan slid his arm around Valerie and eased her out of the line of fire. If someone was going to get hit again tonight, it damn sure wasn't going to be her. Even by accident. "Stay out of this, okay?"

"No." She started to move toward her brother.

Logan clasped his hands around her waist and set her back behind him again. "I'm not kidding. If he comes at me, I don't want you to be in the way. Just stay here and let me handle it. Promise me."

"Logan."

"It'll be fine. I just want you safe."

When she sighed and crossed her arms, indicating that she was reluctantly agreeing to stay there, Logan spun around to face Brett like a man. He rubbed one hand over his face and approached him slowly. "Look, I can explain—"

The two-handed shove came out of nowhere. Well, actually it came from Brett. But either way, Logan hadn't expected it and wobbled back, a little off-center. He thought for sure he'd be able to get at least a sentence out before the violence started.

"Just listen to me for a sec—"

A sharp right jab caught Logan in the nose, stunning him. He winced at the pain, and his eyes watered instantly. He wiped at his nostrils and checked his hand for a sign of blood. There was a little, but nothing worth crying over. "Fine. Damn it. I deserved that one."

"Oh, you deserve a hell of a lot more where that came from," her brother sneered, rolling up his sleeves.

Logan shook his head. "I'm not going to fight you, Brett."

"Then you're going to stand there and get your ass kicked. Either way works just fine for me."

Logan sighed. "Damn it. We were going to tell you."

Brett threw another punch but it only grazed Logan's jaw since he dodged to the side to keep it from connecting with his face. That only seemed to piss Valerie's brother off more. "Stay still, you little punk."

"This is stupid. Would you just stop and listen?"

"No." Brett threw another punch.

Unfortunately, Logan couldn't get out of the way fast enough. He took the full brunt of that forceful blow in his face and stumbled back. White-hot pain lashed through his cheek, making his entire face hurt. He shook his head to clear his vision. "Goddamn it. Knock it off already."

"Make me."

Logan groaned. *Again? Seriously?* First Max, then Paul, and now Brett. Why the hell were all these grown-ass men still using the *make me* line? They weren't kids, for Christ's sakes. "Brett, stop and listen. This wasn't just some fling...for either of us. You know I wouldn't take advantage of your sister like that."

"Yet you still did," he said, coming toward Logan again.

"It wasn't like that. I wasn't using her for sex, if that's what you're thinking."

Brett paused. "So then you were only sleeping with her because you needed a fucking bartender? That's even worse."

Before Logan could even answer Brett's question, the guy's short fuse detonated again. He let out a fierce growl and lunged for Logan, knocking him back into the dance floor's wooden banister before driving a hard fist into his stomach. The breath whooshed from Logan's lungs, and he winced at the ache in his back. Christ. He was going to have one hell of a bruise tomorrow.

Brett had a short, compact body but he was lightning fast and could be as mean as a snake when he wanted to be. Most guys took one look at his bulky frame and got the hell out of the way. Apparently, they were the smart ones.

"Brett, stop it right now!" Valerie yelled, coming closer.

Logan shook his head and held up a hand to stop her forward motion. "No. Get back."

Brett grasped on to the collar of Logan's shirt and came nose-to-nose with him. "Don't tell my sister what to do, asshole."

"She's *my* girlfriend. I'll tell her whatever the hell I want."

"Wanna bet?" Brett held him up against the dance floor banister and landed another hit.

A flash of pain exploded in Logan's jaw as the metallic taste of blood filled his mouth, and his gut rolled with nausea. *Sonofabitch, that hurt.*

"No, stop it!" Valerie shouted, her voice straining. Ignoring Logan's request for her to stay away, she ran over and grabbed Brett's bicep, yanking as hard as she could. "That's enough. This is stupid."

Logan glared at her. "Damn it, Valerie. I told you to stay out of it. This is between me and your brother."

"What the fuck did I just tell you? Don't talk to my sister like that."

Valerie pushed against her brother's shoulder. "Leave him alone, Brett. He's your friend. And he didn't do anything wrong."

He rolled his eyes. "Oh sure. Stick up for your lover boy."

"I'm not. I just want you to stop being ridiculous before someone gets hurts."

Logan groaned under his breath. If the tenderness in his face and the soreness in his body were any indication, it was a little too late for that suggestion.

Brett reared back to hit him again, but Valerie squeezed in between them. "Move," he ordered.

"No. This is done. If you want to hit him, then you're going to have to go through me."

Logan couldn't believe she was blocking him with her body. "Jesus Christ, Valerie. Just fucking move and let him hit me again."

That comment had Brett blinking. "You really are a stupid bastard if you're wanting me to hit you again."

"I'm protecting her, you dick."

Brett glanced around the room. "From who? There's no one else here."

"God, you're an idiot. I'm trying to protect her from *you*."

Brett shook his head furiously. "I'd never hurt my sister, jackass." He hesitated for a moment, but then let go of Logan and stepped back. The anger twisting his features didn't subside though. "This is over as of right now. Do you hear me? You're done seeing Valerie."

"I'm old enough to make my own decisions," she told him. "That includes who I want to be with...and I want to be with Logan."

"Damn it, Val. He's not the right guy for you."

She thrust her hands onto her hips. "Why? Because you say so? Who the hell made you God?"

"You don't know the kind of shit he's done in the past. He's not the guy you think he is."

"I *do* know. He's told me what kind of trouble he's gotten into over the years. And none of that matters to me. I need him, Brett. He's the one for me."

"You're not thinking clearly."

"I need her too," Logan said.

Brett glared at Logan. "I'm not playing, man. From now on, you're going to stay the hell away from my sister."

"I can't do that," Logan said. "I've tried. For years I've tried. It's no longer possible. I'm sorry." Then Logan glanced at Valerie, who was standing there with tears clinging to her lashes. And he couldn't end things on that note. "No. You know what? I'm not fucking sorry." He looked his best friend square in the eyes and breathed out a hard breath. "I'm in love with her, Brett."

"The fuck you are."

"I am. I don't give a shit if you believe it or not. But she needs to know how I feel." He glanced at her. "I'm in love with you, baby."

She sniffled and wiped at a lone tear trailing down her cheek. "Good. Because I love you too."

Brett threw his hands in the air. "Well, that's just fucking great," he said, pacing in a circle. Then he stopped and glared at his sister. "You're in love with a fucking coward. He didn't even have the balls to tell me that he wanted you. He had to sneak behind my back to do it."

Logan shifted his weight against the wooden banister. "It wasn't like that. My relationship with Valerie has nothing to do with my friendship with you."

"The hell it doesn't. Did you really think we would still be friends after you stabbed me in the back like this? Don't think so, buddy. You made your choice the moment you betrayed me. I hope the sex was worth it, asshole."

Without looking back, Brett stormed out the door.

Fuck. They'd obviously handled all of this really

badly, and Logan didn't have a clue what to do. He gazed up at Valerie. "Are you okay?"

"Me? You're the one who's hurt." She helped him over to the nearest chair and looked over his injuries. "Do you need to see a doctor?"

"No, I'm fine. Just a few bruises. I'll live." He glanced toward the door and then back to her. "I'm more worried about your brother. He's upset and pissed off, which isn't a good combination."

Valerie's lips trembled. "He's just hurting right now. I'm sure after a few days of cooling off, this will all blow over, and he'll come around."

Logan rubbed his sore jaw and sighed. They both knew Brett well enough to know that this wasn't going to blow over in a couple of days...and that he'd probably never calm down. There was only one thing Logan knew for certain right now and that was that he just lost his best friend. Forever.

"It doesn't matter, Val. Even if he never forgives me, there's at least one good thing that came out of him catching us together. Everything is now out in the open, and there won't be any more lies."

Chapter Eighteen

Valerie hadn't spoken to her brother since Saturday night.

Though she'd driven by his house and phoned him multiple times, he was never home and hadn't bothered to return any of her calls. She'd even tried to catch him at work on Monday, but he'd had his boss cover for him and tell her that he wasn't there...although his car was in the parking lot and she knew damn well that he was.

If he wanted to be like this, then fine. There was nothing she could do about it. She had way more important things to do than worry about Brett and whether or not he would get over his aggravation about her and Logan being together. Like figuring out why Logan had called her to come into work earlier than usual.

It was Tuesday, and thank goodness Leah had already gotten home from her honeymoon. Otherwise, Valerie wouldn't have been able to cut out from the bakery in the middle of the day.

The front door to the bar was unlocked, but it didn't appear that anyone was there. Strange since she'd seen two vehicles in the parking lot, one of which belonged to Logan. "Anyone home?" she called out.

Within seconds, Logan stepped through the swinging doors. "Hey, princess. Thanks for coming in early on such short notice. I hope it wasn't a problem."

"No, Leah was there so I asked her to watch the store for me. She had some paperwork to catch up on anyway since she'd been away for the entire weekend so it worked out."

"Well, thank her for me too."

Valerie nodded. "I will, but why did you need to see me? Your message sounded urgent. Did you talk to Brett or something?"

Logan shook his head, his lips straightening into a grim line. "No. But it's not for a lack of trying. I've called him a dozen times since Saturday night, but he's avoiding or ignoring me."

"Same here," she said, her voice softening. "I really thought he would get over it by now, but he's taking this pretty hard. My mom is out of town this week, but when she gets back, I might have her try to talk to him for us and see if she can't get through to him. I don't know what else to do."

He put his arms around her and hugged her to him. "I'm sorry, baby. I know this is hurting you."

"It is. But it's because *he's* hurt. I don't know. Maybe he just needs more time. It's not like I can force him to forgive us."

"There's really nothing to forgive. You're grown, and he needs to stop trying to run your life."

"I know. But he's done it so long that I don't think he knows how to let me go." She sighed. "Doesn't matter. You obviously didn't have me meet you here to talk about my brother. So what's going on? Why am I here?"

"Paul came by here earlier today."

"He's out of the hospital? And he's doing okay?"

"Yeah. He got out this morning. He had emergency surgery on Saturday night to remove the glass fragments from his side and stop the bleeding, but he seems to be doing all right."

She gazed up at Logan warily. "So then what did he want? Did he stop by to apologize?"

"Uh, no." He shook his head. "More like he came by to let me know that he's thinking about suing me."

"For what?"

"Medical expenses, pain and suffering...you name it. He's claiming I assaulted him for no reason, and he's threatening to find a lawyer to take his case, but I'm not all that worried about it. There were plenty of witnesses to corroborate my story."

"Okay, then I don't understand. Why did you have me rush over just to tell me about something that you aren't even worried about?"

Logan smiled. "That's not why you're here. I called the insurance adjuster on Monday, and he wasn't supposed to come out until next week. But he got an opening in his schedule and asked if I could meet with him today instead. It was perfect timing since Paul had threatened me with a lawsuit this morning. I told him that my insurance would cover his medical expenses, which I think will appease him." He gestured to the back room. "The claims adjuster is in my office right now going over the police report I picked up this morning and the medical records Paul gave me."

"Paul gave you copies of his medical records?"

"Well, yeah. He wants to be paid off and providing me copies of his medical records would help speed up the claim. If we had to go through other channels to get them, then it might take a lot longer. That's why I'm pretty sure Paul will just settle for having his medical expenses taken care of."

"What about the damage inside the bar?"

"The adjuster assured me that my liquor liability insurance will cover the damages for most things: the damages inside the building, the medical expenses, and any legal fees incurred, if necessary. We just need to finish up with the last few details."

"Which are?"

"He needs to verify your account of Saturday night. That's why I called you in. Paul claims that you sold him a drink after he arrived, and since they consider this a liquor-related incident and you were the bartender who served him, the insurance adjuster needs to talk to you."

She nodded. "Okay, sure. That's not a problem."

An older gentleman in a brown suit came out of the swinging doors, carrying a briefcase in one hand. He was tall with light brown hair and sported a pair of small, round reading glasses with black frames. "Hi, you must be Miss Carmichael. I'm John Palmer."

She stuck out her hand. "Nice to meet you, sir."

Likewise, young lady," he said, giving her a quick shake. "I'm glad you're here. I was just going through your employee records, and I noticed that your TABC certification isn't on file."

Valerie cringed, but before she could say anything, Logan spoke up. "Oh, that's because I hired Valerie in a pinch. It was completely unexpected, but she'd just moved to a new apartment and didn't know where her certificate was at the time. I forgot to get it from her later."

"Well, since Miss Carmichael is the one who sold Paul the liquor consumed during the accident, I'll need her to provide me that as soon as possible. Today would be ideal. In fact, if you could run home and get it right now, then that would be even better. I won't be able to move on with the claim without it."

Logan nodded his agreement. "That's fine. You can do that, right, Val?"

Her heart beat so hard that she thought it would jump out of her body. God. She couldn't believe this was happening to her. She was backed into a corner and had no choice but to tell him the truth.

Valerie turned to face Logan full-on, ignoring the persistent ache in her chest. She closed her eyes for a moment and tried to calm her erratic pulse. "I...um, can't."

"That's okay. If you need help searching through boxes for it, I can call James to come in and sit here with Mr. Palmer while I run and help you find it."

Damn. She wished she could run away and hide right now. The last thing she wanted to do was tell him that she lied. Especially right in front of Mr. Palmer. But she didn't really have much of a choice. "No. That's not what I mean." She swallowed. "I can't get you the certificate."

Logan looked confused. "Why not?"

"Because...I don't have one."

His eyes widened. "What do you mean you don't have one? Where is it?"

"I've never had a TABC certification."

His eyes darkened and narrowed, pinning her in place. "But you told me you did."

"Um, no. Actually, you just assumed I did...and I didn't correct you."

Fire flashed in his eyes as he growled out, "That's the same damn thing, and you know it. Why the hell did you lie to me?"

Valerie wrung her hands together, not knowing what to say. But she knew it was best to just tell the truth. "Because I wasn't entirely sure you would let me work here if you knew that I didn't have the certification."

"Val, you could have gotten one. It's a one-day course that lasts only a few hours."

She lowered her head. "I know. I looked it up the night you hired me. But they have limited classes, and the closest one was three hours away. Working two jobs, I didn't have time to get it done. And even if I could've found the time to sneak off and take the course, you would've noticed the date on the certificate and knew I fibbed about the whole thing. I couldn't take that chance."

"So you just lied about it this whole time?"

Valerie nodded. "I was already in way over my head, but since it was only supposed to be a temporary position, I figured no one would know."

"Damn it, Valerie. You should've come to me and told me the truth. I could have helped you resolve it. Why didn't you just say something when I asked you about the certificate the first time?"

Tears invaded her eyes. "I overheard you tell James

that you couldn't hire anyone without bar experience. So when you assumed I had some, I kept my mouth shut." She sighed heavily. "I really wanted to work here to help you out of the bind you were in, and part of me wanted to see if the bar industry was something I wanted to do in the future."

"So you just kept it from me? Even after we started seeing each other?"

"Yes. I'm sorry. I didn't say anything because I figured you'd be mad at me." She reached for his arm.

He jerked away from her. "Oh, you mean like right now?" Logan fixed a hard gaze on her before glancing over at Mr. Palmer, who wasn't saying anything, and then he shook his head. "This isn't a good time to discuss this. We'll talk about it later. After I finish up with Mr. Palmer."

"Uh, actually..." the man began, "I'm sorry to say that you have a much bigger problem on your hands now."

Logan ran his hands through his hair. "What do you mean? What problem?"

"Well, this is sort of a gray area actually, but your liquor liability insurance isn't able to cover your claim after all."

Stunned, Logan's eyes went wide. "What? Why the hell not? I've paid all of the premiums, and I haven't been late a single time."

"I understand," Mr. Palmer replied. "But let me explain. While technically bartenders and servers are not required to have a seller's certification, the establishment is required to have a TABC-trained and certified staff."

"I don't get it. What's the difference?"

"Basically, by indirectly requiring the TABC certification, it's the way for the establishment to show due diligence in the court's eyes and that sometimes might help lessen the liability if this ever became a civil case. Which is very well what could happen if the young man who got injured decides to follow through with his threat to get a lawyer and take you to court."

Logan let out a frustrated breath. "I'm not following you. What does any of this have to do with whether or not my insurance covers the claim?"

"Unfortunately, the terms of your contract with the insurance company clearly state that the insurance will not cover claims arising from the sale of liquor in a manner that violates the law or terms of your contract."

"Since the bartender, which in this case was Miss Carmichael, wasn't legally certified by the Texas Alcoholic Beverage Commission to sell or serve alcohol to the complainant, then the insurance won't cover the alcohol-related incident."

"B-but I didn't know," Valerie said, her words stuttering out.

"I understand that. But whether or not you were aware of the coverage terms or not, that doesn't change the conditions of his contract with the insurance agency. He would still be responsible for all the damage, medical bills, and court fees that may occur surrounding this incident."

"You've got to be fucking kidding me. So let me get this straight. You're saying the insurance isn't going to pay a damn dime on any of this all because my bartender doesn't have a TABC certification?"

"Yes, that's exactly what I'm saying. I'm sorry, but

since Miss Carmichael isn't certified to sell alcohol out of your establishment, she has basically voided out your insurance coverage."

*   *   *

Logan couldn't believe it. Any of it. "You've got to be kidding me."

The insurance adjuster shook his head. "I'm sorry. I wish I were. If there was some way I could help you, I would. But according to Paul's statement and the police report, it's already on record that Miss Carmichael was the one who served the injured party a drink right before the incident occurred. Nothing I can do will change any of that."

"Great. So now what am I supposed to do?"

Mr. Palmer paused thoughtfully. "Well, I don't normally give out legal advice in situations like this, but I've been doing this a long time and know all about risk management. I've seen enough to know that you're in a tough position."

"What exactly does that mean?"

"If the person who was injured in your bar takes you to court, you could be held criminally responsible for his injuries. You would most likely have to hire a criminal defense lawyer to help you with your case, which is not cheap by any means. And if you lose, your legal fees alone would probably be upward of fifty grand." Mr. Palmer set his briefcase on a nearby table and opened it, pulling out a card. "I can give you the name of a good lawyer, but honestly, your best bet is to settle out of court with this guy as quickly as possible to avoid him suing you for everything you're worth."

"You actually think Paul might have a case against me?"

"It's possible. But if you can get him to agree to just accepting a lump sum that would cover his medical bills, you would save yourself a ton of money…and wouldn't be possibly facing jail time."

"Jesus. This can't be fucking happening right now." Logan rubbed a hand over his face. "What does this mean for the bar?"

Mr. Palmer shook his head dismally. "Unfortunately, there are some stiff penalties for things like this. Chances are good that the Texas Alcoholic Beverage Commission will suspend your establishment's alcohol-selling permit for a period of sixty to ninety days or maybe even permanently for violating a provision of the code."

Logan blinked. "Say that again, only more slowly this time."

Mr. Palmer repeated himself while Logan hung on every word.

"That's what I thought you said. So in other words, they're going to close me down?"

"Yes. I'm sorry. I wish I had better news for you."

"Well, that's just fucking great. Guess I'm pretty much screwed." He glared at Valerie.

The insurance adjuster closed his briefcase and lifted it from the table. "Look, I have a few contacts over at the TABC office. I can give them a call and put in a good word for you," Mr. Palmer said. "I can't guarantee it will help in the long run, but some favorable words from me on your behalf might be enough to keep them from canceling your permits on a permanent basis. It's not much, but it's something."

"Thanks. I appreciate it, Mr. Palmer. Anything you can do to help would be great." Logan shook his head and led him to the door.

Once the insurance adjuster left the premises, Logan spun around on Valerie with heat blasting through his entire body. Knowing she'd orchestrated this entire lie from the beginning and hadn't bothered to come clean hurt him deeply. He couldn't believe she'd do this to him. Yet she had.

Valerie turned to face him with tears in her eyes. "Say something."

"There's nothing left to say."

"Logan."

He shook his head. "No, I don't want to hear it. We both know I'm in a world of trouble, thanks to you. There's no way I can afford to pay some big damage claims out of my pocket right now. If I don't pay ten thousand dollars to the bank by Friday, my mother loses her home."

"I understand that. But you heard what Mr. Palmer said. If you don't settle this with Paul now, he's probably going to sue you. And that might end up costing you more than what a new home would be worth. I think it would be smarter to—"

"No. I won't lose my mother's home. With my dad gone, it's the only damn thing she has left."

"That's not true. She has you."

"Not good enough," he said, shaking his head.

"No, what you're saying is that *you're* not good enough. And that's the biggest load of crap I've ever heard. Damn it, Logan. You're not your father. You didn't get her into this mess. *He* did. And you've done nothing but try to help her fix it."

His eyes narrowed. "No, that's not what I'm saying at all. I know better than anyone that I've been working my ass off so that I don't end up like him. But now you've come along and..." His words trailed off.

She blinked at him. "And what? I came along and screwed everything up? Is that what you were going to say?"

"Doesn't matter. This is my problem, not yours."

"I—I'm sorry."

"Oh, I'm sure you are," he ground out, taking his frustrations out on her. "But the only thing I don't know is whether you're sorry that you ruined my business or sorry that you got caught in a lie."

Anger flashed through her eyes. "It wasn't like I did any of this on purpose. You have to know that."

"Maybe not, but you lied to me more than once about that damn certificate. If you would've stopped to think about what you were doing, then none of this would've happened. But you didn't think. In fact, you never do. It's like as long you get what you want, nothing else matters." Logan's jaw tightened, and his stomach clenched. He remembered saying those exact words to someone else years ago. "I guess that makes you more like my father than I am."

Valerie's expression hardened. "No, there's a big difference between the two of us. Your dad purposely deceived your mom, whereas I didn't intentionally hurt you."

"Yeah? Well, from where I'm standing, it doesn't feel all that different."

She winced. "I know you're pissed at me, Logan, but you don't have to be a jerk."

"Oh, okay," he said, rolling his eyes. "You lie to me for the past two weeks and somehow, *I'm* the jerk? Figures."

Temper flared in her catlike eyes. "No, you've always been the jerk. I'm only just now pointing it out."

Anger consumed him. Just where the hell did she get off? It wasn't like he was the one who'd screwed her... at least not in the way he meant it today. "Don't push me, Valerie. I mean it."

She flipped her hair off her shoulder and stuck out her chin. "Or what?"

Logan's eyes connected to hers. He was still way too pissed off to be talking about any of this right now. But he couldn't seem to stop himself. "You have some fucking nerve getting all haughty on me. I just lost everything because of you: my best friend, my bar, and now probably my mother's house."

Valerie flinched. "Damn it, Logan. That isn't fair."

"Yeah, well, neither was you lying to me, but that didn't seem to stop you from doing it."

She glared at him and then turned and walked toward the door without a word.

"So that's it, huh? You don't like what I'm saying so you just walk away?"

She swung back around and threw her hands in the air. "Well, it's a better option than standing here and listening to you go on and on about a stupid little lie I told."

Little? That "little" lie fucked up his whole life. No, actually, *she* did. His hands fisted at his sides. "I can't believe I didn't see how selfish you really were. Not everything revolves around you."

"I never said it did. But I already told you that I didn't mean for any of this to happen. You just aren't listening."

"Oh, I'm listening. You didn't mean for any of this to happen? Good. Then maybe we should go back to a time before it did and forget everything...including us."

Her mouth fell open slightly. "You don't mean that."

"Yeah, I think I do. And one more thing. You're fired."

Chapter Nineteen

Valerie couldn't breathe.

When she'd numbly walked into the bakery, Leah took one look at her pale face, flipped over the CLOSED sign, locked the bakery door, and hugged her friend so hard that Valerie thought she would break in two. And God, she practically did.

Sobs ripped from her chest as her shoulders shook with heartbreak. Pain clawed its way through her until there was nothing left but a desolate trail and the disturbing knowledge that she'd brought all of this onto herself.

Concern filled Leah's eyes. "Are you okay? What happened?"

"Logan broke it off with me."

"What? He called you to come in to work early so that he could break up with you? That doesn't make any sense. Why would that idiot do that?"

Valerie sniffed and rubbed her raw nose. "Because he

found out that I've been lying to him. It's my own fault, but I didn't know any of this would happen."

"Let's go sit down, and you can tell me all about it."

Valerie shook her head. "You can't just close up your bakery and not make money because I'm having a personal crisis."

"The hell I can't. I'm the owner."

"I'm being serious, Leah."

"So am I. You're my best friend. I would close my doors for you any day." She nudged Valerie toward one of the chairs near the front window. "Now sit down and tell me everything."

So she did. And she cried the entire time.

Finally, after the hiccupping sobs began to fade, she swiped away the remaining tears. "He's so mad at me right now that I'm not sure if he's ever going to get over it."

"He will," Leah assured her. "You just told me this morning how he told Brett that he loved you. Do you think he can just turn that off?"

Valerie swallowed the lump in her throat. "I ruined everything for him. His whole life is messed up because of me. That's what he said. There's no way he's ever going to forgive me for that."

Leah rubbed her hand over Valerie's slumping shoulders in slow, comforting circles. "Honey, he was mad and hurt when he said that. Trust me, he didn't mean it. This is just like the situation with Brett. Logan needs a day or two to cool down. Once he does, he'll come around."

"But what if he doesn't?"

"Then I'll send Sam over there to kick him in the head."

Normally, she would've laughed at something like that. But Valerie wasn't in the mood. She lowered her gaze to the floor. "How can this be happening?" she said, more to herself than to Leah. "After all the years I spent waiting on Logan to come around, he finally did. And then what did I do? I went and screwed up the best thing I ever had."

"Everything will be okay," her friend promised. "You'll see. Just give it time."

Unable to do much else, Valerie took a deep breath, her chest hurting from the effort. *God. Please let Leah be right.*

The doorknob rattled.

Valerie glanced up, tears still in her eyes. "Leah, someone's at the door."

"So." Leah shrugged.

Someone knocked on the door. When neither of them moved to answer it, the soft knock turned into manic pounding.

Valerie sighed. "You have to open it. If it's Mrs. Howard, she's going to think I locked her out again."

"Again?" Leah asked, her eyes widening. "You locked Mrs. Howard out of the bakery?"

"Well, I tried. But she got in anyway."

Leah laughed. "You're going to have to tell me *that* story for sure." She headed to the door, unlocked it, and swung it open.

Max filled the doorway, his eyes flitting back and forth between them. "About time you opened the door. Why the hell is it locked?"

"We were having a private conversation," Leah told him. "Ya know, girl talk."

He gazed at Valerie and took in her swollen, tearstained face. "Do I need to go kick his sorry ass? Because you know I will."

Valerie tried to smile though she was sure it didn't reach her eyes. "No, it's okay. Thanks for the offer though. With my brother not talking to me and Logan breaking up with me, I was fresh out of men who were out for blood."

Max stepped over to her, tipped her face up, and kissed her cheek. "Sweetheart, I don't think you'll ever be out of men who are willing to kill each other over you. Now stop this crying shit and tell me what the fucker did to you."

She laughed. Leave it to Max to put a smile on her face. "He didn't really *do* anything."

"So then you're crying because he's leaving town?"

She blinked. "What do you mean he's leaving town? Who told you that?"

"No one. I just thought that he was moving or something."

"Not that I'm aware of," she replied. "Did you hear something?"

Max pulled out a chair and spun it backward before straddling it. "I didn't hear anything. On my way here, I drove by the bar and saw the asshole putting a FOR SALE sign up outside."

"What?" Valerie exchanged looks with Leah and then glanced back to Max. "He's selling the bar?"

"Apparently. And he's selling it cheap too. Only asking ten thousand dollars for it. He'll sell it fast at that price. It's bound to be worth a hell of a lot more."

Valerie couldn't believe what she was hearing.

"Damn it. He's only selling it for that price because that's how much he needs to get his mom's house out of foreclosure."

Leah gasped. "Oh no! Mrs. Mathis is going to lose her home? That's terrible. I hadn't heard."

"No one has. They've been keeping it a secret. But Logan is trying to help her get the mortgage back on track. That's why he needs the ten thousand dollars. God. This is all my fault."

Max raised a brow. "How is it your fault that his mother didn't pay her mortgage?"

"No, not that," Valerie said, shaking her head. "On Saturday, when we got back to the bar after the reception, Logan got into a fight with his ex-bartender named Paul, who was seriously injured. Logan's insurance would have normally covered the incident and paid Paul's medical bills, but because I served him a drink, Logan's insurance won't cover the damages."

Max looked even more confused. "But aren't you the bartender? Who else is supposed to serve the drinks in that place—the doorman?"

"No, no. I mean, I was a bartender who was supposed to serve drinks. But I lied to Logan about having a TABC certification and ended up accidentally canceling his insurance coverage for the bar. So now he's going to have to pay for Paul's medical bills out of pocket, which means using the money he was saving for his mom's house. That's why he's selling the bar. To get the money for his mother's house."

"Damn, that sucks," Max said. "He's in a tough spot."

"Yeah. Because of me." Valerie scowled. "But you know the really messed-up thing about all of this? Since

I've been living upstairs in Leah's old apartment and working two jobs, I've been able to stockpile a good amount of money. If I thought for one second that he would let me help him..." She sighed.

Max grinned. "Maybe you should buy the bar from him." Then he burst out laughing. "Or I could do it. That would really piss him off after I goaded him at the reception."

Leah glanced at Valerie, and they both stilled.

When Max realized he was the only one chuckling, he stopped. "Um, sorry. Too soon? I wasn't trying to be insensitive or anything. I was just kidding around."

Valerie smiled. "Um, actually, I think your idea has merit."

"That you should buy the bar?"

"No. *You* should. It's brilliant."

Max squinted at the two of them. "Have you two been smoking something? Logan isn't my biggest fan. He's not going to sell me his bar. And even if he would, I don't want it."

Leah giggled. "No, silly. You would buy it for Valerie. That way she can keep him from selling it to someone else as well as help him to pay off his mother's foreclosure. Win-win."

"I can't do that. It's dishonest."

Valerie rolled her eyes. "Like you care? You're all for this kind of stuff, troublemaker."

Max grinned. "Well, it keeps people on their toes around me."

"So you'll do it?"

"Hell yeah. Why not? Sounds like fun."

Valerie gazed over at Leah. "Can you call Sam?"

"On it," Leah said, heading for the cordless phone hanging on the wall.

Max frowned. "Sam? I thought you wanted me to buy the bar from Logan. What the hell do we need Sam for?"

"Oh, come on, Max. You didn't really think I would unleash you on Logan without having someone there to keep you in line, did ya?"

"One could only hope," he said with a wink.

True. And right now Valerie hoped that she wasn't too late.

* * *

Logan glanced up when a knock sounded on the door. "Bar's closed," he yelled out, but the door opened anyway.

"Then you probably should've locked the door, smart guy," Sam said, stepping inside with Max on his heels.

Great. Valerie's cheerleaders were here. "We don't know each other very well, fellas, so I'm going to say this as nicely as I can. If you're here for what I think you're here for, then I'm not in the mood." Unless Max was looking to fight. Then he would get in the mood for that real quick.

"Just came in for a drink. Know where we can get one of those?" Sam said, gesturing to the glass of top-shelf whiskey in Logan's hand.

Logan tossed it back and poured himself another. "Yeah, at an open bar." But he grabbed two extra glasses and filled them anyway. "So you two didn't come by to talk about Valerie?"

They grabbed seats at the bar as Sam shook his head. "Nope."

Logan's brow arched in curiosity as he slid them each a drink. "Then what are you doing here?"

Sam took a big swallow of his whiskey. "Well, I thought you could use a friend. Since Brett still isn't talking to Valerie, I figured he probably wasn't talking to you either. Or am I wrong about that?"

"Nope. You nailed it right on the head."

Logan nodded toward Max. "So what's he doing here then?"

Max grinned. "I'm here to buy your bar."

The words were like a bucket of ice water dumping over Logan's head. He held his breath as his heart seized in his chest. "You're kidding me, right?"

"Nope. I don't kid around about money. I've got ten thousand dollars burning a hole in my pocket right now."

Logan took another shot of whiskey, letting the burn numb him from the inside out. "You're serious?"

"I said I was, didn't I?"

"Do you even know how to run a bar?"

Max downed his drink in one gulp. "What's to know? Just hire some people to run the place and then show up and drink."

Logan rolled his eyes. *Idiot.* "Yeah, well, there's a bit more to it than that. And you shouldn't drink on the job. You need a clear head to run a bar."

Grinning, Max raised one brow. "Didn't help you, did it?"

"Max," Sam warned, shooting his buddy a dirty look.

"Oh, calm down. I'm just kidding around." He gazed

around the room. "There's a lot I could do with this dump."

A lot he could do? Dump? That asshole. Nothing needed to be done to the place...because Logan had already done it. "I'm asking ten thousand. Cash only."

"Don't trust me?" Max said, grinning.

Logan shrugged. "Nothing personal." Jackass.

Max pulled a huge wad of bills out of his pocket and started counting them out on the counter. When he finished, he stacked the cash into a pile and shoved it toward Logan. "Ten thousand dollars."

"You aren't going to look around first? Or ask to see the books?"

"Don't need to. I've been in here before, and this place hasn't been open long enough to maintain good books."

"Okay, fine. But since I just put the FOR SALE sign up a few hours ago, I haven't had the time to draw up a contract for the deed. And I don't think either of us trust one another enough to do a gentleman's agreement."

"Why not? It's legally binding in Texas."

"I think we'd both prefer something a little more concrete than that." Logan grabbed a pen from next to the POS system and wrote up a mini-agreement on a bar napkin and then copied it on a second one. "Just to keep us honest," he said, shoving both of them across the bar at Max, along with the pen.

Max checked them both over and then signed at the bottom of each next to Logan's signatures. "A copy for each of us?"

"That's the idea." Logan nodded. "But I'll need a week to clear out my stuff. And you'll need to find new staff since I've already let mine go."

He nodded. "That's okay. I'm betting I know at least one who will be more than willing to come back to the bar."

Now he was just trying to push Logan's buttons. "Yep, probably. Might want to make sure she has her TABC certification though. And I wouldn't take her word for it. She's been known to lie."

Max's gaze heated. "You might want to watch what you say about—"

"Max," Sam interrupted, "now that your business with Logan is concluded, why don't you go ahead and take off? I'll catch up with you later."

"Don't have to ask me twice." Max slid his empty glass back to Logan. "Thanks for the drink...and the bar." He grinned and then strolled out the door.

Logan shook his head. "You really like that guy? He's a prick."

Sam grinned. "Yeah, he's a bit of an instigator. But he's also a damn good friend. If anything, I imagine you can understand that. Given that you're friends with Brett. I get along with him, but he's not always the easiest guy to be around."

"Well, to hear him tell it, we're not friends anymore."

Sam shook his head and laughed. "Max tells me that every time I threaten to fire him. He hasn't left my side yet." He hesitated and then said, "So about this thing with Valerie..."

Logan laughed. "I knew you had an ulterior motive for being here. You said you were here for a drink, you liar."

"That too," Sam said, tossing back the rest of the contents in his glass. "But if while I'm drinking, you need to talk about what's bugging you, go ahead. I'll listen."

"There's not much to say. Valerie lied to me. Within a matter of days, I lost my best friend, my insurance coverage, and my bar. And almost my mom's house."

"And Valerie."

"Huh?"

"You forgot to include Valerie in that list. You lost her too, didn't you? Although I'm pretty sure that was your own fault. She didn't leave you. You left her, right?"

"Well, yeah. But what else was I supposed to do? If she hadn't lied about having a TABC certification, my liquor liability insurance wouldn't have been canceled and I wouldn't have had to pay a settlement to Paul, my old bartender. That lie of hers cost me a lot."

"Really? Because I thought it was you who threw the punches at Paul, not her. I'm betting that if you hadn't done that, then none of this would've happened. Am I right?"

Logan took another swallow of his whiskey and grimaced. "Okay, Sam, you're really not helping matters."

"I don't know. I think I'm helping a lot. I'm making you think."

"I don't want to think. I want to drink."

Sam chuckled. "Look, I get it. She lied. You're pissed. But I think we both can agree that she wasn't the only one who made mistakes. And you know she didn't intentionally screw you over. Valerie would never do something like that. The girl doesn't have a malicious bone in her body."

"Maybe not. But it still doesn't change the fact that I'm completely screwed."

"Again, that isn't Valerie's fault. At least not completely."

Logan sighed. Yeah, he was well aware of that. But he didn't know what to do about it. "Okay, enough said. I get your point. But I don't know where Valerie and I go from here, if anywhere. So let's just sit here and drink so I can try to figure it out."

Sam grinned. "You got it, buddy."

Chapter Twenty

Valerie wasn't willing to put up with it any longer.

Her older brother had gone several days straight avoiding and ignoring her, and she'd had enough of the big baby's temper tantrum. She'd hoped he would come around on his own, but he apparently was even more stubborn than she'd given him credit for. But enough was enough, and all of that was going to end today.

It was time for her to face off with her brother, once and for all. Whether Brett liked it or not. And knowing him, he probably wouldn't like it one bit.

Oh well.

Valerie rapped on the door with her knuckles and waited, but the door didn't open. So this time she banged on it harder with the palm of her hand. Still the door remained closed. "I know you're home, Brett. You might as well open up. I'm not leaving until you do."

Complete silence.

Valerie sighed and leaned against the wall, her hand landing on the black mailbox mounted near the door. She grinned. She'd forgotten all about the hidden key that Logan had used to let them in after picking her drunk ass up from Rusty's Bucket. And she would bet it was still there even now.

She ran her hand beneath the mailbox, and her fingertips roamed over a small, flat metal object with ridges on one side. Bingo! The key had a small magnet glued to its head, which was what kept it on the mailbox.

Without hesitation, Valerie slid the key into the lock and quietly unlocked the door. She didn't want to tip Brett off. The idiot was liable to hold the door closed or barricade it with something heavy to keep her out. But she couldn't wait to see the reaction on his face when she went barging in. *Teach him to mess with me.*

She threw the door open and quickly stepped inside. "Ah-ha!" Her eyes immediately found her brother sitting on his couch...in his underwear...eating Cheetos.

Brett's mouth fell open. "What the fuck, Val?" There was a flash of white as he went scrambling toward his bedroom as fast as he could.

Cringing, Valerie covered her eyes and turned away. "Oh God. I'm so sorry."

"What the hell are you doing here?" Brett's hostile voice echoed down the hallway.

"I, um, wanted to talk to you."

"Well, I don't feel like talking. Go home." Having slipped into a pair of cargo shorts, Brett came back into the living room.

"No. Not until we work this out."

Brett plopped back down on the couch and tossed the

open bag of Cheetos onto the coffee table but didn't say anything.

She lifted a brow. "You eat Cheetos in your underwear often?"

"Well, yeah. When I'm wearing them."

Ew. "I'm never eating anything at your house ever again."

"Good. I didn't plan on having you over here anymore anyway," he said, obviously still angry. "You wouldn't be here now if you hadn't committed breaking and entering. In fact, I should probably call the cops on you and have you arrested."

"Go ahead. I didn't break in, dork."

"Oh, really? Then how the hell did you get inside? I know damn well that door was locked."

"I used the key under your mailbox."

His eyes widened. "How did you even know about—never mind. I forgot you were sleeping with the enemy."

She didn't mean to get emotional, but tears sprang into her eyes. "Actually, I'm not. Logan broke up with me a couple of days ago."

His hands clenched into fists. "Damn him. I knew he was going to end up hurting you. I tried to warn you, but you wouldn't listen."

She shook her head. "It wasn't like that, Brett. This was all *my* fault. I hurt Logan, not the other way around."

"Is that what he told you? Man, now I'm going to have to kick that fucking prick's ass all over again."

Valerie rolled her eyes. "Um, I don't think you can call it kicking someone's ass when they refuse to fight back. That's basically the equivalent of beating up a couch pillow."

"Whatever. He's still a dead man."

"No. You have to stop this. I didn't come here to cry on your shoulder so you'd go beat him up. He didn't do anything wrong. I'm the one who lied to him so he has every right to be pissed at me." She moved closer and sat on the edge of the wooden coffee table, facing her brother. "You, however, don't."

Heat flashed in his eyes. "How do you figure? You lied to me too."

"My relationship with Logan wasn't any of your business. I didn't owe it to you to tell you anything until I was ready."

"You're my kid sister, Val. Everything you do is my business."

She shook her head furiously. "That's where you're wrong, Brett. I know I should've put my foot down with you a long time ago, but I'm not going to tolerate your intrusion into my personal life any longer. I love you, but if you can't respect me enough to let me make my own decisions, then you can just stay out of my life from this point forward."

"You know I can't do that."

Her eyes narrowed. "Then you're going to lose your only sibling."

"Damn it, Val. You don't mean that."

"The hell I don't," she snarled, getting angrier by the second. "I don't know what your problem is, but I've had just about enough of you trying to dictate my life and always telling me what to do."

Brett shot to his feet and crossed the room. "Do you think I wanted to be fucking responsible for you all these years? To watch over you? I'm only four years older than you. God, Valerie, I was just a kid myself."

"Well, if you didn't want to, then you shouldn't have. I sure the hell didn't ask you to."

"Damn it, I promised Dad—" His voice cracked, and his head lowered.

Valerie cringed. She hadn't meant to bring any of this up. She stood and walked over to him. "Brett?"

He broke down, sobbing, pinching the bridge of his nose with one hand, and the anger and frustration she felt quickly dissipated. She reached for him, but he turned away from her.

"It's okay," she said, placing one hand on his shoulder.

"No, it's not. It's never been okay," he said, shaking his head. He'd never been one to show much emotion, but when he turned back to face her, there were tears shining in his eyes. "Do you remember the last time we visited Dad at the hospital?"

"Y-yes. I was only eight, but I remember...all of it. It was the worst day of our lives." Her own tears caught in her throat, and she swallowed hard. "His last stroke had been a bad one. Daddy was hooked up to all those machines and barely able to talk."

Brett rubbed a hand across the back of his neck. "You went with Mom down to the vending machine, and before y'all returned, Dad went into cardiac arrest."

Visions of him lying in the hospital bed and then in a cherrywood casket ran through her head. Tears fell onto her cheeks, and she quickly dashed them away. "I...don't want to talk about this. It hurts too much."

"I know. But it's important. I need you to know something." He led her to the couch and motioned for her to sit. Then he pulled an ottoman up directly in front of her and sat facing his sister. "After you and Mom left the room, Dad called me over to him. He had a hard time talking, but he told me he wasn't going to be around much longer and that I would need to be the man of the house. He asked me to take care of my little sister just like he..."

When he paused and closed his eyes, Valerie's hand shot out to grab his. "You don't have to tell me any more, Brett. I already know what happened that day."

"No, I need to say it. I've been carrying it around inside for so long because I didn't want you to know." He shook his head. "Dad asked me to be there for you just like he would. He asked me if I would walk you down the aisle on your wedding day. Then he told me that he loved me, loved all of us, and how proud he was to call me his son."

His hand trembled, and Valerie held it tighter. "He loved you, Brett. He loved all of us so much."

"I know, but...then he just died. His eyes rolled up in the back of his head, and the machines went crazy. He just died on me...and I didn't even get a chance to tell him that I loved him too."

She gathered him in her arms and hugged him tightly. "Daddy knew. You didn't have to say it out loud for him to know that." She pulled back, and with one hand locked on his neck, she looked him square in the eyes. "He knew. He never had any doubt."

He shook his head. "You don't know that."

"I do know it. I saw the tears shining in his eyes when he said good-bye to you."

Brett's head snapped up. "What are you talking about? You weren't even there."

Tears began free-falling from her eyes. "I was there

the whole time. I didn't want to go to the vending machine with Mom so she said I could stay with you and Dad in the room. So I came back. But when I walked in and heard what he was saying to you, I stood in the doorway and stayed quiet. I didn't want y'all to know I was listening."

"Y-you watched him die too?"

She nodded, her lips trembling.

"God, Valerie. Why didn't you tell me? Why didn't Mom?"

"I don't think Mom even knew. When she heard them call a code, she rushed back down the hallway and found them working on Dad, trying to revive him. I was standing right there, and she screamed and ran past me, but I don't think she even saw me. Then a nurse took me to the waiting room down the hall. They brought you down there a few minutes later. Mom was so distraught that I don't think she realized either of us had been in the room with Dad at the time."

"But you never told her?"

"No. I didn't want to talk about watching my father die. Or how the last words he ever spoke were to make sure I was taken care of." She wiped her fingers under her eyes and smiled at her brother. "Besides, that moment belonged to you and Dad. It wasn't my story to tell."

Brett rubbed a hand over his distraught face. "Look, I'm sorry, okay? I know I didn't do a great job at taking Dad's place. I tried my hardest. I really did. But I just can't do it, Val. I'm not him. I'll never be him."

"I don't want you to be him. You were only twelve at the time, Brett. Although I know you meant well, I don't think this is what Dad meant when he talked to you about stepping into a fatherly role for me. Besides, I want you to be my brother, not my father. But either way, you have to stop treating me like I'm something fragile that's going to break. I'm not eight years old anymore. All I want is for you to try to give me some space. You did a great job in helping raise me. Now trust me to make the right decisions."

"You're right. I know that. And I'll try my best to work on it. But it might take me some time to get used to just being your brother again. I'll try my hardest though. I can't lose you too, Val. You and Mom are all I have left."

She squeezed his arm. "You're not going to lose me. But from now on, I'm making all of my own decisions... and that includes who I want to be with."

He squinted at her in confusion. "I thought you said Logan broke up with you?"

"He did. But I refuse to let the only man I've ever been in love with walk out of my life forever... whether you like it or not."

Brett sighed heavily. "Does he love you back? I know he told me he does, but do you believe him?"

"Yes, I do. But he's hurt that I lied to him about having a TABC certification when I didn't. That stupid stunt voided out his liquor liability insurance so Logan had to put the bar up for sale."

"Shit. That sucks. He loved that place."

"I know... which is why I bought it from him."

Brett's eyes widened. "Logan sold you his bar?"

"Not exactly. He sold it to Max, who used my money to buy it. So technically he sold it to me. Just indirectly. And Logan doesn't know that yet. But I had to do something. If he lost his mother's house because of me, he would never forgive me. Hell, I would never forgive myself."

"You knew Logan wouldn't take your money."

Well, yeah. But what was Logan going to do—be mad? He was already pissed at her as it was. None of this would change anything. "I'm guessing you probably don't want to hear about Logan anymore..."

"I might be a little pissed at him for sneaking around with you behind my back, but he's still my best friend." Then Brett smirked. "But don't think for one second that means I won't kick his ass if he hurts you. Because I will. I'll fuck him up so bad that he—"

"Brett."

He paused. "Oh. Right. Sorry."

Time. It was going to take some time. But at least it was a good start.

*　*　*

Logan let himself in through the front door. "Mom?"

A sweet, feminine voice drifted to his ears. "I'm here. In the kitchen, dear."

He walked in that direction as the warm, familiar scent of freshly baked sugar cookies mingled with the smell of the vanilla potpourri his mother had kept hidden around the house in strategic places for years. Her house always smelled great.

She stood in front of the white Formica countertop, her brunette hair standing out in stark contrast, though lighter gray streaks had begun to show through. She had on her BEST MOM IN THE WORLD apron today, which meant she was in baking mode. And she usually only did that when she was stressed out. Like right now.

"Good morning, son," she said as she transferred cookies onto a wire rack to cool.

"Hey, Mom," Logan said, kissing her cheek as he snatched one of the warm cookies.

She swatted at him. "Not yet. They're still too hot. I just pulled them out of the oven."

He popped the whole thing into his mouth and grinned around it. "They're perfect as usual."

"Well, thank you. So what brings you by this morning?"

"I need to talk to you about something. Do you have a second to sit down at the table with me? It's important."

"Of course." She sat down across from him at the small breakfast nook and folded her hands in her lap. "What do you want to talk about?"

"This." Logan slid a document across the table in front of her.

She gazed at it warily at first, but then her eyes widened and a smile slid firmly onto her face. "You're kidding? Is this what I think it is?"

"Yep. You're out of the danger zone. Your home is officially off the foreclosure list, and your mortgage has been reinstated."

"Oh my God," his mother squealed. "You did it? You actually did it? I can't believe this." She stood and rounded the table, wrapping her arms around his neck and giving Logan a big hug. "Thank you. You don't know how much this means to me."

"Yes, I do," he said, squeezing her back. "You love this old house."

She pulled back. "But how did you—"

"Does it really matter?" he said with grin.

"Well, no. But I would like to know how my son came up with such a large chunk of money in such a short period of time." Her suspicious eyes raked over him. "I hate to ask, but you aren't hustling pool again, are you?"

"No. Of course not. I told you a long time ago that I wasn't going to do that anymore. And I meant it. I've kept that promise, Mom. I swear."

"Good. I'm glad to hear it. Especially since that was the exact way your father got his start into gambling. I don't want you to turn out like him."

A strangled sound left Logan's throat. "I think it's too late for that. I already am like him."

Her eyes darkened, and she shook her head. "Son, you may look like your father, but you are nothing like that man."

"Mom, I'm sorry to tell you this, but I think you'd be surprised to know how much like him I really am."

She gazed at him curiously and then took her seat once more. "Okay, then tell me. In what way?"

"In every way apparently. I sold my bar for next to nothing to get the money to save your home. I'm a complete failure."

Her eyes went wide. "Please tell me you didn't really do that."

"I can't. It's true. I did it."

"Darn it, Logan." That was her version of cussing him out when he made her angry. "I never wanted you to give up on your dreams just to save my home. This is exactly why I didn't tell you about the foreclosure in the first place."

"It's fine, Mom. I can start over."

She shook her head. "But you shouldn't have to."

"Well, neither should you. But Dad didn't leave you with any other options."

"Sure he did. Years ago, he gave me *you*. That was the best thing that man's ever done. I couldn't ask for a better son."

Logan smiled. Moms had to say stuff like that about their kids...even their grown ones. "You're only saying that because you're stuck with me. I'm the only son you have, and you've got no choice but to make the best out of a bad situation."

"Hush your mouth. I don't want to hear you talk about yourself like that ever again. Even if I could've hand-picked my one and only son, you would still be the one I chose."

"That's sweet, Mom, but you don't have to say that."

"Why not? It's the truth. I admit that I worried about you when you were younger and always getting into some kind of trouble. But even back then, I was proud of you. And then you changed for the better. You went away and got yourself together, and I'm so proud of the man you've become."

"Mom, are you even listening to me? I'm a failure. I couldn't even keep my business running for a month before I had to sell out."

"You only did that to save my house though. That doesn't make you a failure. That makes you a hero, as well as the best son in the world. You sacrificed something you loved in order to help someone else. It was kind and thoughtful and selfless...three qualities that your father doesn't know a thing about."

"That man never deserved you."

She nodded in agreement. "You're right. But he never deserved you either. And you definitely didn't deserve to have a father who cared more about his craps game than his own family. Seems like we both deserved better."

"Yeah, maybe."

"Now if I can just convince you to find a nice young woman to settle down with, I could get some grandchildren out of the two of you," she taunted him with a smile.

"Actually, I was dating someone, but we just broke up a few days ago."

Her eyes brightened. "From here? I hadn't heard a thing about it. Who is this mystery woman?"

"Valerie Carmichael."

His mom grinned wide. With Brett as his best friend growing up, his little sister had never been far behind them, and Logan's mom knew her well. "I always wondered if the two of you would find your way to each other. Valerie is a very sweet young lady. If you don't mind me asking, why did the two of you break up?"

He didn't really want to throw Valerie under a bus, but since his father was such a liar, Logan always made it a point to tell his mom the truth no matter what. That's how she knew about all the trouble he'd gotten himself into in the past. "Valerie lied to me about something. It wasn't a huge lie or anything, but it had a domino effect and caused a lot of damage."

"Ah, I see. Yes, lies have a way of doing that. I should know. Your father never told the truth about anything. So I take it that you broke up with her then?"

"Yeah."

"Was she against it?"

"I think so, but it wasn't like I gave her much of a choice in the matter."

His mother paused. "Well, is there any hope that the two of you will get back together?" Her mouth held an optimistic smile. Apparently, she hoped so.

He shrugged. "I don't know. Besides the lie, there are some other issues. Like how Brett's no longer speaking to me since he found out that Val and I were involved with each other."

His mother grimaced. "I was wondering how well that went over. Brett has always been a bit of a loose cannon when it came to his little sister. I guess I can't really blame him. She's a pretty girl. When you kids were younger, I saw how you looked at her. I worried about whether your friendship with Brett would withstand the rift that a relationship with Valerie might cause."

Logan grinned. "Well, I can tell you now that it didn't. He says we're not friends anymore."

Sadness filled his mother's eyes. "That's too bad. I've always liked Brett a lot. I do, however, think you and Valerie would be perfect for one another. Maybe it's not too late to salvage your relationship. And then maybe her brother would come around after some time passed."

He shook his head. "She deserves someone better than me. Someone who can give her what she needs."

"And you can't do that?"

"No."

His mother squinted at him. "Son, what is it that you think she needs?"

"I . . . I guess I don't really know. I just know that I can't give it to her."

"Why not? You spent the last eight years keeping yourself out of trouble and on the right path. You grew up and matured into a fine, responsible young man. You're good looking, honest, and caring. Any girl would be lucky to have you."

Logan sighed. "I didn't grow into a responsible person. It was my fear of becoming like my father that kept me on the right path. I was trying my hardest not to be like him."

"Who cares what put you there? The only thing that matters is that you found your way. You made it. And I couldn't be happier for you."

"But that doesn't mean I'm good enough for someone like Valerie, Mom."

His mother smirked. "Well, from what you're telling me, it seems that Valerie disagrees with that statement."

"Doesn't matter. After the way I spoke to her, I doubt she'll ever want to see me again anyway. Even though she apologized for the little white lie she told, I was angry and said some pretty unforgivable things."

"Like what?"

"I basically told her that I thought she was selfish and how it was all her fault that I lost my best friend, my business, and your house. At least that's what I thought at the time." Then Logan cringed. "And I, um, may have accused her of being like Dad."

His mother gasped. "Well, that was a rotten thing to do."

"I know."

Her lips pursed in annoyance, and then she sighed. "So what did Valerie do after that?"

"She told me I wasn't being fair and called me a jerk."

A smile flitted on his mother's lips. "Good for her."

"Hey, whose side are you on here?"

"I'm always on your side, son, you know that. But I didn't raise you to talk to women like that. Brett has lorded over Valerie for years, always trying to control her. She has put up with a lot out of him, but she's always treated him with nothing but love and respect. So if she had the mind to call you a jerk, then I have no doubt that you deserved it."

Logan grinned. "Yeah, I deserved it," he admitted, leaning back in his chair. Then he realized something and cringed. "Honestly, I probably deserve much more than that. I hate to say it, but I haven't treated her much differently than Brett has. I've been just as controlling and almost as overbearing. I'm not even sure why Valerie put up with me as long as she did."

His mother shook her head in disapproval. "Logan..."

"You don't have to say it. I know. I've been acting like an idiot."

She gave him a knowing smile. "You're in love with her, aren't you?"

"Yes."

"Have you tried to talk to her since you split up?"

"No."

The anger seemed to come out of nowhere. His mom stood up and fisted her hands on her hips. "Logan Mathis, I didn't raise a dumbass for a son, nor did I raise a coward. If you're not going to fight for that girl, then you know what? You're absolutely right. You don't deserve her."

Logan blinked in shock as his mother spun away from him and stalked across the room and back to her cookies. He couldn't remember a time that his mother had ever cursed at him. At least until now. But that just showed how serious she was.

But God, she was right.

He'd stupidly screwed up the one good thing he had in his life—his relationship with Valerie. He knew he'd overreacted the day he broke up with her. The anger he'd unleashed on her that day had stemmed from his unresolved issues with his lying-ass dad, a man who never took responsibility for his actions. But Valerie wasn't like that. She'd never been like that. Yet he'd treated her as if it had been his father standing in front of him.

Okay, so maybe he wasn't a perfect guy. He made mistakes. He screwed up. He was only human. But he could be enough for Valerie, couldn't he? Hell, he'd be willing to be anything she wanted if he could just have her back in his life. He needed her. Felt empty without her. And he wanted to try to be the kind of man that she needed too.

But would she be willing to take him back after he'd hurt her? That was the question. One he should figure out the answer to. "Um, I should probably get going."

His mother cleared her throat but said nothing.

He was pretty sure she was still irritated with him, but he thought he might test the waters. "You think I can have a few cookies for the road?" God, he sounded like a four-year-old.

Her gaze landed on him, and her brow arched. "Depends. Are you going to talk to Valerie?"

"Yes. I'm going to apologize to her and see if she'll give me another chance. And this time, I'll show her the love and respect she deserves."

She smiled. "Then I guess you can take as many as you want."

He strolled over to his mother, grabbed a handful of sugar cookies, and then kissed her temple. "Love you, Mom. I'll let you know how it goes with Val. Wish me luck."

"I love you too, son. And I do wish you lots of luck. Now go be the man I know you are and win back your woman."

He grinned. His mom would always be his biggest supporter. "You got it."

Chapter Twenty-one

Although Logan had told his mother the truth because he *did* plan to go see Valerie and beg her forgiveness, he had something important he needed to deal with first.

He banged hard on the front door with his fist.

Chances were good that, the moment Brett opened it, a hard fist would fly toward Logan's face and pummel him into the ground. But he didn't care. He was going to say what he came here to say whether his buddy liked it or not. And if Brett even dared to slam the door shut on him, Logan planned to use the key under the mailbox to let himself in and finish what he had to say.

Because enough was enough, damn it.

When the door opened, Logan braced himself for a punch. But Brett just stood there staring at him with his mouth hanging wide open. He looked like an idiot. "We need to talk. Now." His tone was firm and demanding, making it clear that Brett didn't have a choice in the matter. They were going to talk even if Logan had to sit on him and hold him down to do so.

"And just what the hell is it you think we have to talk about?"

"Valerie." Logan moved forward to go inside.

Brett blocked the doorway with his body and crossed his bulky arms before raising one suspicious eyebrow. "What about her?"

"I just came by to tell you that, even though she's your little sister, you're going to have to share. Valerie is my woman... whether you like it or not."

Brett chuckled under his breath. "Really? Because I heard you dumped her... and from my experience, when you dump a girl, that pretty much is the equivalent of her not being yours."

Logan sighed heavily. "I wasn't in the right mind-set that day. I was upset and hurt and angry. But I didn't mean for things to go that far."

"Then they shouldn't have."

Logan shook his head. "Really, Brett?"

"What?"

"You caught us together and went ballistic," Logan said, glaring at him. "But whether you like hearing it or not, there was way more to us than just having sex. I wasn't 'fucking your sister' as you so sweetly put it. I was falling in love with her, you jackass."

"Are you trying to make me sick?"

"If that's what it takes to make you back off of Valerie, then yes. Neither of us have treated her with the respect she deserves. She doesn't have to answer to either of us and doesn't need our permission to live her life the way she sees fit. And that includes being able to choose who she wants to be with. Got it?"

Brett grinned maliciously. "And what makes you so goddamn sure that you're the one she wants? You aren't the only stallion in the pasture, buddy. She has other options, you know."

Logan frowned. "What other options?"

"Well, there's always Max, for one. After seeing how much he flirted with her at the wedding reception, I'm sure he would love a shot at her now that you're out of the picture."

Anger swept through his veins. "I'm not out of the picture, dickhead. And Max is not getting a shot at Valerie. Not if I have anything to say about it." *God. I'm sounding like a demanding prick again.*

"But you don't. You broke up with her, remember? Pretty harshly from what I hear. I should kick your ass just for that alone."

Logan's hands clenched into tight fists at his sides. "You want to take another swing at me? Fine, go ahead. But I'm warning you. I'm not just going to stand here. I will hit you back this time."

Brett laughed. "Got tired of being a couch pillow, huh?"

Couch pillow? "I don't even know what the hell that means."

"Because you're an idiot."

Logan grinned. Yeah, Brett knew how to push his buttons. But he also knew how to push his buttons right back. "Yeah? Well, you're a dipshit mechanic who wouldn't be able to put an alternator on, much less a tire."

Heat flashed in Brett's eyes. "Take that back, asshole."

Logan smiled and said, "Make me." Then he cringed at the words. *Sonofabitch. Not me too. What the hell is wrong with us men?*

Brett chuckled. "Yeah, I'll make you all right." Then he grinned. "Ya know, it took you long enough to finally grow a pair."

Keep pushing those buttons, jerk. "Though I'd love to sit here and argue with you, I don't have time for this shit. I need to go find your sister and rectify this situation between us. But before I go, I have one last thing you might want to know."

"Yeah? What's that?"

"I plan on asking your sister to marry me...no matter what you have to say about it. So deal with it."

Brett grinned and nodded with approval. "Okay."

"Okay?" Logan's head spun. "That's not quite the reaction I expected. So you mean you're all right with me being your brother-in-law?"

Brett shrugged. "Why not? Better you than Max. Besides, we've been practically like brothers since we were kids. Now you're just making it official. But if you hurt my sister, asshole..."

"I'm not going to hurt her. I just need to go find her and tell her what an idiot I am."

Brett chuckled. "Don't bother. She already knows."

Logan stared at him, confusion eating at his brain. What the hell was he talking about? Then Brett stepped aside to reveal Valerie standing behind him in the living room with a stunned expression on her face.

* * *

Valerie sat there in stunned silence, her heart galloping in her chest at the sight of Logan standing in the doorway. Her throat was tight, her stomach jittery. After a moment of hesitation, she finally spoke. "Did you mean that?"

Logan shifted his weight from one foot to the other, as if he was nervous. "Which part?"

"All of it."

His eyes pierced into hers. "Yes. I meant every last word."

She searched his dark eyes and found nothing but sincerity and warmth. "You want to be with me again?"

"I never stopped wanting to be with you, princess. I was just mad and didn't handle any of it well. I'm sorry for everything. I should never have spoken to you like I did. There was no excuse for it, and it won't ever happen again. Please forgive me and say you'll give me a chance to prove it to you."

Tears filled her eyes, and she swallowed a lump in her throat. "There's nothing to forgive," she said, wiping her eyes. "I'm pretty sure I deserved what you said. Most of it anyway."

"No, baby. You didn't deserve any of it. I know I upset you, and I plan on making it up to you. Every day if you'll let me. I don't want to see that pained look on your face ever again. And to know I'm the one who put it there only makes me feel worse."

She stepped past Brett and joined him on the porch. "I'm sorry. I know I hurt you by lying to you, but I didn't mean to. You had every right to be upset with me."

"But that didn't give me the right to take out my frustrations on you. My irritation stemmed from issues with my father. It was a gut reaction, one that didn't have anything to do with you. I'm not perfect, and maybe I'm not even the right man for you. But I want to try and be the kind of man you need. One that you'll be proud to call yours."

"You already are that guy, Logan. You've been that person for years."

He placed one hand on her cheek, and his eyes softened. "There's something else you should hear. I know you don't like it when I call you princess. But you're just going to have to get used to me getting on your nerves. Because you are a princess. *My* princess. And I wouldn't have it any other way."

"Oh my God. Dude. That's pure cheese." Brett rolled his eyes. "You two are seriously grossing me out right now."

Valerie giggled. "Shut up and go inside, Brett."

Thankfully, he did. Definitely an improvement over the old Brett. Maybe there was some hope for the guy after all. The moment her brother closed the door on them, Valerie sighed. "Logan, there's something you need to know before this goes any further. I was dishonest about something else, and although my intentions were good, it might change your mind about wanting to be with me."

He looked a little worried, but said, "Nothing is ever going to change my mind about wanting to be with you."

She pulled the bar napkin from the front pocket of her jeans and held it up for Logan to see. "Do you recognize this?"

His eyes focused on the napkin and then widened. "Where did you get that?"

"Max gave it to me."

"Why?"

"Because the money he gave you for the bar wasn't his. It was mine."

Confusion filled his eyes, and he shook his head. "You bought my bar for Max?"

"No. The bar doesn't belong to Max."

"It does now. I wrote up that agreement, and we both signed it. It's legally binding."

She grinned. "I take it you didn't check his signature?"

He grasped the napkin, glanced down at the bottom, and burst out laughing. "The fucker signed his name as Snow White?"

"Yeah, Max has sort of a weird sense of humor." She released a hard breath. "I'm sorry I deceived you again. I wanted to help you save your bar and your mom's house, but I knew you would never accept the money if you knew it came from me. So I asked Max to give it to you."

"That was a lot of cash to trust in someone else's hands. He could've taken you to the cleaners."

"Max isn't like that. I know you probably won't believe this, but Max is a good guy. Sure, he's mischievous and a bit of an instigator, but he really is a great friend."

"I trust your opinion, Valerie. If you say he's golden, then that's good enough for me." He smiled at her. "So I guess since the money was yours, then *you* were the one who bought my bar."

She shook her head. "Actually, I was hoping we could look at it more like an investment or a buy-in. I was going to come talk to you about it once you stopped being so mad. I love working in the bar industry and thought maybe we could be business partners."

Logan shook his head. "I hate to tell you this, Val, but the last thing I want is to be business partners with you."

Her heart sank, and her head lowered. "Oh." She never considered for one second that he would turn her offer down.

He lifted her chin and smiled. "I'd much rather make you my wife."

Tears pricked her eyes. "Really? You mean that?"

"With everything I am," he said, taking her into his arms. "Is that a yes?"

"Yes!"

Logan bent his head and took her mouth. But this wasn't a slow burn. The hot, openmouthed kiss lifted her onto her toes as fire blasted through her system, rushing straight to her core. A strong erection pressed against the seam of his jeans, and she rubbed herself against him, wanting to feel that hard ridge pressing between the apex of her legs. "Logan," she whispered, her voice filled with need.

He pulled back from her and took a gasping breath. "I know, baby. I want to be inside you. I've been going crazy not having you. You want to get out of here?" he asked, hope blooming in his eyes.

God, she missed this. Missed him. "Hell yeah, I thought you'd never ask."

He led her out to his truck. "One more thing though. We'll need to make a quick stop before we get to my place."

"Okay. Where are we going?"

"We need to stop by the bakery and see Leah and Sam."

She bounced in place with excitement. "Oh, you want to tell them that we're getting married?"

"Sure, but that's not the only reason we're stopping there."

"What's the other reason?"

Logan grinned. "I want to borrow a drill so I can put a hole in my bedroom wall. There's still one more thing on your naughty list that we haven't gotten around to doing yet."

Valerie tossed her head back and laughed. "You're so dirty."

He wrapped an arm around her waist and pulled her closer. "I know. And you love every second of it, princess."

She smiled up at him. "You're damn straight I do."

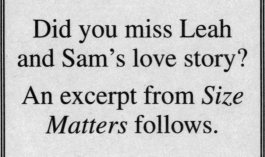

Did you miss Leah and Sam's love story?

An excerpt from *Size Matters* follows.

Chapter One

Leah Martin nearly choked on her beer.

"What do you mean *just pick one?*" Her eyes scanned the entire bar before settling back on her friend. "Pick one what?"

"A guy, of course."

Yeah, because it was just that simple. For Valerie maybe. Even though they were close in size, Valerie always wore her weight better and turned heads everywhere she went. It probably helped that she had expressive doe eyes, wavy platinum blond hair, and looked more like a cutesy toy poodle any guy would give their right testicle to take for a walk.

"I hate to tell you this, Val, but that only applies to women who look like you." If Leah had to classify herself in that same frame of reference, she'd accurately describe herself as a bulldog. Not only did she have the breed's innate stubborn streak, but she also had the matching broad shoulders, wide hips, large chest, and —if she didn't lose a few pounds—probably the same short life span. "Hippy brunettes with body image issues and smudged eyeliner don't get the luxury of *just pick one*."

"Oh, shut up," Valerie said, rolling her eyes. "Your eyeliner looks fine."

Yep, that about sums it up. My eyeliner is the only thing that looks decent on me tonight.

The little black dress she wore was just that—too little—and was slowly squeezing the life out of her. Especially after packing on ten extra pounds in the last few months. The sheath of fabric clung to every curve, as well as every bulge. Thank God they lived in Texas instead of Alaska or an Eskimo might've mistaken her for a seal and tried to skin her.

"So what's your pleasure?" Valerie asked, not giving up. "Plenty of gorgeous men in here tonight."

"Sure, if I squint."

"Okay, stop being negative. You're gorgeous, and lots of men love curvy women. I should know. Now pick one."

No point in arguing with her. Once Valerie set her mind to something, she didn't stop until the mission was accomplished. But the only time Leah had ever had her pick of anything was when she stood in front of the doughnut case at work, deciding between a chocolate éclair or a cream cheese Danish.

"How am I supposed to know who to pick? It's not like they wear signs on their foreheads saying, I DIG FAT CHICKS."

Valerie shot her an exasperated look. "We'll just establish a baseline for the kind of guy you want."

"The kind of guy I'd want wouldn't be hanging out in a bar called Rusty's Bucket. In fact, I wouldn't be here either if you hadn't forced me to come."

"Leah, you got dumped. Happens to all of us sooner or later." Valerie's voice softened as she reached for Leah's hand. "It sucks, I know. But you're always at work or upstairs in your apartment, which means you never leave that damn building. It's not healthy. You can't hide out forever."

"I'm not *hiding*. I've just…been busy. I never imagined I'd be this swamped only a month after grand opening, and I've had to put in a lot of extra hours." Leah caught Valerie's *I'm not buying it* expression. "Come on, Val. The wedding is tomorrow night. Everything has to be perfect because…well, you know."

Valerie rolled her eyes. "Why does it even matter?"

"Because my reputation is at stake. It's *my* cake the happy couple will be stuffing into each other's mouths. They can choke on it for all I care, but it's going to be the tastiest damn wedding cake they've ever eaten while keeling over. Everything has to go as smoothly as possible, and I have a million things to do before tomorrow night. I still need to—"

Valerie raised her hand to stop her from continuing. "What you need is a break. Let's find some guys to dance with and have a few hours of fun before you lock yourself up in the cave again. Just humor me, okay? Now, what would you say your dream guy's most attractive quality would be?"

Leah sighed. "A pulse."

"No vampires. Check. What else?"

"I don't know. This is stupid." Leah caught the disappointment in Valerie's eyes and groaned. "Okay, fine. I guess I'd want..."

Her gaze sifted through the crowd, landing on two men at the bar. While the one standing motioned to the bartender, the other rolled up the sleeves of his blue button-down shirt, drawing Leah's attention to his tanned, muscular forearms. When he finished, he bumped his elbow against the other man's ribs and said something that made them both laugh. The warm, amused smile he wore sent a zing of pleasure through Leah, like she'd been given an intravenous shot of serotonin. *Him. I'd want him.*

Leah smiled. "I guess I'd want someone who could make me laugh."

"That's great and all"—Val groaned with annoyance—"but you're killing me here. What would he *look* like? That's what I want to know."

"Tall, dark brown hair, well-toned forearms, killer smile, a bit of scruff on his face, and a light blue shirt," Leah said automatically, still eyeballing the man across the room.

"Um, okay, wow. That's pretty specific."

Leah gazed back at Valerie, shaking her head to clear the man's image from her mind. "Sorry, it just sort of...popped out."

"No, no, it's good. Gives us something to go by. At least now we have a starting point. Okay, so let's see," Valerie said, peering around the crowded room. "Ah, there's a guy in a blue shirt." She nodded toward a man sitting four tables away.

He wasn't looking in their direction so they waited for him to turn around. Then they both cringed.

"Well, I guess two out of seven isn't bad," Valerie said, crinkling her nose.

"Two? The blue shirt is a given, but I doubt he has a pulse. Definitely pale enough to be considered a vampire, though...well, if he had any teeth."

"Okay, what about...*that* guy?"

Leah glanced in the direction Valerie pointed. "Oh, come on! Give me a break. Even I'm not that desperate."

"What's wrong with him? He's exactly what you described. I'm all for being picky, Leah, but you're just going to dance with him, not marry the guy."

The man at the bar noted their attention and swiveled his stool around to get a better look at his captive female audience. He took an extended pull from his longneck, swept his thick tongue across his bottom lip, then set it down before giving them a not-so-sexy wink.

"I'm glad you think the best I can do is a guy who actually has teeth, but I never said I wanted a guy in stained overalls and white rubber boots. If you like Shrimper Bob so much, then *you* go talk to him."

"Wait. What? No, not him." Valerie grasped Leah's head and turned it a fraction of an inch to the right. "Him!"

Leah didn't know why she was surprised. She'd given Valerie his basic description, which was the equivalent of placing a flashing neon sign above his head with an arrow pointing down.

Granted, she'd left out some of the other noticeable details. Like how his large hand wrapped strongly around his beer, yet brought it to his mouth slow and gentle, as if he were touching his lips to a woman's breast. Or how the muscles in his back bunched beneath his shirt while leaning over the bar, as if a satiated woman lay limply beneath him.

Leah wouldn't have minded being that woman. But when he shifted on his stool and his eyes met hers, then darted away, she got the message loud and clear. *Not interested.*

"You're totally eye-humping him," Valerie shrieked, smiling at the new mission she was about to partake.

"No, I'm not."

"Yeah, right, Leah. I can see the drool dribbling down your chin."

Insecure about whether her friend was telling the truth, Leah nonchalantly wiped the back of her hand across her face.

"See?" Valerie said, laughing. "You *do* think he's hot. Know what else? It wouldn't surprise me if you had described him from the start."

"Shut up, Val."

She laughed again. "God, I love it when I'm right."

"I didn't say you were right."

"No, but you always get defensive when I am. Why didn't you just point him out to begin with?"

Leah shrugged. "Not my type."

"Oh, please. A guy like that is every woman's type. What you're actually saying is that you don't think you're *his* type."

"It's the same thing, no matter how you put it. Either way, he's not interested."

"Oh, so now you're a mind reader, I guess. How do you know what he's interested in? Maybe he's waiting for you to ask him to dance."

Leah grimaced. "You've seen me dance, and it's not

pretty. If he isn't interested now, he definitely won't be after seeing *that*."

Valerie giggled and leaped out of her seat. "Guess we're about to find out."

"No, Val. Don't go over—" *Damn it.*

* * *

Sam Cooper wasn't about to turn around.

In the mirror behind the bar, he watched as the yappy blonde in his ear made a play for his buddy Max. Not only had she flirted with him, but she touched his biceps—Max's second favorite part of his anatomy—and cinched the deal. Within seconds, she had him promising to join their table, offering to buy her and her brunette friend a drink, and eating out of her slick little hands. The lady was damn near professional. *The sonofabitch never had a chance.*

After she finally walked away, Max turned to Sam. "I need you to stay a little longer and be my wingman."

"Nope. You're on your own, *Rico Suave*. I told you I was leaving after this beer."

"Yeah, but that was before the dark-haired girl caught you checking out her rack and her friend invited us over to join them."

Sam grinned. He had noticed the well-endowed piece of real estate on the pretty brunette across the room, but that wasn't what grabbed his attention the most. It was the way her expressive eyes flickered over him as she licked her pouty lips. That alone did more for his libido than her oversized breasts—not that those weren't nice to look at too.

But... "I'm not interested."

"Even though you're single now?"

"Doesn't matter," Sam said, shaking his head. "I just broke up with one crazy broad. Last thing I need is another one breathing down my neck."

"Oh, come on. You only dated Sylvia for a month. How much damage could one chick do in such a short amount of time?"

"She wanted to get married."

Beer spewed out Max's mouth as he burst into hysterics. He reached for some bar napkins and wiped at his tear-filled eyes before cleaning up the spray on the bar. "Sorry to hear that," Max said, still chuckling.

"Yeah, the sympathy is rolling off you in waves."

His buddy suppressed his lingering smirk by running a hand over his face. "No, I mean it. I really am sorry to hear that. But I'm a little confused. Just last month, you said it was time for you to settle down. It's fast, but if she wants the same thing... well, I guess I don't see what the problem is."

"I told you. She's crazy."

Max shrugged his brows suggestively. "Like crazy-in-bed kind of crazy?"

"No, crazy as in crazy-as-a-loony-tune. She had the whole thing planned out. First she'd meet Mr. Right—which apparently was me—and then she'd marry him and have a white picket fence, a dog named Spot, and exactly two-point-five kids. The woman had goddamn charts."

"Fuck."

"Yeah, tell me about it. That's why women are off my radar for now. I don't need or want the complication. The hell if I'm going to marry someone because they have a schedule to keep."

Max motioned for the bartender, ordered four beers, then turned his attention back to Sam. "Look, I'm buying this round. Come on, take one for the team. You know I'd do it for you."

"I wouldn't need you to."

"You cocky bastard," Max said with a laugh. "I just need you to entertain her friend while I make my move."

"I'm surprised you're even interested in the blonde. I thought you only liked women so skinny you could pick your teeth with?"

Max grinned. "Let's just say I'm willing to make an exception on a case-by-case basis. Now, come on. Do a good deed for your buddy. You know you want to."

Sam groaned and glanced at his gold watch. "One hour. If you haven't worked your magic by then . . . Well, you're going to owe me. Big time. By the way, you're buying my beers the rest of the night too."

Max paid the bartender, picked up two beers, and headed across the room with a smile on his face and an eye on the blond yapper. *Poor bastard.* Against his better judgment, Sam grabbed the other two beers and followed.

The women had their heads together whispering but stopped talking the moment they approached. The blonde smiled up at them, but the brunette kept her gaze lowered, and her cheeks blushed fiercely. It almost made Sam want to check and see if his zipper was down.

While introductions were being made, he forced himself to keep his eyes on hers because staring at her glorious chest or that delicious mouth implied a strong sexual interest he preferred to avoid. But when her glistening green eyes lifted to his, he decided her forehead was a safer bet.

Sam hadn't even gotten out a single word before the blond Chihuahua beckoned his friend toward the dance floor with a sexy come-hither wiggle of her hips and a crook of her finger. Max smiled and glanced over at Sam, who shrugged and took a seat across from her friend. Hell, maybe an hour was generous. At this rate, he'd be heading home in twenty minutes. *Thank God.*

He slid a beer across the table. "So, Leann…"

"Leah," she said, her brow wrinkling a little. "My name's Leah."

Shit. "Sorry."

"It's okay," she said, though her tone conveyed otherwise.

Sam ran his fingers through his hair. "Well, I guess the two of them didn't waste any time ditching us."

"Yeah, I guess not." She hesitated but then continued, "You'll have to excuse Valerie. She's not very subtle."

"That's okay. I like when a woman goes after what she wants." *Damn. Why did I word it that way?* He made the mistake of glancing at Leah's mouth, which curved into a delighted smile.

Disturbed by the pleasant sensation it gave him, he fastened his eyes back to her forehead and kept them there. But he couldn't stare at her head for an hour straight. If he didn't do something soon, his eyes would eventually work their way back down to her face. Or worse, her cleavage.

"Maybe we should go out on the dance floor and show them how it's done." When she didn't respond, he said, "Well?"

"I, uh...I can't dance."

"Everyone can dance."

"No, I mean I *really* can't dance. Last time I tried, someone called 911 because they couldn't figure out if I was possessed or having a seizure."

Sam laughed and accidentally lowered his gaze again. Her wide eyes and pinked-up cheeks told him everything he needed to know. The girl was terrified of embarrassing herself again, and for some strange reason, the desire to relieve her of that mental anguish washed over him. "If you can walk, then you can two-step. I'll teach you." He rose to lead her to the dance floor, but she didn't move. "Come on," he said, coaxing her out of her chair. "I promise not to let anyone call an ambulance...or a priest."

She stood and smoothed out the wrinkles in her dress by running her hands over her curves. Sam shifted his gaze and blew out a breath. *Don't look at her, you idiot, or you won't be going home alone.*

He held out his hand—one she reluctantly accepted—and then pulled her onto the crowded dance floor. He settled her left hand on his right shoulder and wrapped his free hand around her waist.

She stiffened.

"Relax," he said, offering her a comforting smile. "This is supposed to be fun." He quickly explained which leg to start on and the tempo of the dance, while she sighed nervously and forced her body to loosen. "Okay, ready?"

She nodded hesitantly, and he moved toward her, dancing her backward to the beat of the music. At first, she stumbled to keep up. She bit her bottom lip and concentrated intently on her foot placement, but she didn't quit. Sam liked that about her, even if her jerky movements were throwing him off as well.

To help her keep the rhythm, he pulled her closer, forcing her to look over his shoulder instead of down at her feet. Then he lowered his mouth to her ear and whispered, "Quick, quick, slow. Slow."

She improved instantly, and her movements lined up with his, matching the pace he'd set to the music as they glided across the dance floor. He was sure she was chanting the mantra over and over in her head and probably still wore a tense look of concentration and determination, but he hesitated to pull back to see for himself. Mostly because her soft skin emitted a sweet, delicious aroma, and he couldn't get enough of it. Like the woman had bathed herself in vanilla-scented sugar. *God, she smells incredible.*

Her unexpected laugh had him wondering if he'd spoken out loud, but then he noticed her friend across the dance floor with a huge smile, giving them a thumbs-up. Not only was Leah dancing, but she was doing a fairly decent job at keeping up. Sure, her form could use a little polish, and she stepped on his foot every now and then, but he had to give the girl some credit.

"Your friend seems nice," he said, making small talk to pass the time as well as smooth out the awkward silence.

"Valerie's great, even under all that toy poodle cuteness."

Sam let out a hearty laugh. "A poodle—that's it! I had her pegged more as a Chihuahua, but I think you nailed it. All she needs is a large, obnoxious pink bow in her hair."

"She stopped wearing hair ornaments after I made the reference last year," Leah said with a giggle.

"She keeps staring over here. Why does she look so surprised to see you dancing?"

"Because I can't dance," Leah said evenly.

"Oh, really?" Placing his hand on her hip, Sam pushed her out, spun her around twice, and pulled her back to him in one smooth motion. "Looks like you're doing a fine job to me."

"It's you," she said, looking him square in the eyes with a heavy-lidded gaze that stole his breath. "Y-you make me look good."

The song ended, and although they stopped moving, they didn't separate. Silently, he stared at her face, taking in her features one by one. Emerald jewels stared back him, glistening under the strobe lights. She licked her plump, ripe lips nervously, coating them with a glossy sheen of moisture. Rosy cheeks, heated by the spike in body temperature, clearly had nothing to do with dancing. For a moment, Sam lost his wits.

"I don't know about that," he said, allowing his eyes to drop lower for a delicious view of her nicely rounded curves. "I think you look pretty damn—"

"Excuse me," someone interrupted, tapping his shoulder. "Do you remember me from the other night?"

Sam and Leah both turned toward the black-haired beauty standing behind him. The young woman's red leather pants clung low on her waist, displaying a midriff pierced by a sparkly diamond on a silver chain. Her top— if you could call it that—resembled a sexy push-up bra with rhinestones.

"Sorry to interrupt," she said, glancing at Leah and

then back to him. "But I saw you when I walked by and couldn't help myself." She giggled and blushed a little. "After all, it's not every day a girl gets picked up and taken home by a stranger."

Sam knew she referred to the innocent ride home he gave her when he found her on the side of the road with a flat tire and no spare, but he stiffened a little anyway. Anyone—including Leah—could easily take the girl's comment out of context. And judging by the irritated expression on Leah's face, she had done just that.

He could've told the truth. Hell, maybe he should have. But remembering what he was about to say to Leah made him rethink his position. The interruption had to be some sort of divine intervention. Otherwise he'd have his mouth trailing all over Leah's body until morning. And that couldn't happen. He meant what he'd said to Max. *No women. Not even this one.*

"Amy, right?" Sam asked the young woman and waited as she nodded in confirmation. "Would you like to dance?" Out of the corner of his eyes, he monitored Leah's reaction. Her green eyes widened, and her mouth fell open before she snapped it closed. "You don't mind, do you, Leah?"

"No, of course not." She smiled briefly, but the disappointment was apparent in her lackluster eyes. Without another word, she pivoted and marched away, leaving him with an overwhelming amount of guilt in her wake.

"Give me a second," he told the young woman and then rushed to catch Leah before she vacated the dance floor. "Leah, wait!"

She spun on him, her fierce eyes punching him straight

in the gut. She was pissed and rightfully so. And that only made him feel more like a heel than he already did.

"Leah, it's just that..." He should explain it all, if only to keep her from thinking he was a jackass. But he couldn't. Not without leading her on, which wouldn't be fair to her. The last thing he wanted was to get involved with her—with anyone, for that matter. And as cowardly as it was, the simplest solution was to let her think whatever horrible scenario she'd conjured up in her mind was true. "I'm sorry. You're just not my type," he blurted out.

Leah glanced across the floor, her eyes scrolling up and down Amy's skin-baring, leather-clad figure. Then she peered down at her own voluptuous body and pursed her lips. "It's okay, Sam. It's not like I didn't see it coming." Then she turned and walked away.

He cringed. Not only was what he said the farthest thing from the truth, but the thoughtless brush-off sounded more like a fucked-up insult. *Smooth, asshole. Real smooth.*

ABOUT THE AUTHOR

Alison Bliss grew up in Small Town, Texas, but currently resides in the Midwest with her husband and two sons. With so much testosterone in her home, it's no wonder she writes "girl books." She believes the best way to know if someone is your soul mate is by canoeing with them because, if you both make it back alive, it's obviously meant to be. Alison pens the type of books she loves to read most: fun, steamy love stories with heart, heat, laughter, and usually a cowboy or two. As she calls it, "Romance...with a sense of humor."

To learn more, visit her at:
authoralisonbliss.com
Facebook/AuthorAlisonBliss
Twitter @AlisonBliss2

Fall in Love with Forever Romance

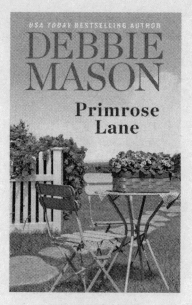

PRIMROSE LANE
By Debbie Mason

"[The Harmony Harbor series is] heartfelt and delightful!"
—RaeAnne Thayne, *New York Times* bestselling author

Finn Gallagher returns for a visit to Harmony Harbor only to find that the town's matchmakers have other plans. Because it's high time that wedding planner Olivia Davenport gets to plan her own nuptials. And finding true love is the best reason of all for Finn to move home for good.

Fall in Love with Forever Romance

COMEBACK COWBOY
By Sara Richardson

In the *New York Times* bestselling tradition of Jennifer Ryan and Maisey Yates comes the second book in Sara Richardson's Rocky Mountain Riders series. When Naomi's high school sweetheart comes riding back to town, this self-sufficient single mom feels something she hasn't felt in years: a red-hot unbridled need for the handsome cowboy who left her behind. As much as Naomi's tried, a woman never forgets her first cowboy...

Fall in Love with Forever Romance

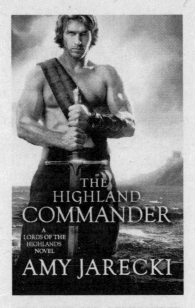

THE HIGHLAND COMMANDER
By Amy Jarecki

As the illegitimate daughter of a Scottish earl, Lady Magdalen Keith is not usually one to partake in lavish masquerade balls. Yet one officer sweeps her off her feet with dashing good looks that cannot be disguised by a mere mask...Navy lieutenant Aiden Murray has spent too many months at sea to be immune to this lovely beauty. But when he discovers Maddie's true identity—and learns that her father is accused of treason—will the brawny Scot risk his life to follow his heart?